The Mule Tamer III

Marta's Quest

Mule Tamer III — Marta's Quest
Copyright ©2012 by John Horst
ISBN-978-1478153061 (CreateSpace-Assigned)
ISBN-10: 1478153067

Cover art by Kevin Moore
Editing, Composition, and Typography by
www.ProEditingService.com

Special Note: This edition of *The Mule Tamer III – Marta's Quest is* designed to provide entertainment for the reader. It is a work of fiction. All the characters, organizations and events portrayed in this novel are either products of the author's imagination or are used fictitiously.

Our views and rights are the same: You are responsible for your own choices, actions, and results.

For Peggy and Kate, Again

Be kind, for everyone you meet is fighting a hard battle

Contents

Forward

The story of Mexico is a tragic and tumultuous one. From the time of the Aztecs until the period of our story, the peoples of Mexico—the natives—have been abused and misused, dispossessed and trampled upon. First by the Europeans, with the eventual overthrow of the empire of the French emperor Napoleon III in 1867, to the homegrown abuse meted out by Porfirio Díaz for more than thirty-four years.

During this period, the "president" who'd never been voted out of office, allied with the land monopolists, the corrupt hacendados, to further a process whereby the rich and powerful flourished and the poor found it difficult to simply survive.

It was during this period that Tienda de Raya, the company store, came into existence, in which workers on large estates would be paid in vouchers or tokens that were redeemable only at the stores belonging to the landholders. Debts accumulated by a worker would be passed to his children and would continue to move through the generations until fully paid, which rarely—more likely, never— occurred.

This made it impossible for peasants to travel to lands that might afford a better opportunity, and they were subsequently made—literally—captives on the land of their oppressor, oftentimes forced to live in squalor; live without even enough to eat. For the ones who tried to break the bonds, the rurales were summoned to track them down and return them to this prison home.

When sugar became the big cash crop, the peasants could not even plant enough corn to survive as every bit of useful land would be used to maximize the profits. It was just not lucrative to let a peon have a few feet of land to keep his family alive.

In addition to this subjugation, the Díaz regime also dispossessed the peasants of their lands, lands handed down from one generation to the next through honor and a handshake but without proper documentation. These lands were handed over to the hacendados and because of this, a long and unbreakable kind of serfdom reigned. Finally, in 1910, with the aid of Francisco J. Madero, the chains of the Díaz regime were broken. The peasants finally had a voice.

But old habits die hard and over the many years of this totalitarian dictatorship, monsters were bred and nurtured and permitted to flourish. People such as General Victoriano Huerta inevitably came to be and, with the aid of the United States Ambassador to Mexico, destroyed the Madero democracy in its infancy. They, in addition to international interests, could not bear to see Mexico become a free and democratic society where the native peoples, the Indians, could be considered something more than sub-human; more than just a pack animal or beast of burden to be used.

This is the setting of our story, which is fiction. It is important to note this out of respect for the real players of the time. Many of the characters in this story are based upon real people, but they are fictionalized. Additionally, timelines have been altered to fit the age or the moment in history for our characters. The author begs the indulgence of the reader in this respect, as well. It is not meant to give a false account of history, but rather to make the story flow in such a way as to entertain and provide a believable escape into a fascinating and tragic time.

—John Horst, 2012

I Stonefields 1911

"Ah, I theenk I have eet almost clean, señorita!"

"Stop, stop!" The girl's screams echoed off the curved sides of the porcelain bowl as the children stood agog, mesmerized, not certain what to do.

"Someone should find Rebecca."

The young Mexican woman pulled the girl's head out of one toilet and moved her to the next. "I theenk these a one is a little dirtier, señorita. I will get eet nice an' clean for you!"

The young woman struggled, unable to free herself from the Mexicana's grip. She was furious and frightened and humiliated.

"Stop it. Stop it, let me go!" Her long pretty hair swished about the toilet bowl. Thankfully, headmistress had a good housekeeping staff or the experience would have likely been much worse.

Marta looked up, saw Rebecca arrive, breathlessly, an underclassman holding her hand, pulling her anxiously along. She smiled at her sister weakly.

"Ah, seester, you are jus' een time. La niña rica wan's us fregonas to make everything nice an' clean."

Rebecca Walsh knew better than to command her sister to stop. It would only encourage her to continue. "Marta, why are you talking this way?"

"Ay, chingao, we are Mexicana trash, seester, we musta' obey the reech girl."

She finally allowed the girl to stand upright on her feet. She looked the red-faced child in the eye as the toilet water ran down her face. She gave her rosy cheeks a squeeze, then patted her face.

Marta lost her cruel smile. "Next time, think twice before you open your mouth, dear."

The student ran off, humiliated.

Marta wiped her hands as she looked into a mirror and straightened a displaced lock of hair. The little girls surrounded her, scared, awed and mesmerized by the wild upperclassman. One spoke up.

"Gosh, Marta, you're in for it now."

Marta smiled. "Sweetheart, I have only one term to go. What is Madame going to do to me now?" She looked at Rebecca's reflection in the mirror. "I suppose we'll be seeing Abuelita sooner rather than later, Rebecca."

Rebecca suppressed a grin. Before she could answer, a fourteen year old looked her in the eye then glanced back at Marta. "That new girl was very cross. Marta tried to make her stop but she wouldn't. She saw Marta and said it was nice that we have live-in maids. Marta tried to get her to stop and she kept on, making bad comments about Marta's color. Then Marta turned her upside down and used her head to scrub the toilets."

Rebecca patted the girl softly on the shoulder. She looked at the girls all around them. "You all go on back to your rooms. You make sure you were somewhere else when all this occurred, okay?"

They nodded obediently and ran off. Rebecca always made things right and she'd keep the girls, all of them, out of it.

She looked at Marta's face in the mirror and smiled broadly, shaking her head from side to side. "You are incorrigible, girl. Simply incorrigible."

The two old ladies sat in the headmistress's office, one on either side of the big oak desk. They loved each other and had been friends for more than sixty years. Abuelita sat, back straight, her egret feather hat draped over one eye giving her the appearance of a lovely lady buccaneer. She finally spoke up.

"How much, dear?"

Madame Boutin sat back and tapped the desk blotter with a pen. She looked at Alice Walsh and chose her words carefully. Alice was her best friend in the world and was the reason Stonefields existed at all.

The school's mistress had a title and education, but nothing more than the clothes on her back when she arrived in America many years ago. Alice gave her the big break, even got her to change the spelling of her name from Button, to Boutin.

She remembered that recommendation as if it happened only yesterday, *'Sounds like you'll be training seamstresses, dear. Can't have it, you must sound more exotic than all that.'*

And Alice, of course, was right. Alice Walsh was, it seemed, always right and as good and loyal a patron as anyone starting and running a boarding school for refined young ladies could ever find.

"The gymnasium needs a new roof." Alice Walsh smiled and calculated the cost in her mind. Her Marta was an expensive child.

"What of the new girl? Will there be trouble?"

Madame Boutin blew air through pursed lips. "Bah, the family hasn't a pot to piss in. They only put her in here because they had to flee the debt collectors in Europe. She's gone and good riddance; would not have likely gotten a penny from them, anyway."

"And I am putting a roof on the gymnasium because… ? Sounds like Marta should be receiving a reward of some kind for saving you a lot of trouble."

She didn't receive an answer because, just then, they were interrupted by the secretary who placed a box on the desk between them and just as quickly left the room. Madame Boutin began to remove items, one by one, as Abuelita leaned forward to see what she was up to.

The headmistress first placed several packets of cigarettes between them. Alice Walsh picked one up, removed two cigarettes and handed one to her friend. They smoked.

Madame Boutin took out the remaining items, including a pack of playing cards, a book of naughty limericks, ticket stubs to the Gaiety theatre, and a folded envelope with a picture of a rooster on it.

"Coq de la Promenade." Abuelita read the cover with great interest. "She has condoms? What sort of school are you running, dear?"

Madame Boutin smiled coyly. "Not con*doms*, darling. Just one." She breathed her answer with her smoke. "What kind of granddaughter are you raising, dear?"

They finished two more of Marta's cigarettes and sat silently for a while.

"Alice, what's going to happen to Rebecca?"

Alice didn't look up. She knew what her friend meant. She nodded her head gravely. "There's nothing to be done. Rebecca and Marta are as one. They might just as well be Siamese twins."

"You know Marta can't do these things when they go to Smith next year. You know that. They won't put up with Marta there and she'll hold Rebecca back."

"What do you propose?"

"Nothing. Nothing, it's just a rhetorical question, dear. There's nothing to be done, is there?"

"Would you do it if there was? Would you want to change her?" She smiled at the school's mistress.

"I would change nothing about that girl, Alice. You know I wouldn't change a thing. I just worry over Rebecca." She shifted the items on the desk and threw the condom and book of limericks in the trash. She looked at Alice. "What do you want me to do about this fellow from the mining company?"

Alice Walsh blew a plume of smoke the size of her hat. "What does Marta say?"

"She doesn't want any help. She's been corresponding with Mr. George. She says what he says goes, but the mining representatives want to meet with her, nonetheless, and she's consented to do it."

"Well, why not see if you can sit in with them? She might allow it. I know she won't let me, or my lawyer." Alice leaned forward in her seat. "She'll be nineteen this year, by our best guess, and she's smarter than any lawyer I've ever known. Let her deal with it as she sees fit. You know she's been running the ranch in Mexico, in absentia, for the last three years. I think she can handle a mining company."

The last child's hair was plaited and the two young ladies sent their charges off to bed. A straggler loitered, needing help with her Latin. Marta was a good teacher, surrogate mother and confidante. The youngest looked back at Marta. "Did you really clean the toilets with the girl's head, Marta?"

"I did, darling. But that does not mean you should do such a thing. Violence is never the answer. I should be ashamed of myself for what I did. I should be very sorry." She kissed the girl on the forehead and sent her on to bed. "Did you clean your teeth?" She called after her and nodded.

They were in their beds now, alone. "Was Abuelita very upset, Rebecca?"

"No."

"I worry about her. She will be ninety-one this year. Am I aging her?"

"No."

"You're quiet tonight."

"I'm tired, Marta. Let's go to sleep."

"They took my things, you know."

"You'll get more cigarettes. You always do."

"But my books, and cards."

"Those limericks weren't even funny. And you'll get more cards easily enough."

"They took the overcoat."

Rebecca was drifting. "You have no need for it. You aren't going to do it."

"Well, I might. I might just do it and then where will I be? Do they want me to get a disease or get knocked up?"

She'd lost her. Marta knew by her breathing that her sister was asleep. She wished she had a cigarette but she, too, soon fell asleep.

"Young lady." The man stood up, smiled weakly but did not extend his hand. He did not shake hands with women or children and especially not with dark ones.

Marta sat at headmistress Boutin's desk. She had graciously refused the old woman's presence at the meeting. A young man sat next to the representative. He was a bit older than Marta, likely mid-twenties. He had a nice face, pale, like her father, with lovely blue eyes. He smiled at the pretty young woman.

Being a normal young man, he liked pretty women and was pleased to be in her presence. He stood up a little straighter than his companion and extended his hand, reaching across the width of the desk to accommodate her. "Robert Curtin, ma'am." When he took her hand, he bowed at the waist.

Marta sat down and looked over the papers in front of her. She did not speak. She'd been reading a lot lately, books on negotiation written by an aggressive new-money rich man to help the up-and-coming young working class. She had studied the author's writing and knew it well. She had decided to use this meeting to practice what she'd learned.

Marta had arranged the curtains behind Madame's desk so that she was backlit with glaring sunlight. She also arranged the chairs in such a way as to place herself six inches higher than the two men on the other side of the desk.

They were forced to squint, were disoriented and uncomfortable. They were unable to make out the expression on Marta's face. Her actions had produced the desired effect. The older man squirmed, then coughed, then cleared his throat. Marta looked up at him, into his eyes. She still said nothing.

"Young lady."

"You may address me as Miss Del Toro." She didn't look up as she spoke. She continued, "Unless you want to persist in this ridiculous manner, in which case, I'll refer to you as old man."

"Ah, Miss Del Toro, of course. Beg your pardon. We are here at Mr. George's request."

"Yes, I know. Dan and I have been in communication about your proposal. I don't understand, though. He knows what I want. Why are you not dealing with him?"

"With due respect, ma'am. That Indian is a bit dis…"

Marta cut him off. "That Indian?" She cast her eyes at the young man who looked mortified at his aged companion. He did not expect this from his colleague.

Marta looked back at the old man. "I am sorry, but why would you say such a thing? I don't call you that Caucasoid, do I?" She did not wait for his response. "I am sorry, mister, what's your name again?"

"Tolkenhorn."

"An unusual name. Not really a very common name, is it?"

She looked at Curtin and could now tell that he was not an ass, and knew full well that his companion definitely was. She looked back at the lawyer. "I'm guessing some sort of a bastardization of an eastern European name. You're not a bohunk, are you?"

The young man snorted, suppressed a laugh and nearly fell out of his chair as his arm slipped off the armrest. He quickly recovered. She was magnificent.

The older man was outraged, but dared not say anything. His face reddened and he looked at his hands. She did not let him reply.

"I've been over these documents. Frankly, Mr. Talking Horn, I believe you should fire the law clerk who proofed them. Disgraceful."

"Young lady, uh… Miss Del Toro, I drafted the documents and proofed them myself."

Marta looked over at the young man. "Well, at least you didn't do it." Curtin blushed.

She returned her gaze to the lawyer. "Mr. Talking Horn, there is no such word as 'irregardless,' you'll need to strike that. You've also written, let me see, one, two, three, four, five, six times the wrong use of the word 'council,' I'm guessing you meant counsel." She looked further and stopped herself, like an impatient schoolmarm. "No, no, here," she pushed the papers toward him. "I've circled all the errors, to include the use of waive instead of wave, you can take it back and rewrite it."

She sat back in her chair and looked the men in the eye. "Are you self-taught or a morbidly ignorant product of our public school system?" She wondered suddenly if she'd gone too far and tried to change the mood.

"Either of you gentlemen smoke? I could use a cigarette right now."

The young man jumped to his feet, offering her a cigarette from his case. He quickly lit it for her. She smoked while she considered the two men. She looked at Curtin replacing his cigarette box and wiggled her finger, commanding that he surrender it to her. He complied and she emptied it of most of the cigarettes. She returned it to him.

"I'm still not clear about why you two are here. You're based in California and could have resolved all of this with Mr. George in Arizona, yet you've traveled the continent to speak to a nineteen-year-old Mexican. What do you want?"

"Miss Del Toro, it is a matter of land use versus outright purchase. We want to purchase your land, not just use it. But Mr. George wouldn't hear of it. It's quite unstable down there right now. There's no telling what will happen; anarchists, socialists, anything could happen. Why not just sell us the land outright? We are prepared to give you one hundred thousand dollars for it."

"One hundred times its value." She looked seriously at the men.

"Yes, madam, and enough for you to live comfortably for many years. On your own, with your own funds."

"I see. And why are you being so good to me? Is it my lovely disposition, or are you just smitten?" She batted her eyelashes at them and blew a plume of smoke over the older man's head.

"Miss Del Toro, it is a gamble. We won't deny it's a great gamble. We know it but we know that you are a savvy businesswoman. We won't deny, either, that our studies have been promising. We believe we could extract upwards of a million dollars in oil from the land."

"Hah! More like ten or a hundred million or more. And, while I am thinking of it, why is nothing mentioned in that pathetic excuse for a contract you've shown me about gas rights or minerals?"

"Gas rights? Don't know that there's ever anything in the contracts about gas rights, Miss."

"Oh, you've not heard of the Coal Lands Acts? Are you actually in the oil business, Mr. Talking Horn, or is this some sort of hobby for you?"

"Miss Del Toro!" He finally stood up. He'd had enough. "I have been patient with you. My company has offered a generous compensation for some, frankly, worthless grazing land in the middle of a country in the midst of a revolution. You've done nothing but insult me and my associate since we arrived."

"I have actually not insulted him. He's been a perfect gentleman, and he's handsome." She gave him a wink. "You, on the other hand, have attempted to go around my lawyer and steal the land that my poor late uncle spent a lifetime robbing, marauding and rustling to make into a proper little empire. Now you want me to sell it to you for a fraction of what it's worth in oil and gas and, likely, gold. Well, that is not going to happen, sir. Not to mention what would happen to the people who call the land home, anyway. I have many families who rely on the place. I can only imagine what you'd do to them if you had full control of the property."

She finished her cigarette and her speech. She looked at the young man.

"May I have another?" Curtin looked down at the pile of cigarettes on the blotter in front of her, grinned, and opened his case again.

She took one and lit it and blew smoke onto Madame Boutin's desk. "Sit down, gentlemen. Let's work this out." The old man did as he was ordered.

"It's very clear, crystal clear. I've made it perfectly clear to you that the land is not for sale, so there's an end to it. I don't want to hear another word about it. However, I have a great interest in leasing gas and oil rights to you, exclusively, if you still want them."

The man spoke into his lap. "We do."

All right, then. Take this back and rework it." She patted the document in front of them. "Make it right and get it to Dan George. He knows what I want and he'll complete the contract. This way, you can go back to California and save yourselves another trek across the continent."

She stood up and walked around the desk. She stood before the old man as he and his companion quickly rose. She extended her hand. He shook it. She looked at the young man and extended her hand to him. "You don't look like a lawyer or a clerk."

"No ma'am, I'm an engineer." He smiled broadly at her.

"It's rich, isn't it?"

"Yes ma'am." He saw his companion stiffen out of the corner of his eye but didn't care. "It's rich as all hell, ma'am."

Curtin looked at his watch. Six o'clock, right on the money. Thankfully, the old man was always in his cups by six. He could get away from him then. Tolkenhorn was especially drunk this evening. He was hissing at his companion who looked around as the old fool was particularly animated.

"That little bitch." He glared at Curtin, eyes fierce, not yet bleary, but bloodshot and angry. Called me a philistine! Me!"

"Bohunk."

"What?"

"Bohunk. She called you a bohunk, not a philistine, she said you were… "

"Enough. Don't care. Little bitch. I was trying to do her a favor."

Curtin stood up. He usually put the man to bed but he didn't feel like helping him this evening. He looked around the lounge of the Emerson Hotel. It was a grand place. He was going to have a good dinner, a good cigar, and go to bed. The young woman had put him in a good mood. He stood up and walked away from the old man.

Robert Curtin would be twenty-nine on his next birthday. He had planned to be a millionaire by thirty, but that had not yet panned out. He was a happy man, nonetheless. He'd worked hard, nearly made a fortune in Alaska and almost lost his life. He loved traveling and adventure. He was fearless but unimpressive looking. He was handsome but not manly. He was quiet but not shy. He'd rather listen than be heard.

He swore off adventuring after nearly meeting his Maker, then just as quickly changed his mind and jumped at the opportunity in Mexico. It was an exotic land; full of excitement, in the throes of revolution, civil war and strife. The people were exotic and interesting and he thought it might be the place where everything would come together for him. He loved it.

He made a choice from the menu and, while he ate, thought of the young woman. What a live-wire. She was incredible, beautiful, saucy, articulate. He was pleased that he'd be working for her, even if he'd likely never see her again. Her land was good from an oil perspective.

He liked the big Indian lawyer in Bisbee, too. He was a good lawyer, a good judge of character and Curtin knew that he hadn't painted the young engineer with the same brush he'd used on the old man.

That was a peculiar quality about Curtin. Even though he had to associate with the fool Tolkenhorn, no one seemed to treat him as if he was the same kind of colossal ass. And it was also why he was sent everywhere with the old man. The fellows at headquarters knew Tolkenhorn well enough, and they knew that Curtin, a man almost one third his age, could keep him in line.

Not that Curtin liked or trusted the headquarters men, either. He essentially trusted no one. It was interesting that a man who was so young should be so cynical. He learned early on that the only one looking out for him was him.

He trusted no one. He knew their games. He knew most of the big mining outfits would sell you down the river for a dollar. It's how he nearly died. They sent him on a suicide mission and he gladly went along, too young and too green to know any better.

Well, he knew better now, and he didn't care what they liked or didn't like. He was a good engineer; he could find work wherever he wanted. He certainly wasn't going to let them take advantage of him again and he'd be keeping an eye on the young woman's situation, as well. Not that she needed his protection. It was very likely, to his mind, that woman never needed protecting by anyone.

He wasn't really surprised about the young woman. He had known what to expect and she did not disappoint him. That dope, Tolkenhorn, was both surprised and disappointed. He thought he'd waltz right in there, get some silly, frilly, self-absorbed rich girl to hand the place over to him just by waving a few dollars in her face. The old fool paid no attention to anything. He was clueless.

But Curtin learned, observed, and knew all about the young woman. He learned about her while he was working at the hacienda. He definitely knew. He'd seen enough of the culture down there to know that she was one-of-a-kind. He heard it in the reverent tone of the people living on the ranch. He could see the love for her in their eyes. Her people were unique; the way she ran the place was unique. The people were happy, engaged, empowered. If only all of Mexico was run the way the young woman's ranch was run, there'd be no revolution.

He looked at his watch again. He thought about taking a cab, looking her up at the school. Just chat, be in her presence. He wasn't attracted to her in a sexual way and he was surprised by that. And it wasn't because of her age. She was old enough and wise beyond her years.

He was awed by her, by her intense power and control. She was impressive, attractive to him in a way no woman, especially a beautiful one, had ever been. She was something different and he found himself grinning foolishly at the thought.

But he didn't go look her up. Instead, he settled for a cigar and bed. He couldn't wait to get back to the lady's hacienda and start making her millions. In a sudden flurry of energy he got up, dressed, packed, went to the front desk and checked out. He scribbled a note to Tolkenhorn and gave it to the clerk. He'd take a train to New York, get a berth on the next steamer to Tampico and get to work. He couldn't bear the thought of spending time with Tolkenhorn on a train overland.

Winter passed quickly into spring and the girls were having a time. In short order they'd graduate, a year overdue because Madame Boutin and Abuelita had convinced them to stay on to help the younger ones with their French and Latin rather than for their own preparation for college. The reality of it was that the two old matrons couldn't stand to have the girls leave. They had convinced them to stay just one more year.

They planned to spend a leisurely summer in Paris then go on to Smith. Rebecca was giddy with excitement. She loved to travel, loved France and loved to be doing things with her sister. And Marta could relax now, as well. The hacienda was settled. Dan George was making regular visits to check on the overseer of the ranch as well as the men from the mining company. The strikes had been rich and money was flowing generously to everyone. If the Revolution would settle down, all would be right in Marta's world.

Marta had been fairly well behaved through the winter and spring, only slipping off half a dozen times to the seedier streets of Baltimore for a few late night trips to the Gaiety, a couple of all-night forays into the back alley dance halls down in Washington, and a couple of cold nights spent up in New York.

She even took a sleeper train all the way to Montreal with two young college men from Georgetown. Regrettably, according to her journal, nothing happened, though. Most men were terrified of Marta. All in all, despite the inappropriateness of her shenanigans, nothing happened that could get Abuelita's heart rate up—or her bankroll down—had the grandmother ever found out about any of it.

Rebecca was always waiting for her. She'd never be cross, never lecture, never ask questions. She knew her sister had a compulsion as strong as a human being's need to breathe and she'd never try to stop her. She wouldn't try to stop her but she wouldn't go with her, either. Rebecca didn't want to know what Marta was up to when she went away, couldn't bear to be in the places Marta sought out.

Marta possessed an insatiably curious mind and it often sought the lonely, ugly places of the human condition. She was a sort of anthropologist in these matters; objective about them, never caught up or weakened by them. She was searching for some kind of lesson or truth in these forays, and always returned unscathed. It was as if Marta was reliving the days spent with Sombrero del Oro, the days with the savage bandits, and everything she'd endured. Marta once confessed that she was a voyeur, assuring Rebecca that she'd never put herself in harm's way, but was fascinated by the self-destructive pastimes of human beings. She liked to see people on the edge, behaving badly, being dangerous, reckless, squandering their lives. She studied it, analyzed it, used it as her own form of therapy from the degradations she'd suffered in her early life.

The only exception to this was her adventure that spring; sneaking in to ride the Maryland Hunt Cup. It was a fantastic notion, preposterous because the officials would never knowingly allow a woman to participate. Marta did it with Rebecca's help.

They'd bribed the smallest jockey, Jake Spencer, into allowing Marta to ride in his place. It was thrilling and dangerous. The jumps were high—too high—and more deadly than any other steeplechase in history, in the world. Marta ate them up. She and Tippy took every jump as if it was no more than a shrub in Abuelita's back courtyard.

It was a grand little scheme and they pulled it off without a hitch. Marta would have won, too, but she knew her identity would have been revealed at the winner's circle and she didn't want to embarrass Abuelita or Jake. So she held her beloved Tippy back and gave way at the last two jumps, sensing the frustration in her mount. The animal wanted so badly to win, knew they could, and couldn't understand why she wasn't allowed to fly over the last two fences and on to victory.

Marta watched, satisfied, as the much heavier men, with their winded mounts, plodded past her. She could have won the damned thing riding side saddle.

She came in fifth to the delight of Jake who'd never made it as far. He didn't really want to ride anyway, so it was no great sacrifice on his part. He had, the year before, lost his nerve after watching one of his companions break his neck, waste away in a hospital bed and eventually die.

Jake was yet another victim, not of the Hunt Cup, but of Marta's spell. He carried their secret to his grave in France in nineteen-eighteen at the age of twenty-nine.

Basking in the glow of her success, she thought of her mother who would have been proud of her, both for her performance and for her little deception and decided that one day she'd tell her all about it.

It was just the kind of adventure Chica would love and Marta couldn't wait to tell her.

II Letters

March 1, 1911

Dear Marta:

I am pleased to report that the contract with the Northwest and Union Mining Company has been signed per your instructions. I congratulate you on your handling of Tolkenhorn. He was docile as a kitten. I would have loved to be a fly on the wall at your meeting with him and the engineer. Please do not trouble yourself with the details of the ranch. As I am certain you are aware, there is a lot of trouble brewing in Mexico right now and I strongly advise you stay away from it until things settle down in that part of the world. The ranch appears to be far enough north to avoid any harassment and the staff and their families are all well enough. They are, rightly so, on your side, Marta, and I am certain that, no matter what happens with all the talk of land reform, it will remain business as usual at the ranch.

I will continue to make trips down there as required; however, I am convinced that Adulio will continue to maintain things in good order. He is a good man and can, as always, be absolutely trusted. The drilling has had essentially no impact on the ranching and farming, the corn crop will likely be excellent again, barring any revolutionary activity or drought. Let's hope for a good remainder to the year.

When you have the opportunity, please check your bank account. The first check has arrived from the oil company and I am confident that you will find it satisfactory.

Your humble servant,

D. George, Esq.

Sevilla, April 5, 1911

My Dearest Darling Girls:

Mamma sends her love. Spain is lovely but we miss you. We are sorry to say we will not be able to meet with you in Paris. Mamma and I will be in Turkey of all places through the summer. Mamma has met a Count who is an amateur artist. He insists on painting your mother's portrait in his studio in Constantinople, (with clothes on...both). Oh well, it is just one of the things I must endure where your mother is concerned. She attracts the strangest people.

Marta, congratulations on your brief vocation as a scullery maid, however, I must admit that we were a bit disappointed in your initial career path, as we've always thought your education would allow you to aspire to grander things. I understand that the gymnasium will be getting a new roof. Please try your best to behave so that we are not also rebuilding the chapel or the dormitories before you are gone from Stonefields.

Enjoy your graduation, girls. We will be at Smith in September to get you settled in there. Have a wonderful summer in Paris. Marta, please do not dismantle the Eiffel Tower or storm the Bastille while you are there. I will keep you up to date on what effect your mother has on the Ottoman Empire.

Love,

Daddy and Mamma

April 25, 1911

Gentlemen:

Enclosed please find receipts for the travel through March of this year. Please also find the latest reports from the Del Toro estate. It is still our, Curtin's and my, opinion that the outright purchase of this property will be in the best interest of all parties. Forthwith, we will redouble our efforts to affect the purchase of the tract of land. While she is very strong willed, the young woman who owns the land should be rather easily persuaded. Forthwith, we will move forward with this plan. Please advise to the contrary if instructions are to change. Forthwith, we will continue to report our progress.

Please find, additionally, the proposal per my conversation with Mr. Talbert on the 5th of the month last. The contract is straightforward enough, and the understanding is that Curtin and I will receive the increased percentage on the yield when the purchase is legally in the hands of the Northwest and Union Mining Company.

Yours Sincerely,

M. Tolkenhorn, Esq.

April 29th, 1911

Dear Alice:

Just a note, darling, to tell you how much I enjoyed our dinner last week. We must do this more often, dear. I have to tell you that the loss of my two darlings is giving me such anxiety. I fear my heart is breaking. I have difficulty believing that Rebecca and Marta have been in my care for these past ten years. They have been the single significant source of my joy and happiness. I am crying at the writing of this and have given myself a headache over it. Please come to see me, soon. Friday, or as soon as you receive this letter.

Love,

M. Boutin
Headmistress, Stonefields School for Young Ladies

III Scheming

Miles Tolkenhorn made himself comfortable at Robert Curtin's desk. As always, he brought a bottle and two glasses. Only one was ever needed as Curtin did not drink with his colleague. It was just going on five and the old man was not yet drunk. Curtin welcomed him but ignored him. He still had work to do and he kept to it while he listened to what the lawyer had to say.

"Robert." He poured and gulped and smiled at the engineer. "This is bad business about the Indian getting killed."

"You mean Dan George, the attorney."

"Yes, yes, the attorney, of course."

"Don't know that he has been killed. He's only a little overdue. Could have gotten waylaid, could have a little señorita no one knows about. Why would you think he's dead, Miles?"

"Oh, I'm sure of it, Robert. Sure of it." He gulped again. "This is a mess down here. A real mess."

"I'm not so sure about that either, Miles. Now that Madero is recognized as President, he seems to be getting things in order. He's got Zapata on his side, so far. I don't know that things are so bad."

"Well, they are." The old man snapped, then caught himself and smiled at Curtin. "Look, Robert. I've gotten off on the wrong footing with that young lady and the Indian. I know that now, but, well, I'll cut to the chase. We want this land."

"Oh?" Curtin looked behind him for a file, grabbed it and put it on the desk in front of him. He didn't look up. "Who wants it?"

"We, the company. And I'll tell you, Robert, I've arranged it so you and I get a good cut. How'd you like to be a wealthy man in another year?"

This got Curtin's attention. "What do you mean, you've arranged it?"

"With the boys at the home office. I told them you and I get a bigger percentage of the yield."

"I would rather you not talk to them about me, Miles." He saw the old man's face change. "Not that I don't appreciate it, Miles. I do. Thank you. But I'm satisfied with how things are going. This is making good money for the young woman and the company and you and I are doing okay."

"Well, I'm not." He poured and gulped yet again. "I haven't saved for my dotage as well as I should have, Robert, and I don't know how much longer I can work, my liver's probably as big as a watermelon. I need this." He poured another with shaky hands.

"They aren't interested in selling, Miles. That's an end to it."

"But it would be best for everyone if they did. Mark my words, this place is a powder keg. The Indian dying is just the beginning. These natives have been brewing for a fight, anarchy, for years. It's only a matter of time before some corrupt official, or Villa, or Zapata or some other warlord comes in, takes over, and then the girl will be out, we'll be out, or worse."

Curtin grinned. "You sure know how to cheer a fellow." He suddenly stopped grinning. "Why me, Miles? Why are you being so good to me?" He looked on at the old man's reddening face.

"Look, Robert, I'm no choirboy. I want this land for my own personal gain. I'm not doing this for you, or the company, or the young woman. I'm doing it for me. If we can extract the yield we're getting over the next eighteen months, at the rate I've negotiated, you and I might not have to work again for the rest of our days." He looked into his drink, then up at Curtin. He seemed genuine; he seemed to mean what he was saying. He continued. "Like I said, I didn't handle it well with the girl, but I could see you had her attention. She's not a bad looking little thing. A shade or two darker than I like, but..."

"And I'm to go convince her." He smiled at the memory of the strong willed young woman. "Don't know that I'm up to it, don't know that anyone's up to it."

"You are."

Curtin was beginning to become annoyed, and then caught himself. There was no profit in showing Tolkenhorn any more than he had to. Tolkenhorn didn't have to know everything that was on Curtin's mind. He looked back at the papers on his desk, then looked the man in the eye. "What do you have in mind? Nothing illegal and nothing dangerous."

"Nope, neither of the above, and more importantly, Robert, because I know you, know you have an ugly streak of goodness and decency about you, nothing unethical. Just go back East, that's not so hard to do, things are under control here. Take a nice cruise on the ship back there, stretch it out, stop off in Havana and get yourself a few boxes of good cigars, enjoy yourself a little. You never have any fun, lad. You're a young man. You should enjoy this time in your life. God knows, you feel like hell at my age. So don't waste your youth with your nose to the grindstone. When you get there, tell her about the Indian, tell her what we have in mind."

Curtin blew a long breath through his teeth. "Oh, so I'm the one to tell her that her lawyer and longtime family friend is missing, presumed dead? Nice. I knew there'd be a catch."

"It's bad news, but coming from you will help. You two have a connection, she respects you."

"Right." He stood up and stretched his back. Tolkenhorn would be sloppy drunk in another half hour and Curtin didn't want him falling over in his office. He looked at the old man one more time. He became more serious, more serious than Tolkenhorn had ever seen him to be. "Just understand one thing, Miles. I do have an ugly streak of morality about me, but it wouldn't do to get me riled. Understand?"

Miles thought about grinning, then saw the look in Curtin's eye. He shivered a little and looked back at his drink. "Understood."

IV Portent

Adulio waited in the headmistress's office. He stood erect and formal even though he was alone. He fiddled with the pencil curl on his Homburg and ran a finger under each of his moustaches. He was a twitchy man who'd served Alejandro del Toro faithfully for more than twenty years. When Uncle Alejandro died, Marta made the man the caretaker of the hacienda. He was smart and competent and obsessed with work and order. He was neither tall nor short but always looked diminutive; he carried himself small, kept his eyes to the ground. One would suspect that he was a terrible boss, a terrible leader, and that he would never be able to get things done, but he could. It was very strange, but he always got things done.

He had watery eyes and his lips moved in constant conversation, an audible one when he was speaking to another person, and an inaudible one when he wasn't. It was an odd habit and it amused Marta. She liked him, and out of respect for the strange twitchy little man and out of respect for her beloved Uncle Alejandro, never poked fun at Adulio or made him feel uncomfortable. He was likely the only person in the world who saw Marta act respectfully, articulately, and responsibly, always.

Their conversations were invariably the same, never casual, never unimportant, and Adulio would end every interaction with his young mistress with "A*s you please*." It didn't matter what the subject, command or request, and Marta was amused by this as well. She thought that she could tell Adulio to go and find a stout rafter, throw a riata over it and hang himself and he'd bow, jerk his neck downward the way he always had a habit of doing and say, in his crisp, clipped voice, "A*s you please*," and likely go ahead and do it.

For his trip back East he was dressed impeccably in a cheap wool suit and a tie in the custom of his land. He stood out like a beacon on the outskirts of Baltimore, walking resolutely to his destination, despite the fact that he'd carefully shaved just that day, trimmed his long mustaches and gotten a haircut from a real barber instead of one of the ranch hands. He especially picked a grey Homburg out in Tampico for the journey, but it did nothing to make him fit in. He was a Mexican-Indian through and through and his dark skin, dark from his bloodline and years in the sun, could not be made insignificant by the muted tone of his wool sack suit.

Marta came in, not a little surprised to see him. He'd worked for her for many years and they would see each other perhaps one in every two of those. As far as she could tell, he'd never traveled farther than to Tampico, but here he was, standing in the office in Maryland, waiting for an audience with him.

She moved around him as he stood staring at his hands holding the hat's brim. She sat at Madame's desk and waited for him to sit down. She looked him in his watery eyes and he immediately handed over his pouch with tobacco and papers.

As she deftly rolled a cigarette for herself, and then one for him, she sat back and smoked. Adulio waited. She blew a plume at the ceiling and looked at the glowing cigarette tip with satisfaction. She looked over at her overseer. "What is your business here, Adulio?"

"Señorita," he too stared at the end of his cigarette. "Dan George is missing."

Marta sat up straight in her chair. She was concerned; she loved Dan George as an advisor and a friend. "What do you mean?"

"He was due to the ranch five days ago and he has not yet arrived."

"Did you contact his office?"

"Yes, we did and he left the day he said he would. No one can account for him. Señorita, we fear the worst."

Marta smoked harder. She looked on as Adulio continued. "Señorita, the country is in a terrible state down there, and we fear that the lawyer is dead."

She felt a deep pang. She'd learned to feel sorry for the dead over the past many years. She felt it when the old man died and when her uncle Alejandro and Uncle Bob had died. She now felt it for Dan George. She looked again at the watery eyes.

"And you are certain of this, Adulio? Have any authorities been notified?"

"I've made inquiries, but there is no *real* authority. The army is in shambles, all brutes, then there is Pancho Villa who we are not certain can be trusted. But it could not have been him, he is in jail now." He looked at her as she prepared another cigarette. "And there is something else, Señorita." He waited until she looked him directly in the eye. When he had her full attention he continued. "The oil men. I am not trusting them. I am not certain what it is, but something is happening, something that will make all trouble for us."

"The lawyer?"

"And the young one, the engineer." He watched Marta's eyes. She was taking it all in, reflecting, processing, formulating a plan. He continued.

"The young one, Curtin, is coming to see you. I beat him here by one day. He will be calling on you tomorrow. He and the lawyer, Tolkenhorn, are going to try to convince you to sell."

She waved her hand airily. "They know that won't work, they've tried it."

"But Señorita, I am thinking that they are becoming more persuasive."

"Impatient?"

"Sí, impatient. I am thinking that maybe they could have had some hand in Dan George's disappearance."

"I see." She sat back and considered the man for a moment. She always thought that he was a good man. He was dedicated to the hacienda and dedicated to her. "And why have you come all this way when a wire would have served the same purpose?"

"I want to warn you and ask you to come home. This man, Curtin, will try to persuade you to sell the land and move on. He will tell you that Dan George is dead and that the land is in discord and strife and that you will be better off without it, that it is no place for a young lady and that it is too dangerous."

"I see. And you say the opposite, Adulio?"

"Yes. I know you, Señorita. I know your..." he suddenly became embarrassed.

"My what?" She knew what he was going to say, but pushed him nonetheless.

"Your stock." He looked at his hands and his eyes watered more. "You do not scare easily, Señorita, and you love the land and the people. I know this. I believe you are needed back home, back with us. I just wanted to tell you this thing to your face, because I believe it." He waited and then continued. "It is your place, Señorita. It is your land. Mexico is your land and it is bleeding and it needs strong people such as you. It is time. You are a grown woman. A lovely..." he stopped himself as he was becoming more embarrassed, felt himself fawning over his boss and knew it was not the proper thing to do. "Señorita, you can live a life of leisure, I know this. You can go off and live and enjoy yourself and want for nothing for the rest of your days, but something larger is in store for you."

He was talking nonsense now, but it was from the heart. He suddenly looked up again with his watery eyes. "I am sorry to speak so freely, Señorita. I love the land and it is time you take your rightful place as the hacendada. Make the powerful ones see that there are good hacendados, make the anarquistas and the others who want to tear the land apart, tear the people apart, understand that the system can work. Not the way it worked under Díaz, but the way it worked for many years for your Uncle Alejandro," he crossed himself and kissed his fingers, "and the way you have made it work." He watched her tap the ash from her cigarette and continued. "Please Señorita, please come home."

With that he stood up, held his hat brim with both hands now, appearing like an overgrown rodent sitting on its haunches, looking on at something that might do it harm. He bowed reverently and waited, uncomfortable, as if the speech was now over and someone should come in to physically remove him, help him from the stage.

Marta stood up. She considered him. He made her think about the things that had been eating at her for a long time. It *was* time and she knew it.

Curtin was cold. Freezing cold and exhausted as he lay in a snow bank out of the wind. He slept and waited and after a long time the rescue party found him. They bundled him up and rushed him back to base camp and he lived. He lived and warmed up and didn't lose any toes. He regained his vision after two days and began to eat heartily after three. All the men in his party were dead. He was the leader and the strongest and took the initiative to go after help and leave them and his decision cost them all their lives and the preservation of his own.

So, his selfless act was selfish and self-serving and there was not a little whispering around the place. It was a heavy burden to carry for a man who'd not reached his twenty-fourth year.

He got up and closed the window. It was unusually cold for a June morning in Baltimore and as he kicked off the covers, was fully exposed, not used to the cool weather farther north. He had the same dream every time he got a little cold in his sleep. He looked at his watch, four forty-five on the dot; it was the same every day. He could never sleep beyond four forty-five.

He got dressed and ate a good breakfast. The Emerson was beginning to be his favorite hotel. He looked at his watch and read three newspapers. He decided to walk the five miles to the school. By nine he was ready for his audience with the pretty young woman. He checked his papers, they were all in order. He checked on the cigarettes again. He'd gotten her half a dozen packs of what he hoped were a brand she would like.

She was especially cool to him and he didn't know why. She took the cigarettes and thanked him for them, then took one from his case and they smoked together in silence for a while.

In a bold move he got up, walked to the window and closed the blinds. The sun would not blind him now. He walked back to his chair, adjusted it upward so that they'd be looking eye to eye. He sat down and gave her a friendly smile.

"I suppose you're wondering why I'm here, ma'am."

She didn't respond. She smoked aggressively, blew great clouds at him until they were regarding each other through a significant haze. He continued.

"Something is going on, ma'am. Something that I am not certain about, but know it's not right."

"What do you mean?" She sat forward in her chair. This was getting interesting.

"Tolkenhorn's got some scheme going. He wants me to convince you to sell out. He's convinced that he'll make a great fortune and he's trying to convince me that he's got your best interest in mind." He looked at the end of his cigarette and continued. "I'm not so convinced of all that."

"I see." She thought about Adulio's warnings and was a little confused. Whom could she trust now? "And what is in all this for you? You're not just some messenger boy."

"No, I'm not. He cut me in on the bonus that would be paid if we got the land away from you. I'd likely make a lot of money."

"And you don't like money."

"I like money well enough. But that doesn't mean I'm planning to rob a bank or take advantage of you. Don't want to earn my fortune that way, ma'am."

She waved him off, airily, dismissively and lit another smoke. "Stop calling me that. Call me Marta. God, you're not that much older than me. Ten years?"

"Well, not even, not quite." He felt a little self-conscious at that. He felt more akin to her and closer to her age. A ten year difference made him feel like an old man and he still held out some preposterous hope, the kind of primordial or instinctive attraction, that any beautiful women held over a man.

"What do you think I should do?" She commanded.

"I don't know. Frankly, ma'am…Marta, I don't know what to tell you. I don't know what you want."

"What if I were to tell you that I want to go back down there and take my place as the hacendado. Take an active role in running the place and take an active role in the revolution and see if I can try to help bring some order down there?"

"Then I'd say you shouldn't sell."

"Oh, you wouldn't tell me that it was no place for a girl? That I should take the money and live out my days wasting away as do the idle rich, running up and down the Italian Riviera or some other nonsense?"

"No, I wouldn't say that to you, and I don't see you as a girl. And I don't imagine you scare very easily. No doubt this is a dangerous time for Mexico. I'm not going to tell you that you won't possibly meet your end down there, like Mr. George has. But…"

"Do you really believe he's dead?"

"I don't know, but it's logical to think he is."

"What if I told you that I've heard talk that you and Tolkenhorn had something to do with that?"

Robert Curtin thought about that. He knew where she'd heard it and now wondered how much she knew already about all that was going on down there.

"I'd tell you—try to assure you—that I didn't. I can't speak for Tolkenhorn. Frankly, I would put nothing past the man, but I don't know that he has the guts for committing murder."

"And how about you? What kind of guts do you have, Mr. Curtin?"

"Robert. Please call me Robert. I don't know that either, Marta."

"You're not afraid to be in Mexico, though."

"No. Not really."

"Have you ever killed a man?"

He laughed at the question. It sounded funny, a little old fashioned. He responded without hesitation. "I've killed many." He waited for her reaction. She looked up from her cigarette and into his eyes. She was a little impressed. "Alas, Marta, not the way you think. I've never outright killed a man, shot him or stabbed him or bludgeoned him. But I've been responsible for the deaths of a work party." He took a drag on his cigarette. "I was cleared of all wrong doing, of course, not malicious or even incompetent. But that was a long time ago and I've gotta live with it."

"I see." She looked at her watch and stood up. "What are you doing next?"

"Going to New York, taking the next ship back."

"And when is that?"

"Tuesday."

That night in bed, Marta called to Rebecca, lifting the covers for her to crawl in next to her. Rebecca complied and lay next to her sister. It was always the same with Marta. Whenever she had important things to discuss with Rebecca it was always after lights out, and always in bed. Marta felt the weight of it on her and it bothered her considerably all day. They'd not been apart since the horrible kidnapping of Rebecca some ten years ago. They were constant companions and Marta owed everything to her adopted sister. They'd been together so long that Rebecca could read the young woman's mind. She rested her head on the pillow and waited.

"I've got to go to Mexico, Rebecca."

"Oh?" They'd both followed the news carefully since the beginning of the troubles. The whole family had discussed it and it was decided, ordered by Arvel and Chica, that none of them would go to Mexico until things calmed down. They'd even ordered Dan George to stop checking on the ranch but he apparently had not listened, and now he was missing. Rebecca thought of these things as she considered Marta's declaration.

"I've been talking to one of the men from the mining company, and Adulio came to see me as well."

Rebecca sat up, leaned on an elbow and looked into the dark, in the direction of Marta's voice. "Here? He came here to see you?"

"Yes. Strange, isn't it? Didn't know he would ever leave Mexico. That's why I've got to go."

"Abuelita and Mamma and Daddy will be furious."

"They're not going to know. You'll go on to Paris and tell them I'm with you. You'll do this for me, won't you, Rebecca?"

"No." She could feel the energy leave her adopted sister's body. Could just as well feel the look she had on her face. She waited.

Marta breathed deeply, the remnants of the cigarettes still on her breath. She began to speak when Rebecca continued. "I'm not *going* to Paris, darling." She fell back onto the pillow and stared up into the darkness. "Because, I'm going to Mexico."

V Going Home

Rebecca wandered the decks of the Seguranca. They'd arrived at the docks on the East River ten hours before they were to set sail. They didn't want anyone to know they had changed their plan to spend the summer in Paris and that meant arriving as if they were still planning to cross the Atlantic. Their host was a cousin who'd proven at least as naughty and precocious as Marta. She was twenty-three and newly married to an investment banker. She was simultaneously heartbroken and enthralled by the news that the girls were headed to Mexico. She promised to keep their secret and send false news, keep it flowing to both Abuelita and their parents through summer.

Marta had no idea what she'd do once she'd arrived at the ranch, and didn't even know how long they'd be in Mexico. She decided she wouldn't worry about that now. She'd worry about it when it was time to start at Smith in the fall. A thousand things could transpire between now and then.

Rebecca never considered not going along with Marta's plan. Ever since the two girls had met at Sombrero del Oro's improvised camp in the desert after Rebecca's abduction from the train wreck, they had been as close as two girls could be; closer than twins. Rebecca abdicated to Marta's more aggressive attitude about life. She seemingly held back and made sacrifices; at least, what most would consider sacrifices. She, with her fair skin and light blue eyes, only her blue-black hair suggesting her Mexican heritage, could have easily fit in with the upper strata of society in Baltimore. But, with Marta always present, her Indian ethnicity obvious, both girls were spurned by the socialites. Rebecca wouldn't have it any other way.

Now her dark sister was taking her into the bedlam of a country in revolution. To a ranch that was far off the beaten path, far from the comforts she'd known for the past ten years, to a land that had more than likely claimed the life of one of their dearest and oldest friends.

And yet, oddly, Rebecca was excited for the adventure, sad for lying to Abuelita and scared at the thought of what her mother would do when—not if—she found out. Her mother always found out.

Daddy was a different story. He worried about them, worried about them more than anything else worried him in life, but he'd never get angry; never ever had he admonished them for any infraction they had done. He was completely and unrepentantly in love with his girls and determined to support them in whatever they pursued, dangerous or not.

Rebecca leaned out over the rail, looking down at the forward deck. A few other early passengers were milling about. It was a lightly booked cruise and they'd have a lot of the ship to themselves. She breathed in, smelled the sharp pungency of the East River, the tar coating the wood pilings and pier, the fuel burning off from the stacks. She felt the ship under her feet, the slightest motion; she loved sea travel and could not wait to get underway.

As she looked on, a young man caught her eye. He was a fine looking fellow, a bit older, likely late twenties. He was engaged in a lively conversation with a little girl and it made her feel good to see a gringo being so nice to a child that was, from the appearance of her outfit, a Mexican and of very modest means.

The little girl's mother was nearby and could be seen, guarded but pleased, that the man was being so pleasant to her child. She was dressed in the old style, a long rebozo wrapped about her. She opened it momentarily to make an adjustment and a strong breeze off the river caught it, pulling it from her grasp and sending it ocean ward. The young man lunged for it, dramatically, looking silly, caught it and wrestled it to the ground as if it were some fantastic sea serpent thrown up onto the deck from below.

The little girl caught his meaning and laughed at the funny man as he finally got control of the errant material and returned it to its owner. He made a grand bow as he completed his performance, not knowing he had an audience above. He patted the child on the head and pulled some manner of treat from a pocket and was just as quickly on his way.

Rebecca moved about the ship as she waited to leave. She was fascinated by mechanical things. Her uncle Bob inspired her in this respect as he'd early on purchased one of the first automobiles in Arizona. They'd spend hours tinkering with the thing and Rebecca even helped him rebuild the engine once, from some schematics they'd gotten from the manufacturer.

She made her way below decks, heading in the direction of the engine room when she heard a man's voice call out after her.

"Marta?"

She turned to find the rebozo wrestler close behind. He quickly recovered from his blunder. "Oh, I *am* sorry, Miss. From behind, you look like my employer."

He had pretty eyes. Blue eyes, like hers, like her father's. She liked that he referred to Marta as his employer. He had a nice smile. "Mr. Curtin?"

"Yes." He was confused that she would know his name, then smiled sheepishly.

She extended her hand. "I'm Rebecca Walsh. Marta is my sister."

"Oh, oh, I see. So, she's…, you've both decided to go back home."

"Yes." It felt funny to her to think of it as going back home, but it was. It was more so for Marta, but it was for Rebecca, as well. She was half Mexican and it *was* her home.

"I like mechanical things, Mr. Curtin. I was just wandering about, hoping to see the engines. The captain welcomed me to go about as I wished. Would you care to join me?"

They did wander about together and Curtin enjoyed his new companion. She knew a lot about ships and he let her show off a little. He was impressed with her already and he'd known her less than an hour.

At one point he took her hand as he followed her over some steam lines. She was helping him and it felt natural. It felt good and natural to see a woman so at ease in such an environment and he enjoyed feeling good about her obvious ability to handle herself. He momentarily held her hand, feeling the slightest hint of something more than the casual grip of a steadying hand and it was especially nice. He looked her in the eye and she smiled a lovely smile, to the point of distraction. He stumbled, nearly falling over the big pipes, caught himself, and smiled back.

They made it deeper into the ship until they were assaulted by the odor of something horrible, rotting meat or fish, some kind of carcasses in decay. The stench was particularly appalling, overwhelming, as they moved deeper, peering into a cavernous section of the hold. Something was moving about and halting, labored breathing could be heard. Curtin found a light switch and turned it on.

They simultaneously gasped at the sight laid out before them. Row upon row of sea turtles lay on their backs. Their flippers had been pierced and ropes threaded, one after another, through the slits so that they were tied, immobile, upside-down. The pressure exerted on their lovely almond eyes made them protrude painfully from their orbs; the creatures labored just to breathe. They lay there, their great, ancient heads lolling back and forth, awaiting their fate, awaiting relief from the horrible torture. Some had already succumbed to the mistreatment, and these carcasses were mixed among the living, leaking rotting effluvium from their inner shells.

Rebecca looked at Curtin, furious. *"This is an outrage!"* She looked about them and then again at the young man's face. He did not fully comprehend. It simply would not register in his mind. Why would anyone treat creatures in such a way?

They heard a noise and spied a longshoreman coming toward them. He obviously knew what they were thinking and held up a hand to stop the diatribe he knew was shortly forthcoming.

"I know, I know. Think it's a sin myself."

"Why?" Is all Curtin could say.

"They'll die if you put them on their bellies out of water and no one at the Fulton market will buy dead turtles. Can't make soup out of dead turtles. Ah, well, turtles that've been dead for a while. Gotta be killed fresh. It's an ugly business, folks."

"It's an outrage is what it is." Curtin was disgusted. "Why not slaughter the poor beasts when they're caught and sell the meat?"

"Hah! That's a good one, sir. Refrigeration costs money, ice costs money, and that cuts into the bottom line." He looked beyond them at the mess he'd soon be removing from the hold. More turtles than normal had perished and it was going to be an odorous job.

"Please, folks, this is no place for a lady." He held out a hand to Rebecca who allowed the longshoreman to take her out of the hellish place.

On deck she looked at Curtin who had tears in his eyes. He didn't want her to see him so emotional and recovered as best he could. He looked at the man who was already going about his business, preparing to remove the terrible cargo. He was, in a way, the poor beasts' savior. At least in death they would no longer continue to suffer. Curtin called out to him.

"Can you take me to a telephone?" He reached out and shoved some bills into the man's hand.

"Follow me."

Curtin grabbed Rebecca by the hand and followed. In short order they were in a little shack near the loading dock. The man left them there and went on about his business. They were alone now.

Curtin pulled Rebecca into the shack with him. He held onto her hand, wouldn't let it go. They were only inches apart. She could feel him breathe, feel his breath on her face as he waited for the call to go through. As she waited, she realized she didn't want to change her position or move away from him, she wanted to stand in the little shack with him for the remainder of the afternoon.

"Abe? Bob Curtin... Yes... Yes. Good to hear your voice, too, old friend... Yes, yes. Are you still with the papers, Abe?... Good. Good. Can you come down to where the Seguranca's docked?... Yes, right, Ward Line, headed out in a few hours to Nassau then Tampico... Right... Pier..., wait a minute." Rebecca reluctantly pulled herself away, stepped out, and looking down the pier, saw the number.

"Fourteen."

"Pier fourteen, Abe. Got a good one for you. Cruelty to turtles... Yes, yes... I know it sounds silly but you've gotta see this... Okay, hurry, they're taking them off now, heading to the Fulton Market. Hurry, Abe."

He absent mindedly reached out and took Rebecca's hand, pulling her in close, so close that he could smell her hair. He held onto her as he finished his conversation. After he hung up the receiver he looked her in the eye. He could not contain himself any longer and pulled her into his arms, kissing her gently on the mouth.

"I'm sorry." He suddenly thought better of what he had just done.

Rebecca smiled coyly and said, "I'm not."

They returned to the ship. Rebecca felt strange. Her head was fairly spinning from the kiss and the hand holding. This lovely man was so kind and sensitive, yet so decisive in his actions. They stood on deck and the little movement of the ship made her feel ill. She looked at Curtin and smiled weakly; she could see the concern in his eyes. "You don't look so good, Miss Walsh."

"Oh, I'll be all right in a moment. Let's sit for a while."

They found some deck chairs and Curtin got her some water. She looked better now. They sat quietly and Curtin smoked downwind of his companion. He had only just stopped shaking, himself. He gave her a little smile.

"Abe is a friend from school. He's been a reporter for the Times for a while. He did a big piece on cruelty at the racetrack a couple of years ago. I knew right away he'd be the man for this one. I hope he gets here soon enough. Sure he will."

He waited for Rebecca's response. She smiled at him and sat back. She was feeling better now. He took her hand again.

It was clammy, cold despite the warmth of the late spring day. He continued to prattle on. He looked at her again.

"Miss Walsh, I apologize. I was out of line kissing you back there."

"Rebecca, please. And you are Bob?"

"I prefer Robert. Boys at school called me Bob, but I prefer Robert."

She looked at him again. Those eyes. She looked at his hand holding hers. He had nice hands. They were rough, the hands of a laborer, yet he was a gentleman, an engineer. He had the hands of a rancher.

"So, can you forget about my little indiscretion, Rebecca? I'm no cad, ma'am. I don't do that sort of thing. You are a fine lady, a fine person, and I should not have taken such a liberty. It's just…"

"Robert."

"Yes, Rebecca?"

"You talk too much." She leaned over and gave him a long, passionate kiss. Now they were both dizzy. "Mr. Curtin, that was the second kiss of my life. I'm not that kind of girl."

Marta refused the first stateroom offered. It had two individual beds and she preferred one. The girls always slept together when they could. They'd done this since they'd met and slept best when they were together. She had just finished arranging a bouquet of roses when Rebecca finally tracked her down.

"You've gotten us a new room, darling? And it comes with flowers." She walked over to admire Marta's handiwork.

"Oh, no." She looked at her sister. "I see why you're so pale. You're love sick."

"You're silly, I'm not pale." She blushed. How could Marta know she had been kissing a strange man? She looked into the mirror to check as Marta read the card.

"Robert." She grinned at her sister. "How can you be on deck for fewer than six hours and get a man's attention so quickly?"

"It's Mr. Curtin."

"Oh, you little devil. I was saving him for myself. He's a fine looking fellow. And good. He's a good one, dear. How did you get him so quickly?"

"I didn't *get* him." She looked at the flowers and the card, just to make certain Marta was correct. She was.

Rebecca suddenly felt faint. She plopped herself down on the edge of the bed. The color was fading from her face.

"What *is* the matter?" Marta got her a glass of water and began fanning her briskly.

"No, nothing. It's just… we found turtles."

"Turtles? In the river?" Marta was genuinely confused. She began undressing her sister and pushed her gently back onto the bed. She pulled her shoes off and opened a porthole.

"No, down below decks. In the hold. They were transporting them up from the Caribbean. It was horrible, Marta."

"You mean foodstuffs? They are for slaughter?" Marta shook her head knowingly. Her sister had such a kind heart.

"It doesn't matter if they're to be eaten, Marta. It doesn't mean the animals should be treated cruelly. They shouldn't treat any creature in such a way."

"And this has gotten you in such a state?"

"That and the whole issue of lying to Abuelita. She was so happy to see us off and we've lied to her. A big lie. I know you've lied to her over the years, but this is different, Marta." She felt better now that she was off her feet. She looked at the roses. "And, Curtin… he kissed me."

"No!" Marta feigned shock. It was not an issue for her, but she could see it was for Rebecca. "Darling, your first real kiss!"

"Oh, Marta. He's wonderful. He had a tear in his eye because of the turtles. And he made it right. He contacted a friend from the papers. There will be cruelty charges, no doubt." She was beaming now and the color was coming back into her cheeks.

"You rest." Marta kissed her forehead. "We're casting off in another hour. I'm going for a walk." She was gone.

Marta watched New York go by as the ship moved through the East River and up through the Long Island Sound. She had smoked all her cigarettes by the time they passed Block Island to her left. She wandered over to the starboard side and watched Montauk steadily glide past them. They passed through Block Sound and were finally out to sea.

Marta mentally shook her head at the strangeness of the English language. Here they were, setting forth across the sea, yet it was called the Atlantic Ocean. Deep in a secret part of her soul there resided a bit of a romantic and she thought it would be so much more adventurous—okay, even romantic—to say 'going out to sea,' or 'seafaring.' No one ever said ocean faring. One might say ocean bound, but somehow that didn't sound right. Marta was more comfortable considering herself at sea; finally out to sea. Who knows? Maybe they'd touch the edge of the Sargasso? Then they'd really be at sea. They might strike some hidden rocks like in Hodgson's book. Maybe they would encounter sea monsters!

She looked at her watch realizing she was hungry.

She made her way through the service areas of the ship, the area where the ship's personnel would not want or expect to find a lady. She always did that, no matter where she went: on a ship, in a restaurant, at a hotel, she always wandered where she shouldn't. There was something about rule breaking that Marta liked. She soon walked up on several young men lounging on boxes, smoking and shooting the breeze. They were not on guard. She should not have been there to see them doing nothing.

They were startled by her presence and jumped to their feet. She nodded and encouraged them to relax and sit back down. She asked for cigarettes and three men jumped to attention, packs out in extended hands. She took one and let them light it for her, sat back on a box and smoked as she rested a foot on the middle rung of the rail, her skirt, not necessarily by accident, rode up and revealed her leg to the knee. She wore no stockings. She spoke to them in Spanish as they were all

Mexicans. They began to relax and exchange pleasantries with the pretty young lady.

"Any of you boys know where I can get some mollejas?" One of the fellows, a cook in the galley, nodded energetically and excused himself. In short order he had a beautiful plate of gizzards to present to her. The others laid a table for her right out on the deck, replete with white table cloth, silver, and a glass of Fronsac.

The young cook bowed proudly as he presented her the meal, "Mollejas En Chile Verde, Señorita."

She ate with gusto. They were delicious and she hadn't had such excellent peasant food in more than a year. "Gracias, Señor, muchas gracias."

They were enjoying her company until the chef appeared. He was astonishingly agile for such a big man. They once again jumped to attention and waited for his reaction to the unorthodox treatment of their unusual guest.

He looked at each of them in turn and then at Marta. His entire body went rigid, as if he were preparing to have some sort of fit. He then clicked his heels, bowing at the waist. "Madam!"

"Sir!" She reached up with her free hand and gave a little salute.

The chef, a German, scrutinized the food on her plate. He looked into it, stared as if some secret message had been mixed among the gizzards and peppers. He looked the young woman in the eye, then, with a flourish and great pomp, produced a fork from inside his coat. "With your permission."

Marta nodded.

He took up a solitary gizzard on the fork, stared at it, examined it, smelled it, then popped it into his mouth. He rolled it around as if tasting a mouthful of vintage port. He tasted, looked up at the sky, closed his eyes, said nothing. Chewed some more and finally swallowed.

"Is good, madam?"

"Quite."

"You are from the land, madam?"

"I am."

"This is good, madam?"

"Quite."

He looked around at the Mexicans. They were standing, stiff, as if preparing for the gallows. This was their first cruise with the new German chef.

"Who made this?"

He waited. "Come, come, boys, who made this for the lady?"

The cook finally stepped forward.

"You?"

"Yes, sir."

"And the wine pairing?"

"Yes, yes, sir."

The chef stepped back and looked at the fine table laid next to boxes of cabbages. He looked again at Marta who'd now resumed eating.

"And this is good, madam?"

"Very good, Chef. You are a lucky chef." She stood up to shake his hand. "Marta del Toro."

He took her hand and shook it gently. He bowed again and clicked his heels.

"Max Von Mayerling, madam. I am the chef on this vessel. At your service, madam."

"Well, Max. Why don't you join me?" She looked at the cook. "Señor, would you have enough for the chef?"

He did and ran back to the galley. He returned in short order and put a plate in front of the old man and they dined together as the sun set. He was a nice man despite his severe military bearing. The Mexicans all wandered off, except for the cook who stood by to pour wine as needed.

The German looked at Marta, into her eyes and asked, "Madam...?"

"Marta."

"Marta, the boys are afraid of me. Why is this?"

"Are you serious? Come now, Max. Look at yourself. You look like you swallowed two of them for lunch. You're big.

And your name is Max. You're bald. You look like a holy terror."

He grinned. "But I am not."

"These muchachos, they're poor, Max. This is likely the best job they've ever had or could ever get. It is the job of a lifetime. They don't want to lose it."

He smiled at Marta. "Miss Marta, you are not afraid of me."

She harrumphed. "Hah! Course not. I'm a paying customer on this ship. You *have* to be nice to me."

He looked a little dejected.

"But that's not why I'm not afraid of you." She reached over and grabbed his arm. "You're sweet, Max. I could see it in your eyes the moment you came in. You're a big Teutonic teddy bear."

He glowed as he sat back and finished his wine. "You are an interesting young lady."

"And you are a nice big chef." Removing the napkin from her lap, she stood up and reached out her hand for him to shake. "And you have far too many more important things to do than eat gizzards and peppers with me."

She opened her purse and prepared to hand Max Von Mayerling some cash and then thought better of it. She folded the money in half, creased it, and tore it in two. She called to the Mexican cook and handed one of the halves to him. The other she extended to Max.

"Max, you and your Mexican boys take care of my sister and me on this little trip and I'll give you a lot more of this when we get into port." She held up a cautionary finger. "But you share the wealth. Right, Max?"

Max looked down at his half of the note. He had been handed Clark and the bull's rump. The Mexican cook got Lewis, staring off pensively to the east. The German grinned. He liked her little joke and her proposition.

"Of course, Madam, eh, Marta. Of course."

He stood at attention and bowed again. She held up a hand then pointed her index finger at his feet. "No more heel clicking, Max. This isn't the goddamned Kaiserliche Marine."

Rebecca awoke at eight to the scent of her lovely flowers. She felt the queer twinge in the pit of her stomach again. It wasn't the turtles or Abuelita or the moving of the ship. She dressed quickly as Marta breezed in.

She smiled at her sister. "Feeling better I see."

They were ready to dine by nine. Curtin was there, waiting for them. He jumped to his feet as they entered the dining room. Rebecca was radiant in her best dress and Marta enjoyed watching her sister fall in love.

She realized she was a third wheel and, as was her want, determined to remedy the situation forthwith. She looked at a corner table. A marine captain was dining alone and she'd eyed him earlier in the day. She caught his attention and snapped her fingers a few times, beckoning him over to their table.

He looked around, behind him, to his left and right, making certain she meant him. She did and he casually walked to the party. He was not in the habit of responding to snapping fingers, no matter how beautiful the one doing the snapping; yet he complied.

"Yes?"

"Purser, we've a little problem with our room. We'd like you to speak to the captain about it." He stiffened as she expected he would, straightened his back and looked down at her dismissively.

"Young lady. I'm a captain of United States Marines, not an employee of this vessel."

"Oh, I know you're not, Captain. Settle down, I was having a little tease. Come dine with us. I'm Marta, this is my sister, Rebecca, and this is Curtin, Robert Curtin. We're traveling together."

The captain settled in. He did not enjoy Marta's joke as he was not a man who joked. He was not a man who liked to pursue or have fun. He was Puerto Rican and lived most of his life in Maryland, not more than ten miles from the girls, but they'd never met. He attended the US Naval Academy in Annapolis and had been a marine for six years.

"What's your name, Mister Captain of Marines?"

He stood up and announced his name as if certain it would have a terrific impact on them all. "Pedro del Calle, madam."

"You are mighty dark for a US military officer. Sure you're not a Puerto Rican marine?"

"Marta!" Rebecca was embarrassed. She gave her a warning glare.

"Oh, he knows it, Rebecca." She gave him a devilish grin. "My goodness, you're as dark as me. You're not Mexican, though. I'm guessing an Islander of some kind. Cubano?"

He stiffened again. "Puerto Rico!"

"Ah, sí. I can hear it in your accent." She looked at Curtin who had no idea what she was referencing. "What do you say, Mr. Curtin?"

"Oh, I have to defer to you on this, Marta. I'm no expert on the various dialects of the Latin peoples. I'm just glad that I can get by with my rudimentary Spanish." He smiled at the captain who was beginning to relax a little. He was from a prominent family in Puerto Rico and was not used to such informality. "Where are you going, Captain?"

"Vera Cruz." The man grabbed for his cigarette case and opened it, preparing to put one in his mouth as Marta reached over and plucked it from his hand." He stood, jaw agape at the young woman preparing to smoke in front of him. She was scandalous.

"Oh, settle down, Captain. I'm not stripping naked...yet...just having a cigarette. Nellie Taft does it all the time, in the White House, no less."

They ordered dinner and soon found themselves surrounded by little Mexican men. Everywhere they looked a man hovered; each member of their little party had at least two attendants. It bordered on the absurd as no other guests or tables were staffed in such a way.

Curtin and Del Calle looked about, confused. They did not understand why they were receiving such royal treatment. Before they could ask, the chef arrived in his enormous white hat, adding to his considerable height and giving the appearance of being close to eight feet tall. He bowed to the ladies and could be seen, almost painfully, suppressing an urge to click his heels. He nodded to Curtin and Del Calle. Marta introduced them. He was just as quickly gone, back to the galley to continue his duties.

The men looked at Marta, a little surprised. Rebecca, however, was not. Everywhere Marta went, it seemed, she charmed and had people, especially men, doing their best to make her happy. Marta scrunched up her shoulders a little and looked at the fine meal prepared for her special guests. Marta was a force to be reckoned with.

She looked over at Del Calle. "Captain, it is not much of a trick. Just spread a little money around. Everyone likes you, wants to be your friend, when you have money."

The captain looked down at his food and then up at Marta. "That's a cynical view for a person so young."

"Hah!" She grinned. "It might be cynical, but it's the truth."

After dinner the girls went back to their room to freshen up for an evening of dancing. Curtin and the marine sat and smoked. They were met by the ship's captain who greeted them warmly and with significant formality. He sat down next to them and took a cigarette from Curtin.

"Gentlemen, I need your help. We seem to have picked up a masher. He's seduced a woman in third class. Nothing I want to necessarily share with the ladies on board, but I'd ask you to keep an eye out. Do either of you gentlemen have firearms?"

Curtin did but Del Calle did not. The captain asked the marine to report to his cabin and he'd be given the loan of one.

They sat and smoked a little while, chatted about the cruise, the ship, the weather. As the women approached, the captain excused himself and tipped his hat to the ladies. They sat down and Marta grinned at them. "You look like the Cheshire cat, you two."

Curtin grinned. He loved her nerve, loved the way she could read people and anticipate what they would say and do. He started to explain when the marine spoke up. "Oh, we were just discussing the situation in Mexico, nothing you ladies would find of any interest."

"Oh, *really?*" Marta looked coy. "I see." She looked at Rebecca who knew that it was not a good idea to intellectually dismiss Marta. "And what would a Puerto Rican who's spent most of his life in Maryland know about Mexico and the revolution?"

"Ah, well." The marine was becoming embarrassed. "I just never thought it was a discussion for ladies."

"Oh, I see. We have to worry over our clothing and hair, how to decorate our homes. We needn't concern ourselves with such trifling affairs as world events or politics. Or is it perhaps that we lack the intellect?"

She had the marine's dander up a bit. "No, not at all. My mother has discussed world events many times. It's just the issue in Mexico is particularly difficult to reason out."

"Yes, again, you are saying it is beyond the comprehension of a woman." She put up a hand, "It's okay, Captain, it's okay. Rebecca and I won't worry our pretty little heads over it. We won't ponder the socialist and anarchist threat. That's *your* greatest fear, I'm guessing. You crazy soldiers, looking to find socialists and anarchists under your beds. You think Zapata's one, don't you?"

"Well, yes, of course. No doubt." He looked at her as if she was questioning the turning of the earth.

"Ah, next you'll tell me your source is the Imparcial or any of the worthless Hearst rags." She was showing off a little now. "Tell me, Mister Captain of Marines, how would an anarchist suggest that the current hacendados retain a percentage of their lands? A true anarchist or socialist would dispossess all the moneyed people of all property and turn it over to the state."

"Ah, but you cannot discount the influence of Kropotkin or the school teacher, Sánchez." He countered, a little pleased with himself.

"And you studied Greek philosophy at Annapolis. Does that mean you want to overthrow the United States democratic process and turn our country into a collection of city-states?"

She reached into his jacket and pulled out his cigarette case, lit one for each of them and inhaled deeply. "Look at his plan of Ayala. He is more a Jeffersonian agrarian than he is any anarchist. Give Mexico a chance, Captain. Stay out of it. America can help with silent support and not by meddling in the country's affairs."

She stood up, as if the conversation was beginning to bore her. She won and now she was finished. "Take me out on the dance floor, Captain. You learned to dance at some point in your life, I presume."

He had, and he was a good dancer. Marta was so involved in teasing him that she did not until now realize just how handsome he was. He was way too serious and self-absorbed, but he was handsome and reasonably intelligent—for a soldier. She pulled him too close for decorum but he really didn't mind very much. She wanted to try out a new dance she'd learned in Washington.

"Do you know the Cubanola Glide?"

He did. She began humming the tune the band was playing. "That sounds familiar, an old tune. Let's see, how does it go?"

She began singing, a sultry whisper in his ear:

"Pump away Joseph, do;
Pump away Joseph, do.
Be ready and willing, the kettle be filling,
While I make tea for two.
Get there Joseph, do.
Someday I'll pump for you.
Don't stay there and dandle,
But collar the handle,
And pump away, Joseph, do."

He turned red in the face, quite a feat for a man with such a dark complexion and Marta was again, very pleased. She thought that she might be going too far, but then went ahead a little further.

"Or how about this one:

Ta-Ra-Ra-Boom-De-Ay
Have you had yours today?
He laid me on the couch,
and baby's on his way.

My mommy was surprised
To see my tummy rise,
Now baby's on his way.
Ta-Ra-Ra-Boom-De-Ay..."

Del Calle pushed her away. He jerked his head back. She'd indeed gone too far. "Miss del Toro, *really!*"

She grinned. "Oh, come on, you big marine. You've heard bawdier marching tunes." She grabbed his hand and pulled the other around her waist. "I'm not going to hurt you... much. Don't worry. But I do want you to give me a good kiss."

"What?" He was genuinely flabbergasted.

"A kiss. You know what a kiss is, don't you?"

"Here?" He looked around self-consciously.

"Sure, come on." She took the lead and moved them to a poorly lit place in the room away from the tables and other revelers. "Come on, a good, real, passionate kiss. *Not* what you'd give your mother."

He did and enjoyed it and did it well. She liked it and she liked him. "You're good."

"So now what?" He was becoming interested in this wild creature. She'd given him some ideas.

"Now nothing. Look, Marine, I'm not even certain I like men. Let's try it again."

Curtin stood up and looked at Rebecca. He wanted to kiss her now, but wouldn't do so in such a public place. He looked at their companions and smiled. Del Calle had his hands full. He excused himself.

"Where are you going?"

"The captain warned us about a masher on board. He didn't want to alarm you. I've got to check on a lady in third class."

"I'll go with you." Rebecca stood up and smiled, waved her sister over. Marta and the marine were back in due course. Rebecca relayed the news and told Marta of her plan to go with Curtin to check on one of the ladies he'd met earlier in the day. "Do you have your friend, Marta?"

"Always." She looked back at the marine, grabbed him by the hand and led him back to the dance floor. "Now, let me sing for you a couple of tunes I learned at the Gaiety down on Baltimore Street..."

On deck Curtin grabbed Rebecca by the hand. He pulled her into his arms and kissed her passionately. "I missed you." He kissed her again. She grinned and kissed him back. She loved kissing him.

"We just spent the whole evening together."

"But I couldn't kiss you. I couldn't kiss you." He kissed her again, and reluctantly pulled himself away. "Come on," he grabbed her by the hand. "We've got to check on someone."

"The lady with the rebozo?" She smiled as he looked back at her a little confused. "I was spying on you before we met. You were playing with the little girl."

"Yes, our ship's captain doesn't want a panic, and he's likely to keep it quiet, especially among his less important passengers. I don't want her caught unawares."

They wandered down through the decks and moved steadily toward the third class cabins. Rebecca kept feeling his eyes upon her. She looked every now and again and he was beaming, entranced, enthralled. He remembered what she'd said to Marta in the dining room. "What did you mean by *your friend?*"

"Oh, a little gun my mother gave us a long time ago. She told us to always have it when we were among strange men." She winked at him, gave a little sideways glance.

"Really?" He was pleased and reached over to kiss her again. He leaned back and looked her over.

"Where do *you* keep a gun?"

She gave him a sly grin and reached over, whispered in his ear, so close it tickled. "In my garter, way up high." She laughed as he blushed and kissed him again.

Neither of them noticed the figure in the shadows. The attacker was on them at once, knocking Curtin senseless. The bad man now turned his attention to Rebecca, throwing her into a wall. She worked frantically to pull the derringer from her garter but he was too quick. He was upon her, cutting off her air as he steadily began to crush her windpipe. She squirmed to free herself, but he was too big, too powerful.

Curtin leaped on his back. Reaching around from behind, he grabbed the assailant's nose and tore at his eyes. He fought more savagely than anyone would ever imagine he was capable from his appearance. He managed to pull the man off Rebecca, but the attacker knew how to fight as well. Using his significant girth to full advantage, the ruffian threw himself backward, falling onto his back, pinning and crushing Curtin between himself and the ship's steel deck.

They rolled about as Rebecca gasped deeply. She grabbed her hatpin and, pulling it from her hair, jammed it into the man's left eye, pushing with all her strength until it met the significant resistance of the sphenoid bone. He screamed out in pain and fury, driving Rebecca away with a thrust of his meaty hand. It gave Curtin enough time to beat him several more times on the nose. The man buckled and then, with renewed energy, threw himself once again on the young engineer.

They hurtled toward the outer rail, flipping over it and onto the deck below. Rebecca chased after, trying her best to call for help, but could make no sound through her damaged throat. Curtin was holding his own. He had managed to stun the man, but the miscreant was bigger by forty pounds and Curtin was beginning to tire. The man managed to get on top of Curtin, holding him by the throat, clamping down on Curtin's windpipe as he had done to Rebecca. Robert Curtin was going to die and it would be Rebecca's turn next.

Finally getting to the lower deck, Rebecca looked around desperately. She spotted a fire axe on a nearby wall. She knew if she didn't do something, and quickly, her new-found love would die. Grabbing the axe she raised it over her head and drove the pick end into the back of the cutthroat's head. The blow killed him.

Curtin managed to disengage himself from under the bloody corpse. He rose shakily to his feet, clutching his throat, and leaned over the body, dumbfounded. He looked at Rebecca in disbelief. "*Jesus, woman! Jesus!* I thought your sister was the one to watch!"

Reaching out, he grabbed her and looked at her darkening, bruised neck. He kissed her gently. She was going to be all right.

Rebecca looked at the dead man. She'd not seen a body for many years, yet surprisingly, she was calm. She didn't shake and she wasn't sorry she'd killed the brute. She was proud of Curtin. He was not a large man, especially compared to the animal who'd attacked them, yet he held his own. He had tried his best to protect her and he'd put up a good fight. They had fought for each other.

Reaching over, she pulled the fire alarm. Chaos erupted. She was suddenly angry that this had happened, that they'd let such an animal roam freely on the ship.

Marta was there first, the marine in tow. She grabbed Rebecca by the arm and looked her over. She was appalled at the appearance of her neck. She looked down at the corpse draining blood and brain onto the deck. She looked at Curtin, obviously impressed. He read her mind.

He held up his hands. "Not me, Marta." He indicated her sister with the tilt of his head as he handed her his freshly lit cigarette.

"Oh, sweetheart, *bravo!*" She looked down and saw a glint, a shiny metallic object protruding from the dead man's face. With a grunt and a heave, she rolled the animal over onto his back. She reached down and with a great deal of difficulty, plucked Rebecca's hatpin from the corpse's eye. She wiped it clean on the lapel of the dead man's jacket and handed it to her sister. "That's a nice hatpin, no sense in letting it go to waste."

The captain had arrived by now. He looked around, checked Rebecca over and began barking orders. The ship's physician was called in and attended to the young couple. The captain was impressed. "Anything you would like, Miss Walsh, say it and it's yours."

Rebecca looked at the woman from third class. She'd been roused from her sleep, rebozo and all. Rebecca pointed at her and looked at the captain. "The best available room for her and her daughter."

The man nodded.

"And her passage free and everything they can eat and drink."

"Absolutely, Madam."

Little by little, the crowd dispersed. In short order the corpse was removed and all vestiges of the battle scrubbed away. Curtin escorted Rebecca back to her room. He didn't want to leave her but they were both spent, both ready to turn in. He kissed her again, looked her in the eye and gently touched the bruises on her neck. He kissed them gently and bid her a good night. Before he could leave she grabbed him, placed her trembling arms around him and held on as if her life depended on it.

They stood that way for a long time, both needing to come down from the high of battle, neither wanting to be alone. He kissed her again and whispered in her ear. "I wish I didn't have to leave you tonight."

"Don't."

He regarded her, thinking about what she had just said. He waged a silent battle within himself. Go… stay… come to bed with me and hold me. He wanted desperately to stay, to pick her up and carry her across the threshold and make love with her. But another part of him knew he would be taking advantage of the moment and that wasn't the way he wanted their relationship to begin.

"Go to sleep, Rebecca. Go to sleep and rest and I'll be with you in the morning. Go to sleep, darling." He went to his cabin and to bed.

Robert Curtin sat guarding the door to Rebecca Walsh's stateroom. He was unable to sleep and felt the need to be close to Rebecca. Taking a chair to her cabin, he watched the sun rise as the ship cruised steadily south. They were in the gulfstream now and the water went from green to jade to a lovely blue. Porpoises leapt playfully alongside, racing the ship until they grew tired of the game and went on their way. They were a nice distraction as he waited.

The rebozo lady emerged just after six from her new quarters next to the girls. She smiled and walked up to him. Feeling a little self-conscious, she shook his hand. She wandered off to get breakfast for her little girl, too ignorant of the ways of first class to know that she would be served, if only she requested it.

He wrote in his journal until seven, when the door opened and Marta emerged, looking as fresh and feisty as ever. She immediately greeted him as Curtin jumped up and peered around her, trying to catch a glimpse of Rebecca sleeping.

"Is she all right, Marta?"

"Slept like a newborn babe, except that she kept muttering a man's name every so often. Clive, I think it was." She watched Curtin's face fall. "Just kidding, silly. She was saying your name, of course." She reached over and kissed him on the cheek, touching his bruises gently. "I never did thank you properly."

"Oh, it's Rebecca who should be thanked. I just served as the punching bag, kept the big ape occupied 'til Rebecca could finish him off."

"You went to bed so early you never heard. That man the two of you killed attacked a ticket agent for the elevated train two days ago. Luckily, she was in a cage and he couldn't get her. He nearly tore the thing down with a bailing hook trying to get at her. She called for help and he beat the hell out of three Irish whales who were trying to arrest him. He got away and that's how he ended up on the ship. You two did all right."

She laughed as she pulled back the lapels of his coat, patted his chest until she found his cigarette case and retrieved it. She let him light a cigarette for her. "The woman in the cage jabbed him with a hatpin as well, right through the hand. He was a regular pin cushion."

She looked off in the distance at the clear blue sky and the sparkling ocean and then back at Curtin again. She liked him. "Where's that lunkhead of a marine?"

"He was by an hour ago, looking for you."

She reached over and kissed him again. "I'll track him down. We'll be in Nassau earlier than expected, I hear. Seas have been calmer than normal." She began to march away.

Curtin smiled and called to her. "I almost forgot." He handed her a telegram. "This came for you this morning. The boy was going to slip it under the door but I took it."

She opened it, read quickly but did not share. She looked at Curtin as if she was taking inventory. "Very interesting." She walked on, then looked over her shoulder. "You take care of her, Robert Curtin."

"Yes ma'am."

Rebecca peered out the door of her cabin just after eleven. She never slept so late. She saw Curtin sleeping in a lounge chair in the sun. She crept up on him and kissed him awake. He smiled until he saw the state of her throat; then he wanted to cry.

She noticed and did her best to reassure him, happy to see that he cared so much. "I'm okay."

"You're not! That son of a bitch. I'd like to kill him if you hadn't already done so." He kissed her again. "I thought you'd never wake up. I missed you."

"You did?" She looked up and down the deck and made sure no one was around. She sat on his lap and kissed him more passionately. She kissed him the way the characters kissed in the naughty books Marta used to read to her after lights out. She loved kissing him and she thought she might not ever want to do anything else except sit on Robert Curtin's lap and kiss him.

She finally pulled away and looked at his journal. She started to open it. "What's this?"

"My journal."

She closed it quickly. "Oh, I'm sorry. That's personal."

"No, no. Just some silly writing. Nothing really. You can look at it, if you want."

"Don't let Marta know about it. She'll tease you. She'll say you're keeping a diary, like a girl." She laughed at the thought of her sister teasing Curtin.

"Oh, that's okay, too. I like when Marta teases." She reached down and kissed him again.

"Does anything get you riled, Robert Curtin?"

"Not much." He kissed her again. He loved the feel of her body next to his. It was beginning to distract him, taking him back to the same feelings he had the evening before when they had parted at her cabin door. He looked at her as her lovely raven hair shone in the bright sunlight. "How is it that one such as you would have any interest in one such as me?"

"I don't think it's such a stretch." She kissed him again and resettled herself until she was lying next to him. She snuggled against his shoulder and held him tightly. "I don't think you are so terrible."

"I'm not much to look at. And I'm not very manly." He smiled at her. "I certainly don't rate you."

She leaned up and looked him over. "I think you're quite handsome." She regarded his physique. "You're no Olympian god, but that's not what I like."

"Once I overheard the men in Alaska call me *the baby* because I'm so young looking,"

"Oh, like my daddy."

He looked down at her and knew it was a great compliment. "Really?"

"Oh yes, my daddy. Everyone says…, now what was it my uncle used to call him, an old timey name? Oh yes, a *bully trap.*"

"Bully trap." Curtin thought on it.

"Yes, my daddy. My uncle used to say the bully bad men, they thought they'd push my daddy around and then it was like grabbing a tiger by the tail. That's a bully trap."

"Hmm." He kissed her and held her more tightly in his arms. He felt a new confidence at that.

"Where's my sister?"

"Off looking for Del Calle. That poor fellow."

"Oh, I think he likes it. She likes him."

"Really?" He smiled down at the top of her head, breathing deeply. She smelled good.

"Oh, yes. You can always tell when Marta likes someone. She teases them. If she doesn't like someone, she ignores them. She likes Del Calle, all right."

"She's fearless, isn't she?"

"Do you think so, Robert?" She sat up and regarded him, watching as he thought before answering her question.

"I do. I do think so. Why?"

"She's very… frail. I don't know why I'm telling you this." She looked him in the eye again and kissed him. "Or maybe I do. I've never met anyone like you. I feel like I could tell you anything and everything."

"And I, you."

"Marta and I aren't really sisters, you know?"

"No. Well, you don't look very much alike, but I never gave it much thought."

"We have a long and strange history, Robert."

He pulled out his watch, looked at it and wound it. He looked out at the ocean. "I'm not going anywhere."

She lay back down beside him and, snuggling in close, said, "Okay, then. Where to begin. The life story of the Walsh family."

"And the Del Toro family."

"Right, right." Curtin pulled out a cigarette and offered her one. She waved it off.

"I don't like to smoke." He put the pack away. He resolved to never smoke in her presence again.

He leaned back and held her tightly in his arms. "This is good. When I am an old, old man, and lying in a hospital, waiting to go on to the great beyond, and the nurses say, 'Aren't you Robert Curtin, the man who once loved the famous Rebecca Walsh?' I can say, yes, my dear, and let me tell you all about her." He held out his hand, "And here is what I will say."

She felt giddy. He said that he loved her. He didn't say it to her, but he said it and it made her feel weak. "Let's see. Well, it all starts with my grandmother."

"Abuelita." She kissed him for remembering her grandmother's name.

"Yes. My grandmother had the most wonderful son in the world and she taught him to be kind and generous and nice to all people, and he had a fine wife and a child, but sadly, they died."

"Oh, that *is* sad."

"And my daddy became a famous ranger in the wilds of Arizona and he met a wild Mexican woman and fell completely in love with her and they had me."

"Thank the gods."

"And then, in nineteen-hundred, I was traveling on a train and I got captured by a band of horrible cutthroats."

"Now, Rebecca, you're getting silly."

She sat up and looked him in the eye. "Robert, this does sound silly, but what I am going to tell you is true; it's all true."

"I see." He kissed her before she had a chance to put her head back on his chest. "Please, continue."

"I got captured and was taken by force to Mexico. I met Marta there. She's the daughter of the most horrible villain of that time. His name was Sombrero del Oro."

"Not Del Toro."

"No, that's later in the story. Anyway, Marta was around my age. She was magnificent, Robert. She was amazing but she'd not had a good life. She saw many, many horrible things: women and children abused, innocent people murdered. It was very hard for her. I know you think she is fearless and confident, but she has many scars, Robert."

"I see." He shifted and breathed in her hair again. "And your father came and rescued you?"

"No, my mother."

"Really?" He was genuinely surprised.

"My mother grew up like Marta. She was a bandit and she lived among horrible people. Oh, she was a terror, Robert. Actually, she still is a terror." She grinned. "She saved me."

"So, she and Marta are much the same?"

"Yes. My father calls me Light Chica and Marta Dark Chica. That is his name for my mother. Her real name, as far as we could ever tell, is Maria. You'll like her, Robert."

"And she, me?"

"Oh, yes. Oh, definitely yes. You are kind, like my father. She'd, she'll like you very much."

"Will?"

"Oh yes. Will."

"And your father?"

"He will too. My daddy's a good judge of men. Oh, Robert, he's the best of men. He is kind and funny and he is always smiling. Like you."

He sat up and pulled her into his arms. He looked her in the eye. "Rebecca, I'm an engineer. I'm not an emotional man. I like to calculate and make my choices scientifically, not from the heart." He thought hard about what he wanted to say. "I've known you one day, Rebecca. But I can't help myself. I need to tell you…" he faltered.

"What?" She thought for a moment that it was all going to unravel, that he was going to tell her that he was married, had half a dozen children, something that would destroy it all.

"I love you, Rebecca. I loved you the first moment I saw you. I've loved you since that moment. I've…" She stopped him. Pulled him close and kissed him hard on the mouth.

"And I, you."

Marta found Del Calle wandering about, looking important. He saw her and, barely discernibly, dropped his guard. He'd been waiting to see her all morning.

"And where have you been, Mister Captain?"

"Just here." He stiffened. He liked that she wanted to know what he was about. Her antics over the course of the previous evening had him distracted.

"What are your thoughts on suffrage?" She patted him down and found his cigarette case. She took two, stuck one in his mouth before he could speak. She leaned over the rail, placing one leg high on a rail, exposing her leg to the knee.

"There's no reason why a woman should not vote."

She looked at him sideways, grinning. "Really?" She smoked and blew smoke at the ocean. "Del Calle…"

"Pedro." It was his turn to be a little assertive. "My name's Pedro, not Mister Captain or Del Calle. It's Pedro."

"Okay, Pedro. So you think women should vote."

"Of course. It's ridiculous that women should not vote."

"You are an interesting man."

"Thank you."

They looked out onto the ocean and smoked for a while. Del Calle was happy she'd come around to see him. She was vexing. He thought about what his mother would think. She would likely be initially appalled, then would warm up to her. She was a fine looking woman and obviously smart. His mother liked intelligence in a woman above all else.

"How many men have you killed?"

"I'm sorry?" Del Calle was not certain he heard the question clearly.

"How many men have you killed? You're a soldier."

"A marine."

She shook her head dismissively. "You've been in the Banana wars. How many men have you killed?"

"I think that's something I'd rather not discuss. How many have *you* killed?"

"Six."

"Seriously?"

"Yes."

He looked back at the horizon.

"Why?"

"I used to be a bandit, down in Mexico. My father was a brigand, a cutthroat. Rebecca's mother killed him."

"I thought you were sisters."

"Step sisters. Not really that, either." She was restless. "Let's eat." She grabbed him by the arm. "You've got nice arms, Pedro." She reached over and kissed his cheek. He stopped and she looked at him, confused. He resolved to get things straight.

"Marta. You are playing with me and I don't like it."

"I'm sorry." And she was. Marta was not cruel. She was having fun but she lacked the capacity to be intimate with anyone. She was playing this badly and she didn't want to hurt the man. He was more sensitive than she originally thought. She extended her hand. "Just friends."

He shook her hand, disappointed. "Just friends."

"Good," she took his arm again. "You've got to entertain me. My sister is preoccupied with her future husband."

"I thought they only just met."

"Yes, well... now, Pedro, don't be a bonehead marine. You can't see that they are hopelessly in love?"

"I didn't notice."

"You men... this is what I mean by saying I'm not certain I even like men."

"You're not a..."

"A what?"

"A Gertrude Stein?"

"Ha! Pedro, I am impressed with your range. You are quite the polymath, aren't you?"

"Well, no." He was not by his own reckoning a deep thinker. "I just..." He was blushing again.

"I don't know what I am, Pedro. Hell, I don't even know how old I am."

"Seriously?" He was intrigued.

"Nope. When I grew up among cutthroats, it wasn't common to have birthday parties and cakes and sweets. I never had a birthday until I met Rebecca. We just made one up. So, I am listed as having my birthday on April 25th, born in the year 1891." She shrugged.

He suddenly felt sorry for her. He looked at her. She appeared small to him; small and frail and vulnerable. He clamped her hand a little tighter with his arm.

She closed the door behind Curtin and looked around his room. It was smaller, significantly more modest than the one she shared with her sister. It was his room, manly, smelling of Curtin: tobacco and leather from his luggage and engineer tools, and shaving soap. She liked being in his room and didn't care if it wasn't right. She didn't care about anything anymore except being with him. He wrapped his arms around her from behind, nuzzled her neck and she thought she might faint.

She pushed him away, turned and began removing her dress. He helped her. With trembling hands he worked on the fine pearl-colored buttons and she was soon as naked as they day she was born. She worked on his clothing next.

They lay on the bed together, both struggling to comprehend what was happening, assaulted with feelings that neither had ever known. They felt lightheaded with excitement and desperate to consummate the action that is natural, and yet, forbidden to people of their station in life.

He pulled her onto his body, her flesh warm and seductive. She smelled so good and everything he did, every caress, every movement, gave her joy, suffusing her in waves of ecstasy. They were each filled with a basic, primordial happiness that very few human beings are able to enjoy, even though the means to do so is deeply embedded in our genetic makeup. She could not contain the excitement this moment revealed and was not certain she could endure it. She wondered if anyone ever died from such a thing.

Returning to the stateroom she shared with Marta, she crawled quietly into bed. Marta let her believe that she was getting away with it. She waited, listening to Rebecca breathe. Finally, just as Rebecca was slipping into sleep, Marta spoke in a loud, terse voice, "Well! Okay, young lady. You've got some explaining to do!"

"Oh, Marta." She was so happy that her sister was awake; she needed to talk, needed to tell her all about it. "Oh, I can't tell you, can't begin to tell you."

"It was …, how was it?"

"It was like whatever is the best feeling you've ever had in your life, times a thousand." She held her sister's hand and squeezed it gently. "Every time felt even better than the last."

"*Every time!* You did it more than once?"

"Four times."

"My God! Rebecca, you're going to get knocked up."

"I don't care."

"I can't believe you." She was pleased with her sister. Rebecca never did anything wrong and now she had and she didn't even care.

"Mamma's going to kill you if she finds out."

Rebecca smiled at that thought. It didn't make her cringe at all. "Marta, when is Mamma and Daddy's anniversary?"

"September tenth."

"When's my birthday?"

"December ninth."

"Do you really think I had a three month gestation?" She laughed at her little joke, the little secret that everyone knew. She continued on. "I don't care about anything but him. I don't want anything but him. I'm not hungry or thirsty or tired. I don't want anything but him, Marta."

She rolled over and placed her head on Marta's breast. "I love him so much, Marta."

"What was it like?"

"I don't know." She rubbed her temples with her free hand, staring into the darkness toward the ceiling. "It was like the best hug one could ever have. Like the warmest tingly feeling. Remember when we went sledding and we went down that one dip at Mr. Langley's, you know, by the barn?"

"Yes."

"It was like that tingly feeling, way down deep, not in the pit of your stomach, but, you know, further down, times a thousand."

"What does it feel like, to, to have it inside you?"

"Wonderful, wonderful, wonderful."

"It doesn't hurt?" Marta was intrigued.

"No, not at all. It's like an electric shock that doesn't hurt, and it goes all the way through your body. You feel it in your toes, everything, *everything* becomes sensitive and I thought at one point that I was dying. I thought that at one point I would never catch my breath. I even cried."

"You cried?"

"I did, Marta. I cried and it scared him. At one point, at the worst or the best of it, he thought I was ill. He thought that he'd hurt me." She giggled. "That part was pretty funny." She sat up, drew her trembling legs to the edge of the bed, she pointed at them and smiled. "Look, Marta. They won't stop quivering." She didn't know what to do.

She looked at Marta. "I have to go." And in short order, she was back with him again.

She finally returned to their cabin around five. Marta was asleep this time. Rebecca lay beside her sister and listened to her breathe. It was a sound she had heard for over ten years and Rebecca realized, with sadness, that everything was about to change now that Curtin was in her life.

Rebecca looked at Marta lying on her back. She was a beautiful woman and looked happy. Marta was vivacious and feisty and seemed to be filled with happiness, but for those who were perceptive and cared to look, there was a sadness that lurked deep within her being.

Rebecca had a moment of self doubt. Was she being selfish? She was almost always happy. She was one of the rare people who was genuinely filled with a wellspring of delight with life. Her father had said she was a wise, old soul and one of the happiest persons he had ever known.

She thought about her mother, too. Her mother and Marta were two of a kind. It had something to do with what they'd endured as children, she was certain of it. Rebecca even, at one point, studied it, tried to make sense of it, and hoped, in her adolescent way, that she could read from Dr. Freud and figure it all out and make it right.

Rebecca was the one, like her father, who always tried to make everything right. They took care of everyone and their punishment for their good deeds was to be burdened with the guilt of happiness around people who were not capable of being truly happy. Thus there was an undercurrent of worry and self-reproach. And now Rebecca had even more to worry about. She'd soon leave Marta and she worried that Marta could not endure it.

But there was nothing for it; there was nothing she could do. Asking her to give up Curtin would be like asking her to jump overboard. It just could not be done.

She drifted a little, someplace between deep thought and slumber. She thought about her future. She hoped she was pregnant already. She didn't care if anyone thought badly of her. She didn't care if she wouldn't be able to go to Smith. She didn't care as long as she would spend the rest of her life caring for Curtin. Nothing else mattered.

She thought again about what they'd done together. She knew about it from the bad books that Marta read to her late at night, but nothing, nothing could have prepared her for what she had with Curtin. She was clever enough to know that it was special.

She'd heard horror stories of other couples: how the women hated the act, how the men were bumblers, how they didn't know how to do it. That was a funny thought to her. It was instinctive, wasn't it? She thought about how, for some of the unfortunate souls of the world, it was a duty to be endured for simple procreation and nothing more.

Oh, she used to fret over that. She wondered what it must be like to have a man on top of her, one of the ugly men who captured her those many years ago, and how she was terrified of it. And now, her lovely, lovely Curtin was not that way at all. He was loving and gentle and expert. He was so good. She missed him. She held up her arm and sniffed her sleeve. It smelled of Curtin, she was sure. She loved that odor. She loved everything about him.

Marta woke at six, bringing Rebecca out of her trance. "Good morning, my little rabbit." She reached over and looked Rebecca in the eye.

"What are you looking at?" Rebecca stretched and spoke through a yawn.

"You are a real woman now. I wanted to see if you looked any different."

"Do I?"

"No."

Marta reached over and pulled out the telegram. "Now that you are not busy fornicating…"

"Don't call it that."

"It is that. You don't want me to say the really naughty one, do you? Fu…"

"No! Stop it, Marta. You are making me embarrassed. Call it lovemaking. That's what they call it in all the songs, except for the ones you listen to."

She opened the telegram and Rebecca read it:

Dan George lives. Warning, much danger to you and your sister. Take care. Watch the ones who pretend to be your friends. Z

Rebecca looked it over, doing her best Sherlock Holmes. Marta took it from her. "It won't have any clues, silly. The thing was made up in the ship's wireless room. I did find out it was sent from Tampico, though."

"What do you make of it? Do you think Dan is really okay, Marta?"

"I never doubted that he was." She folded it up. "Don't tell anyone about this, okay?"

"You don't suspect Curtin?" Rebecca was a little annoyed at the thought of her sister thinking her love was up to no good.

"No. I think someone is playing with us, with me."

"Are you … are we in danger, Marta?"

"I don't know. It is kind of fun, though."

"It's the kind of fun I don't need. I'm not like you, Marta."

"Oh, *there's* a bit of news." She smiled coyly at her sister who was not looking happy. "Don't worry my little rabbit." She patted Rebecca's quivering leg. She looked down at her and grinned.

"Four times?"

"Six. Two more when I went back the second time."

"Will you be able to walk today?"

Rebecca smiled and pressed her head into the pillow. She stretched like a cat. She was thinking of Curtin again. "I think so."

Marta became serious. "Rebecca, I want to talk to you about something."

"Okay." She waited. She'd only seen Marta like this once or twice in her life, and didn't much like it.

"This Curtin fellow. He seems a good sort. I like him. And, well…" If Rebecca didn't know better, she would think she saw Marta choke up a little. Her sister cleared her throat and continued. "You go on."

"Go on?"

"My God, Rebecca." She was welling up. Marta del Toro was getting tears in her eyes. "Don't make me spell it out for you. Just go on."

"I see." Rebecca reached over and, grabbing her sister, pulled her close. She pressed Marta's head to her neck. She could feel her shoulders getting wet where Marta's head rested. She felt the sadness emanating from her sister and best friend.

"I'll never leave you, Marta. You know that. I'll always be your best friend. We are sisters. You'll find someone, I know it, and we'll all be together. Sisters do that all the time. Sisters get homes right next to each other, and we can too."

"I, I…don't even know if I like men."

"Then you'll get a woman!" She smiled and patted Marta gently on the shoulder.

Marta smiled sheepishly. "I'm not a lesbian. I, I just don't know. I'm confused. I like men well enough. Curtin is a good fellow. Like Daddy."

"They say you look for a husband who is like your daddy, for better or worse."

Marta looked up at her. "So my husband will be another Sombrero del Oro?"

They looked on at each other and burst out laughing.

"No, Marta. Daddy's more your daddy than that fat hog ever was." She lifted Marta's face by the chin. "You know something?"

"What, darling." She was brightening.

"Dan George gave me some advice about you."

"Really?"

"Yes. And you like Dan, right?"

"Love him."

"You know he was an orphan. Didn't have a mother or father, like you. But he didn't have Mamma and Daddy, either. He told me that one day we'd have to grow apart a little. He said we'd both be looking to make our own lives, and he said I had to be careful because you were very special and that you aren't as tough as you pretend to be."

Marta blushed a little. She knew it was a compliment.

"He said you had deep scars and he knew a little about them, because he has them, too, but that they can be overcome.

He said you don't have to suffer from the things that happened when you were young."

Marta regarded her sister. She was humbled by the thought that she and Dan thought so much of her that they would speak about her in such a way.

She suddenly began speaking, words tumbling out of her mouth in a torrent that she couldn't stop. "I, I think about men a lot, Rebecca. I like them, but when I think about them, all I can think of is all the ugly things men did when I was a bandit. It makes me feel sick. It makes me not want to touch another person or be touched. Remember the big redhead? Remember her? They were so terrible to her. And I watched, Rebecca. I watched them. I should have run away, should have shot a few of them, should have told them to stop it. I didn't do any of those things and now, whenever I think of a man in that way, all I see are savages doing horrible things."

"I know. I know, Marta. I've had the same feelings for a long time. Do you remember back at the tent, when we first met?"

"Yes."

"You were cruel, Marta." She held up her hand. "It wasn't your fault; you didn't know how to be decent. It wasn't your fault, but when you told me in such an ugly way what was to be my fate, it scared me so. It made me think that I'd never let a man do that to me. I used to think, whenever I saw a happy mother with her baby, that this would never be the case for me. I would never have a baby because I'd have to do *that*, and I didn't want to."

She hesitated a moment, needing to get up the courage to continue, to tell Marta the most intimate secret she had held for more than seven years. She continued. "Do you know what changed it?"

"What?"

"One time, when I was twelve, I saw Mamma and Daddy doing it."

Marta grinned. "You're kidding."

"No. It was late and I got thirsty and went to get a drink and I heard them. I looked through the crack in the door and they were going at it. My goodness, Marta, they were going at it! And I could tell that it wasn't bad and that Mamma was happy, and Daddy was very happy, and then I realized that it didn't have to be scary and ugly. And that's when I decided that I wouldn't be afraid. And you know what?"

"What?"

"I was right. Oh, my God, I was right."

Marta found a cigarette she'd gotten from Del Calle. She opened a porthole and smoked and blew the smoke out the porthole so Rebecca didn't have to smell it. Rebecca continued.

"So, Marta." She walked over and put a hand on her shoulder. "If you want a man, you should have a man, on *your* terms, and a good man. I know you like to dabble in the darker side of the human condition, and that's fine, but get a man like daddy, not a man like you-know-who."

"Or a woman?"

"Yes, yes." She grinned broadly, "But get one like me, not like mamma. Mamma's too dangerous."

They were anchored in the harbor and a crowd had gathered to watch little boys in a canoe looking up at them. The passengers would throw pennies and the lads would dive for them. It was great sport but Marta found it revolting.

"That's ridiculous." She looked at Del Calle, then at Rebecca and Curtin. "They aren't bloody trained monkeys. It's demeaning."

She reached into her purse and pulled out a handful of change. She then demanded all of Del Calle's. She threw the little pile of coins into the canoe. The boys were no longer interested in diving for pennies. They swiftly rowed away. Marta stood back, satisfied. The onlookers were disappointed and soon began to drift away, off to pursue some other form of entertainment.

In short order, the steam tenders could be seen on their way to convey them to the Hotel Colonial. It was exciting. The hotel was big and beautiful and the grounds were adorned with palm trees and green lawns. Everyone was energized, anticipating the next adventure. Marta stood resolutely near the bow, her foot resting on the gunwale, looking like George Washington crossing the Delaware.

They stepped off and were soon dining on boiled grouper, Terrine de Foie Gras, paté de Gibier and cocoanut ice cream. They'd spend the night here. The girls each got a suite on the top floor. They would have normally only gotten one and stayed together, but Marta knew where Rebecca wanted to be and she didn't want her sister staying in one of the matchbox rooms that Curtin had reserved. It was foolish for him to get a room at all but the men ended up with the more modest quarters near the golf course on the ground floor. They were next door neighbors. They all split up and agreed to meet at three. Curtin didn't bother even going to his room.

Marta waited in the shade of the palm. Del Calle was first to arrive. "What the hell is on your head, Pedro?"

He looked up and regarded the brim. "My hat." It was a big one. The Marine campaign hat of his summer uniform was quite large.

"It looks ridiculous. Take it off."

"No!" He straightened it. He liked his campaign hat. It suited him. "It's part of my uniform and I won't take it off." He was finally beginning to relax around Marta. She didn't confound and outrage him as much anymore. He liked it when she teased him and comfortably defied her commands every chance he got.

"Come on, you big galoot." She hooked her arm in his. She walked to the front desk and got the concierge's attention.

"Yes, madam?"

"Call room seven-fifteen. Let it ring, they'll be busy. Tell them that Marta said that the two bunnies should stay busy until four. Don't come down." The man was writing feverishly. He hesitated. "Yes, bunnies, she spelled it out; b-u-n-n... yes, you got it." She slipped some bills in the man's hand, looked at

Del Calle and winked. "Come on you big brute, we can't have you looking like this."

She took him to a tailor in town. They had ready-made, which would have to do as they were in a hurry. She had him looking smart in a nice two button sack suit, no vest. She got him a stylish straw Panama hat and picked out his cravat. She found him shoes, as well. She liked dressing him and he was especially handsome now. He would not let her pay, though he did concede to letting her buy him the tie.

They were back by four and had cocktails in the lounge as they waited for Rebecca and Curtin. The Colonial was an opulent hotel and Marta was enjoying it all. The beautiful weather, a piano playing, Pedro del Calle looking like a hero from one of her novels and the finely dressed patrons wandering by helped her forget all the stresses of the past days. She was enjoying herself a little, now.

Rebecca, arriving first, touched him gently on the arm to get his attention. "You look very nice, Pedro." He smiled uneasily. He was not used to so much frivolity.

Curtin showed up with drinks for everyone. He handed them round and proposed a toast. He held up his glass. "To good friends." He smiled, then looked at Pedro who was now the happiest he'd been in a long time.

The four of them wandered along Bay Street and found a taxi. Marta wanted to see some of the shoreline, away from the tourists. Soon they found a quiet stretch of beach. They had the place to themselves. Curtin and Del Calle hung back, smoking cigars and enjoying the women as they wandered along the beach a good distance away.

The girls discarded their outer clothes and walked in their bathing suits. Marta had modified hers so that she was bare up to mid-thigh. She'd had it especially made for her, of cotton, not wool. It was especially shear when wet, and plunged significantly at the neckline. Rebecca was certain she'd be arrested the first time she wore it. She never wore stockings. She periodically waded out into the surf.

They came upon an islander, a fit, middle aged fisherman working hard at fighting a shark. He'd been fighting it for some time and it was beginning to tire. Marta found it all fascinating and began asking the man what it was all about.

"Oh, he's a nasty one, Miss. He's a bull shark and he's been breaking our nets, causing all manner of havoc." The man deftly worked the rod. He was getting the creature close to shore.

"Let me help." The man looked at her, at her immodest dress and then into her eyes. He could see that Marta was not fooling.

"Okay, Miss." The shark was close in now. Not more than thirty yards off, just beyond the breakers. He was deadly, scary. He was fat, at least eight feet long and several hundred pounds; certainly big enough to kill a man. Every now and again he'd try to dive and the fisherman would keep his head up, keep him from making a run. Soon the creature was lying on its side. He'd have him beached directly.

"Now Miss. I'll hand you the rod. Have you ever handled a fishing rod?"

"Caught an eighty pound tarpon in the keys on my seventeenth birthday," Marta lied. She'd read about tarpon fishing in the Saturday Evening Post. She'd never been to Florida and the biggest fish she'd ever landed was a two pound trout in the Adirondacks.

The fisherman held the rod out to her and she took it. "All due respect, Miss, don't put it down there." He dropped his eyes to her nether region. "The end of that rod can do you serious harm if he runs again."

She held the rod firmly, feeling the beast on the end of the line. It was thrilling. She managed to keep the rod tip up and kept the creature from sounding. The fisherman went through his kit and retrieved a sisal line. He made a loop, like a makeshift reata, and waded out toward the shark.

Rebecca found her voice and called out. "*What on earth are you doing?*" The fisherman smiled back at her.

"I'll get this around his tail; we'll hoist him in together. Now, don't let him make a run for me, Miss. I need both my legs."

Marta was pleased. A mistake would likely lead to the man losing his life. She liked this little game. She walked up the beach a ways and began slowly pumping the rod, reeling the great fish toward her with every crank of the handle. The animal was sideways now, looking at her with its beady eye.

These were the most ferocious sharks, the bulls. They were powerful and aggressive and did not mind fighting a human being if they had to. Marta cranked more as the fisherman closed in. At ten yards, just as the water was breaking over the creature's back, the fisherman threw his little reata and the shark's tail was now under his control. Marta cheered and the two began backing beachward as the shark moved sideways, nearly beached, nearly in their possession.

Curtin looked on from a hundred yards away. He was focused on the girls when he heard Marta cheer. "What the hell is she up to now?"

Del Calle looked up. He had been enjoying the various seashells and creatures cast on the beach at his feet. He looked at Curtin. "Jesus, she's a damned menace."

They watched as the huge shark rolled in the surf. Suddenly, it shook its head violently in one last attempt at freedom. The hook suddenly rocketed skyward, flying past Marta's head, and the fisherman found himself thirty yards out in the water, being towed toward his beloved nets. The shark was moving fast, his powerful tail shipping back and forth trying to free itself from the line.

Marta dropped the now useless rod and ran for the fisherman. She grabbed onto him and held on tightly so that now the shark had an extra body's weight to work against. Yet they continued to be pulled out, deeper and deeper, until they were a good fifty yards from shore. The fisherman looked at Marta and she read his mind, "Don't you dare let go!" He grinned nervously and held on. He looked at the dorsal fin twenty feet away. If the shark stayed up, they had a chance.

Curtin and Del Calle were finally there. They called out for the pair to let go. Del Calle was removing his new shoes. He threw his jacket to Rebecca and began to wade after them when, suddenly, the animal dove in the deeper water and the fisherman was forced to let go. Fin and sisal line disappeared under the waves.

There was nothing for it, and the two wet anglers began to swim back to shore. Suddenly, the fin appeared, not thirty yards behind them and Rebecca screamed. "Hurry, hurry, he's coming to get you!" They had become the hunted.

Del Calle finally reached them. He grabbed Marta and pulled, getting between her and the approaching fin, pushing her and the fisherman toward shore. By now the water was shallow enough that they were able to wade but the tired shark continued onward. He was going to blood someone.

Curtin called out to Del Calle. "Pedro. Catch!" He tossed a big gaff from the fisherman's kit. Del Calle was now alone, standing firmly between the fleeing anglers and the beast. Curtin waded toward him, closing, but he wasn't as fast as the shark.

Pedro waited, gaff held high. The creature was too tired to make the lightning strike they were famous for. Del Calle, like a matador on a Saturday afternoon, stood poised, ready to drive the acero deep into the bull's back. He would have one chance to end the deadly game. The shark continued onward, Del Calle wishing he was anywhere but in the Atlantic facing down a rogue bull shark. He could see its eyes now and noted the rotation that would enable the most efficient way for the shark to grab and kill his target: Pedro. Time seemed to slow as Del Calle reached out and grabbed the creature by the nose with his left hand. He held on while his right hand drove the gaff home, sinking it deeply into the shark's brain.

It shook and shuddered as Del Calle held on. Marta was suddenly next to him. She'd gotten the fisherman's knife and now joined the attack, plunging it to the hilt again and again until they were both standing in a sea of shark blood. Curtin and the fisherman grabbed the huge fish and everyone pulled it in together. They sank onto the sand as the animal flopped about the beach, the last of its death throes kicking up sprays of red sand.

No one spoke for several minutes. Marta looked at Rebecca who was completely speechless. Marta remembered something and walked over to the fishing rod. She retrieved it and pulled the line in.

"I knew it. The hook failed." She showed them the straightened hook. "I didn't cause him to throw that hook, the hook failed." She was pleased, it was as if she was saying, *"It's okay that the four of us nearly died because I didn't do anything wrong. It's all okay."*

Curtin passed cigarettes around. The fisherman nodded and looked at his with satisfaction. Rebecca even reached over and grabbed one. She smoked as if she'd been doing it all her life.

Finally, Del Calle spoke. He looked at them. He was proud, happy. He liked battle and he had acted well. He behaved as he had in other battles. He was the hero of the hour. He looked down at his new, wet, and very bloody outfit. "Oh, well, guess that's the end of this suit. You don't suppose they'll take it back?"

Curtin rested on the veranda overlooking the seascape while Rebecca dressed. He liked the seventh floor. She brought him a drink and kissed his head as she reached over the back of his chair. He grabbed her hand and held it to his cheek.

"Marta..." He couldn't finish the sentence. He understood the loyalty siblings possessed and did not want to offend Rebecca.

Rebecca smiled and sat down next to him. She reached over and lit two cigarettes. She smoked while he regarded his love. She'd had time to think about Marta's antics from earlier in the day. "Why is it that men can do such things, but when women do them, then it's reckless and irresponsible?" She wasn't trying to pick a fight.

"Such as?" Curtin turned to face her, look her in the eye. They'd already developed a pattern of listening to each other.

"Men can fight bulls, fly aeroplanes, go into battle, ride broncos and it's all fine. But when a woman does it, then it's bad."

"I guess it's imbedded in our brains, somehow. Women are made to have babies. They're meant to be preserved, to continue the species. Men are expendable." Curtin loved her, loved her mind. He waited for her response to his comment and felt compelled to qualify it. "I don't think that."

"Oh, but you don't approve of Marta doing things."

"Because I care for Marta. I also care for Del Calle and if he told me he was taking up bull fighting, I'd not be happy about that, either. It's the person, not the act that I worry over."

"She's a good soul, you know."

"You needn't defend her, Rebecca. I know her type. She can't help it. She's a risk taker; she needs to do these things just as surely as we need to breathe. It's the great; she's the great tragic hero of the ages."

"I do worry over her."

"As you should. But she'll likely never stop. She's the kind of person who goes over Niagara Falls in a barrel. There's no rational reason for it, she just does it, needs to do it."

"You two were grand." She was proud of Curtin, proud of Del Calle.

"Oh, I didn't do much. Del Calle is the man of the hour. He's a good chap."

"And you?" She got up from her chair and sat in his lap. She kissed him on the mouth. "Are you a risk taker, Mr. Curtin?"

"Only calculated risks. Never just for the thrill, always for a payoff of some kind."

She glanced at the bedroom and smiled. He picked her up as she wrapped her arms around his neck. "We have three hours until dinner and I'm not sleepy."

"Neither am I."

After a time, he drifted into a blissful slumber, the kind of sleep that comes after the intimacy they now regularly shared. He thought he heard an operetta a long distance away. He listened in his dream and heard it again; an angelic voice, *la petite mort, la petite mort.* He looked up and saw her there, naked and beautiful, leaning on an elbow and distractedly, as if she, too, were in the same place, softly repeated the verse, *la petite mort.*

He woke and that brought her awake. She looked at him and smiled. "Oh, hello."

"What were you saying?" He reached over and pulled her head down onto his chest. "My French is not good. I mostly slept through all the classes."

"La petite mort. The little death." She smiled. "Marta used to read naughty books to me at night, after the lights were out. We'd make a little tent with the sheets and use a flashlight. I'd hold the light and Marta would read. There was one book, about a woman in love," she hesitated, a little embarrassed.

"Go on, please."

"She would describe things, things we didn't understand. Of course, we knew what they were doing, you know, *it*, but we didn't fully understand. And she said, the character in the book said, she felt la petite mort. Every time it would happen, it was like a little death." She looked up and kissed him on the mouth, moved her hand down over his body and smiled. "And now I know what she meant."

"Yes, yes." He thought on that for a while. "It's sad, there's a sadness to it, isn't there, Rebecca? Like a feeling that is too overpowering, that it is like Christmas morning, but then Christmas morning turns to Christmas afternoon and then there's sadness." He kissed her hair. "That's stupid. That's not what it is."

"No, no, Robert. I know what you're saying. It's like having the feeling and the feeling is so wonderful that you are afraid it doesn't get any better. Or that, having it is somehow so deliciously bad that you will be punished for your sin, your sin of happiness. That no one has the right to be this happy. No one deserves to be so happy, and something has to give. It's almost as if la petite mort, it would be better to just go on and die, and not recover from it, it…" She suddenly looked into his eyes. They were both misty-eyed, overwhelmed, so much in love that it hurt. Their hearts, literally, ached.

She pulled him on top of her. "Oh, Robert Curtin, kill me again."

Curtin watched the big ceiling fan blades turn, gently moving the air over them. He looked about the opulent room, more opulence than he'd known in his life. He looked down at Rebecca resting her head on his chest. He needed to say it. He was an engineer, always planning, always considering all contingencies, leaving nothing undone, nothing left to surprise. "I'm not wealthy, Rebecca."

She smiled and didn't look up. "Then it's a good thing I am."

"How wealthy?"

"Enough." She shifted and turned to face him. She threw a leg over him and smiled. "Not Carnegie wealthy, but enough."

"Do you mind that I'm not?"

"Well, it depends on how well you perform in certain matters." She grinned slyly. It seemed that her experiences over the last two days had transformed her. She was a woman now. She'd learned the things that made it that way and was happy for them. She loved Robert Curtin and felt connected enough to talk about love-making freely.

"My mamma had no money when she met my daddy. She was a bandit, I told you. They've always been happy."

"But *he* was the one with the money."

She thought hard to counter his argument. "Well, my grandmother, *she* had the money, and my grandfather didn't. So there. And my grandmother, you'll love her. She always told me—told us—marry for love, not money or station. She told Marta and me that very thing." She looked at Curtin who was staring at the ceiling again. "Oh, God, Robert. I wouldn't treat you like a kept man. You must work. I can see that. But isn't it nice to think that we can go and do things like this, do things that you would never do on an engineer's income?"

"You talk like we will be together a long time."

"We won't?"

"I hope we will." He became serious. "This is going so fast, Rebecca. I am a true engineer. I do nothing that is not guided by my brain, guided by logic. I'm not one to follow my heart."

"Who says you must? Who says that any of this isn't logical?" He thought about that and realized she was right.

"I would never imagine, have never imagined, that someone like you would want someone like me." He sat back and smiled. "I used to imagine what my wife would be like. I could even create her in my mind and, frankly, Rebecca, she didn't look or act or smell anything like you."

"Is that a compliment?"

"It's supposed to be."

"What was she supposed to be like?" She turned, fluffed up a pillow and sat upright, folding her arms over her breasts and waiting for his answer.

"Well, let's see." He rubbed his temples and looked at the fan above their bed. "I always thought she would be kind of frumpy, really. She would be a big woman; big boned, not fat, at least not initially, but after five or six children…"

"That many?"

"Oh yes. We'd be Catholic, you know." He looked on at Rebecca. "Is that okay? To be Catholic?"

"Oh, yes. It's fine."

"Well, she'd have kind of muddy brown hair that would thin after a few years, turn grey. Eventually she'd be mostly bald." She laughed out loud. "Except for her eyebrows. They'd have plenty of dark, black hair, well—eyebrow—singular. It would grow straight across, you know." He waited for her to stop laughing and turned to look at her a little seriously. "But she'd have nice big breasts."

"Big as mine?" She blushed at her own wickedness.

"Oh, no. A lot bigger. But she'd have forty pounds on you. Big woman, big breasts. You're more of a small woman with big breasts. All relative, you know." Curtin became serious. He looked at his darling girl. "We've done everything backward. I haven't met your parents. We, we've done…*that*."

"Does *that* matter so much?"

"Well, certainly it does."

She sat, resting her hand under her chin. "I didn't think it would."

He smiled. "No it doesn't, really, I guess. I just feel I've cheated you." He suddenly had a thought. He jumped from the bed, pulled her round so that her feet were resting on the floor. He looked at her. Kissed her quickly on the mouth and ran from the room. He was back in a moment. He dropped down on one knee, at her feet. He grabbed her hand and held it in his. "Rebecca, will you marry me? Please?"

With that he slid a cigar band onto her finger.

She held her hand up to the light. "Well, at least it's a Havana." She looked back at the naked Robert Curtin, on the floor before her, kneeling at her bare feet. She pulled him up by the chin. "You know, the poor country people in Mexico, the ones who live away from towns, far from the church, will often be together for nearly a year, will do *that*, for a year before ever getting officially married in the church. Sometimes, they'll have a baptism and a wedding all on the same day when they come down for the annual festival."

"Are you telling me we have to wait a year to get married, Rebecca?"

"No, just making a point. Just saying, it's not so uncommon in our part of the world. It's okay by God in Mexico. It must be okay here, on a ship, in Nassau." She smiled at him. "There's no sin in it. We love each other. I love you, Robert Curtin. I loved you the first moment I saw you." She admired her cigar band ring. "Yes, I would be proud to marry you."

Pedro del Calle slept fitfully through until evening. The battle with the shark had left him tired, exhausted. He slept and dreamed strange dreams. He dreamed of his one battle in the Honduras. It was a debacle. It was all a debacle, really. He hated it. He wanted since childhood to be a marine, despite his parents' wishes. They wanted him to go into law. Only the dull-witted made the military their career, according to his father, and they were too dark for the US military. They were too Hispanic, too Catholic.

But he forged ahead, went to Annapolis and wasted the opportunity there, too. His father told him to at least stay with the Navy. At least in the navy he had a chance at becoming an admiral. The Marine Corps did not appreciate Annapolis men. The marines were the red-headed stepchildren of the US military. They weren't the army and they weren't the navy. The Marine Corps was not for gentlemen, his father would say. No Annapolis man was ever named the commandant of the Marine Corps.

His men and he essentially moved about, protecting US business interests throughout the Caribbean. Whenever the oil companies, or banks, or the sugar industry felt a pinch, whenever the bottom line might be affected, they sent in the marines; and then, always too sparsely. And he was always the one they sent because *he* was one of *them*, they'd say. He knew the lingo, knew how *they* acted and thought, as if *they* were some other form of creatures, subhuman.

He and his men were often outnumbered, used like a bit of meat on a stick, luring the wolves in so that the navy's big guns could reduce them down. He was in exactly one skirmish, and that resulted in the deaths of three of his men. He hated it. The enemy was not much of an enemy either, though they did have real guns, real bullets. The fighting was very real.

So he dreamed of the battle again, how he won the day and at the end, held one of his men and waited for him to bleed out as he cradled the lad who just wanted the pain to go away. He injected him six times with morphine, enough to kill a horse, yet the lad lay there, crying and waiting to die. It was something Pedro thought about every day.

Then he had a very peculiar dream. He was no longer in battle but was now swimming in the Caribbean with his parents back in Puerto Rico. They were swimming and having fun and his wife was there, too, once again alive. Suddenly, a shark fin broke the water and moved toward him very fast. Something wasn't right because they never swam where sharks were. He was swimming, trying to get between the shark and his wife but he couldn't move. He swam and swam with all his might but he couldn't move. Then the shark turned into Marta del Toro. She lifted her head and the dorsal fin was Marta's black hair. She was naked and swam up and grabbed him and kissed him hard on the mouth. He looked back at his wife and she was smiling and waving him on, telling him it was okay.

He got the news that he'd be alone with Marta this night. Rebecca and Curtin would not be with them. He didn't like that much and downed three Manhattans quickly, but that didn't do much to help matters, either. He was irritated with the girl. She was like a spoiled child, annoying and confounding and he couldn't stop thinking of her. He liked kissing her. He liked looking at her long naked legs and her brief outfits and could see her breasts through her clothes and they were magnificent—and he loved her dark skin. He liked dark women, always had. He liked it when she made sexual remarks and he liked that she came to his aid to fight the shark. But overall, he would have been a lot happier if she had never come into his life.

Eventually she was there, beside him. She looked radiant. She'd put on a new dress and her hair was done up in a rather provocative style. She wore clothes that were too revealing and as far as he could tell, no undergarments.

"You look in a foul mood, Pedro."

He didn't respond. They got a table and dined. This would be their last night in Nassau. He wanted it to be over. They ate quietly and now Marta wanted to dance. He accommodated her but was just not in the mood.

"I think I'll turn in, Marta."

"No. You can't." He looked at her. She sounded plaintive, as if a child had spoken in her voice. He looked her in the eye.

"I'm tired. That shark business wore me out."

"Oh, nonsense. I'm sure you've done more dangerous things."

"How are you so sure?"

"You're a marine."

"Not everyone wants to go around trying to kill themselves, Marta. Even marines."

"You liked it. I could see you liked it. We're not so different, Pedro. That's what you like about me."

"Do I?" He knew that was cruel but couldn't help it. She faltered a little, showing a bit of uncertainty. It made him feel sorry for her and he felt himself responding to her.

"I'm sorry." She looked down at the table. She always ran full tilt and often it was too much, too overpowering, especially for men. "I'm feeling a little blue, Pedro. My sister, she's gone, she's gone."

"What do you mean, she's gone?"

"With Curtin. She's gone from me. Let's dance."

She held him closely and they moved about the floor. She gripped his hand tightly and he could feel her breath on his face. Once she reached up and kissed him gently on the cheek.

It was getting very late but she talked him into taking a walk. It was a bright night with a full moon and it reminded him of his home in Puerto Rico. Her melancholy was contagious and he, too, was in a somber mood. She seemed to sense it and gripped his hand tightly. Soon they were kissing under some palms, next to the golf course. He liked kissing her and at the same time, hated it. He didn't want to do this, wasn't ready for it, couldn't deal with it now.

"May I stay with you tonight, Pedro?"

It was the first time since he'd met her that she actually asked for anything. She was always demanding, ordering, in charge.

"No."

She was hurt. "Don't you like me?"

"Yes, frankly, I do and that's why I'm saying no."

"So, if you didn't like me, you'd let me in your bed and we'd make love."

"Yes, maybe, probably not."

"But you do like me, and that's why you won't make love to me."

"Yes."

"Even if it's just between friends."

"Especially for that reason."

"But I've never tried it. I want to try it. Have *you*?"

He smiled weakly. This was a ridiculous conversation to have with a beautiful twenty year old girl. "I had a wife, Marta."

"Oh."

"She's dead."

"Oh."

"She died in child birth, a hemorrhage. They couldn't stop the bleeding. She was only twenty. It was two years ago."

"And the baby?"

"Fine, fine." He brightened at the thought of his little girl.

She kissed him again. "I really need you, Pedro."

"No you don't, Marta. You need to think about this, think about your sister and think about what will make her happy. You are close, and that is a good thing, but you are grown women now, it is time you lived your lives separately. Let her go."

"But it's too hard." He thought she was crying, but it was her temper coming through. He put his hands on her shoulders and kissed her forehead.

"Your sister is a very lucky young lady, and you are a very lucky young lady. Good night, Marta."

Before she could say another word he was gone.

Curtin awoke to Rebecca watching him sleep. "Good morning." He kissed her. "How long have you been awake?"

She scooted up next to him and rested her head on his chest. "Since three." It was nearly seven.

"Since three? What made you wake up?"

"You. I was thinking of you and it gave me some ideas and I wanted you but didn't want to wake you." He lay quietly for a while; said nothing.

His demeanor suddenly changed, became serious. "Rebecca." He sat up, leaning on an elbow. "We need to talk."

"Oh?" She didn't like his tone.

"From now on, whatever I'm doing, wherever we are, no matter how tired I am or how soundly I'm sleeping, you *always*, and I mean *always* tell me when you want me." He smiled at her.

"Even in church?" She climbed on him and he started to lose his train of thought.

"Yes, even in church."

"When we're having dinner with your parents?"

"Yes... well, my parents are dead, but if they were, alive, yes, even then."

"At a dinner party, with guests all around and with you carving a roast or a turkey or a ham?"

"Yes, even then."

"I love you Robert Curtin." She moved some more. "Now, shut up, I'm busy."

Marta showed up at the pier as requested and Del Calle helped her onto the sloop. She looked it over, interested. She'd done a little sailing, but only as a passenger. She watched Pedro work and prepare to shove off. She could see he was a capable sailor and knew that this was his peace offering. He looked at her when he was set. "All ready?"

"Ready."

She helped him push off and they began moving steadily to sea. He looked the sails over, made adjustments here and there, sat down beside her and brushed a lock of hair from her eye. "Sleep well?"

She smiled a little weakly, felt embarrassed to answer, "I haven't been to bed yet." He let it go.

"She's a nice little sloop, we have her until noon."

Marta leaned back and began to doze. The silence of the craft and the steady movement across the waves made her sleepy. She leaned onto Del Calle's shoulder, relaxed. It was the most relaxed he'd seen her, but it didn't last long. She shook herself a little, like a toddler who wanted to keep awake. "Can it go any faster?"

"A little."

"Make it go."

"Nope." She looked at him, a little surprised. He was the only person, other than her adopted mother, who told her no so often.

After some time passed during which Marta had a brief nap, he dropped the sails and then the anchor. It was pleasant out here, too far out to hear the holiday makers on the island, and far enough away from the sea lanes so as not to be a bother.

Marta awoke and looked about as Pedro opened a picnic basket. "Let's see what we have here." He had a happy look on his face, a kind and fatherly look, and it made her think of her adopted father. He pulled out cold chicken and champagne, some fruit and cheese. He poured some champagne for both of them. She ate and felt better, more awake.

"So, this is nice." She felt a little self conscious. "Kind of romantic for just friends." She didn't look up.

"Oh? I don't know. Friends can go sailing."

"Would you take another marine sailing, with champagne, let him sleep on your shoulder while underway?"

"Why do you want to fight with me all the time, Marta?" He wasn't being mean or angry, he wanted to know.

"Why do you want to be nice to me all the time, Pedro? I'm not nice to you. I tease you and demean you and I'm just a plain little shit to you."

"I don't know." He poured another glass and sipped it. "This is good champagne, it usually tastes like vinegar to me."

"Did you bring me out here to finally make love to me?" She looked down into the cabin. It was furnished with a bed in the bow. It would serve as a fine little bordello.

"I don't make love without love. I already told you that."

"What if I told you I don't need you to, now?" She could see him wince a little. "What if I told you I found a man last night, after you left me?"

"Did you?"

"No."

"When are you going to stop trying to commit suicide, Marta?"

"What do you mean?" She was a little annoyed at the implication. "That's a sin and a crime."

"Yet you're doing it."

"Am not."

"You know what the sin and crime is in suicide?"

"Sure." She shrugged as if it was a stupid question. "It's self-murder."

"Yes, but the victim of the crime is not the one who dies." He waited for her to look up at him. "It is a crime against the ones left behind; those who loved the one committing suicide. In your case, Rebecca and your grandmother and now Curtin, your parents, and me."

"You're talking nonsense. I don't want to die. I like a little excitement, want to try things, there's nothing wrong in that."

"And you want to push the limits, take chances, put your heart out on a limb for the thrill of sensual pleasure. You are a conqueror, need to have something to prove. What is it, Marta? What is it that has made you hate so much?"

"Hate! I don't hate." She looked at him, angry now. "What are you playing at? What business do you have asking me such things? You're not Sigmund goddamned Freud. Take me back."

"Not until you tell me."

"I'm about full up of you telling me no! No one tells me no, goddamn you. Take me back."

"Tell me first." She was furious now and threw the basket overboard, along with the champagne and her glass.

"You goddamned men. I *hate* you. I hate all of you! I'm sick of you always being so goddamned smug, looking at me like I'm some kind of weak kitten. You want me, yet you don't have the guts to take me. Take me." She began to unbutton her dress. He stopped her.

"No."

"Fine, then."

She pulled away from him, got the boom between them and stripped down. "I'll swim back." She dove in on the port side and had to swim around the stern. She began making her way to shore. It was five miles and Pedro could think only of the shark from the previous day.

"Marta, please." He thought about what to do, found a line and threw it, got it over her and pulled hard, dragging her back. He grabbed her, manhandling her and pulled her back into the boat. She was really furious now.

"You son of a bitch!" She rubbed the rope burns on her legs. "Look at my legs, you goddamned brute bastard." She wanted to hit him and he kissed her, held her tightly in his arms and kissed her again. She finally broke, crying and holding onto him and began pouring out the emotions that she'd bottled up for years. Pedro waited, holding her and saying nothing. He let her cry. It was cathartic and he just held her.

"I'm sorry." She finally got hold of herself.

"No need to be."

"I never cry."

"You should. A good cry is good."

"Yeah, good for little weak girls."

"I've had a good cry."

"You have?"

"Many, in fact."

"When?"

"When my wife died, dummy. When do you think? And when one of my men died. He was gut shot, bled all over me. I cried. It took him so long to die."

She held his face between the palms of her hands.

"I did bad things, Pedro."

He smiled and wondered at what she could have done that was so bad. "I can't imagine what."

"Oh, you can say that again. You cannot imagine, Pedro. There is no way that you could imagine, not even with the imagination of a madman, could you imagine."

"Then tell me."

"Rebecca and I, we aren't sisters. I was a bandit. I lived with bandits for the first half of my life. The men were savages. They raped, murdered, and I was part of their band. I did things, Pedro. Things that people hang for. I've never been punished. And, I don't know..." The color drained from her face and she looked at Pedro with a sadness he'd never seen before, sadder even than his mother's face when his wife had died. "I watched men rape and torture and just be horrible, and when I think of, you know, *that,* all I can think of is those men." He got up and threw a towel over her shoulders, got her something to drink and gently dried her hair.

"So, this was, let's see, when you were a little child? Perhaps ten?"

"Yes." She dried her face as Pedro helped her with her dress. He got a couple of cigarettes and lit them, handing one to her. She smoked and it seemed to calm her down a bit.

"And Rebecca, she told you it isn't horrible, that it's a good thing, and you are losing her and everything is unraveling."

"Yes." She looked out at the water and the tears ran down her cheeks. "I've never been punished and this, I guess, is God's way of punishing me." She looked at Pedro, into his eyes. "I'm so unhappy. I'm always, always unhappy and angry and just miserable, Pedro. And I make everyone around me that way, too."

"Except Rebecca."

"Oh, she's lucky. She's been stuck with me for ten years. I've made her life hell. Now she'll be rid of me, God bless her. God bless her for Curtin. I'm so dark, but she could pass for a white. She could have been the belle of Baltimore but she was stuck with me, her Indian nigger pretend sister."

"Stop it!"

She looked at him. She wasn't used to so much force in his voice. It must be the voice he used when he commanded his men and it got her attention.

"Now you listen to me, Marta."

He sat down next to her and took her hand. "Do you know why children are not punished as adults?"

"Yes."

"Do you? Do you know why?"

"Because they are not responsible for their actions. I understand, Pedro, I appreciate all that. But…"

"Stop! Just shut up, Marta. Shut up for a minute and listen." He took a breath and let it out. "I know a little more about you than you realize. Curtin told me. He told me what Rebecca had told him about you. She said you were once a savage but you saved her life.

"Look, I don't know why you did some things and not others, but you are judging yourself as if you were grown up. You were ten years old, Marta. God bless you for what good you did. That is remarkable, a miracle, a triumph! You did fantastic things. You saved many lives and you should be proud."

She was embarrassed now. She didn't know that she'd been spoken highly of by others. She shrugged her shoulders, self-conscious, just as she used to do as a child.

"But I watched them. I watched them." She teared up again.

"And it was horrible, but it wasn't you. You must remember that, Marta. It was them, not you. It was them. And it wasn't love-making you saw." He thought for a moment, held up his hand. "What's this, Marta?"

"A hand."

"What's it now?"

"A fist."

"What's the difference? I'll tell you. It's the actions of the person behind the hand, not the hand. You can use a hand to caress, heal, or punch and choke, that's the point. The sexual act is the same. What you saw was rape, ugly, brutal rape. That is not the same thing as lovemaking. And there is even another level, fornicating and lovemaking. Many, many people get caught up in that; fornicating instead of lovemaking. It's empty, sad, and I don't want you to fall into that trap. The two are not the same thing, Marta. Trust me, especially not the same when you love your partner. I can tell you that. I can tell you that for certain." He felt a little foolish now, being the confessor. It was not in his nature to be tender and so expressive.

"You loved your wife."

"Every day." It was his turn to cry now. "I miss her so much, Marta."

She cried again and looked up. "Why are you so good to me? Why is everyone so good to me?"

He kissed her on the head. "Because you are good, Marta. You've got a big heart and you're smart and funny and very beautiful. Remember, men are mostly fools when it comes to a beautiful woman. They'll do anything for a woman who's beautiful."

At that, she managed a smile, then a grimace. "I'm so tired." And she was. She was exhausted from fighting and crying and being up all night. She had a terrible headache. He led her to the bow and got her to lie down. She slept while he sailed back to the hotel.

VI Subterfuge

The last leg of the trip, to Tampico, was spent in her room. She'd exhausted herself, slept fitfully, awoke often and every time she did it reminded her of the fact that Rebecca would never, ever share her bed again. It was inevitable but, nonetheless, she'd never prepared herself for this time. They were always together and Rebecca was the main reason why Marta enjoyed some relative happiness since her freedom from the bandit gang.

Del Calle understood and gave her the space she needed. She was awestruck by him, especially how he handled the incident on the sailboat. She could tell that he knew she was strong. He also sensed that she was in the crisis of her life and, most importantly, knew that leaving her to work it out on her own was the best thing for her now.

She wondered at his absence, though. She wondered why he hadn't knocked on her cabin door. She missed him desperately.

She had so much self-doubt these days. More than when she first went to live in Maryland with Abuelita and at the fancy girls' school. That was a terrifying time, too. The other girls were so far along in their studies and Marta was so ignorant. She was ignorant in academia, ignorant in the ways of polite society and she stood out like a beacon with her dark skin.

She knew she didn't fit in the Walsh's world, yet they welcomed her, protected her and did so in such a way that she felt like family, not some charity case; not like she was some sociology experiment.

She remembered reading about little monkeys rich ladies kept as pets to occupy and entertain them back in the old days; she often felt like that. She was Rebecca Walsh's little trained monkey. She also knew that was all in her mind. No one in the Walsh family ever looked upon her as anything less than one of the family. She loved them all so much and never stopped appreciating what they'd done for her for all these years. Yet, at times, she still felt like a burden and an outsider.

And now her Rebecca was going to leave. Rebecca was the strong one, not Marta; Marta pretended, Rebecca lived it. And Rebecca never abandoned her adopted sister. Rebecca was loyal to her all through the years. In looking back, Marta realized there had been many opportunities that Rebecca didn't take because of her loyalty to Marta. Rebecca had been invited to San Moritz but, because Marta hadn't been, Rebecca declined. There was the time Rebecca had been invited to Rome—without Marta—and she chose not to go. She never said that if Marta wasn't welcome, then she wouldn't participate. She always had a plausible reason for declining the many invitations and never indicated by word or action that she believed Marta was holding her back.

Marta looked at the empty pillow and cried thinking about what life would be like now that Rebecca was gone. She thought about living in adjoining houses, being together, finding a husband and settling down and raising her family with Rebecca's family, but it didn't seem good enough. It didn't seem that it could ever fill the void that she was feeling now.

Marta fell into a light sleep and dreamed a little; some were good dreams. She dreamed of Del Calle. He was a good man. She felt ashamed of calling him a galoot. He was not a galoot, he was smart and sensitive and kind. She had dreams of all the good men in her life, there were so many good men in her life. She thought about all of them, first the old man, then her uncle Alejandro del Toro, and especially her adopted father, Arvel Walsh. And uncle Bob, and Dick Welles, and now Curtin and the strange aborigine man, Billy Livingston, and the handsome as all hell, Dan George.

They were men. And she didn't hate them. But why, when she fantasized about doing *it* could she only see the rapes? Why?

She knew that love could be tender and good. She held up her opened hand and then made a fist. Del Calle was right, sex could be bad and it could be good; he was right, she knew he was right. But to think about the act made her ill.

It was like awakening from a bad dream, and then, every time she closed her eyes, all she could see was the same ugly dream. It was not really awakening from the dream at all, it was just a continuation; the dream was a nightmare that lasted a lifetime and made her want to never go to sleep. This is what she was feeling about being with men.

She thought about having a baby. Rebecca was going to get pregnant, no doubt about that. No one could do it that many times and not get pregnant. She worried about Rebecca so much. When she was with the bandits, they had so many babies and so many were sick and the mothers died in childbirth. The curandera was mostly to blame. Her rituals were absurd: forcing the women through childbirth, applying her potions, carrying out her ridiculous mindless acts. She caused more deaths than anything else.

She'd forgotten so much about her bandit life and now, in the past three days, it was all coming back to her. The terrible memories rushed in from the place in her brain where she had buried and suppressed them. They scared and worried her.

Del Calle's wife died giving birth. Did they have a curandera at the birth? Did they have curanderas in Puerto Rico, or was his baby born in Maryland? Maybe she had died at the naval hospital where there was the best medical care. She had still died.

She was so afraid for Rebecca now. She suddenly hated Curtin, sticking that thing in her. The bastard! He was going to impregnate her and she'd give birth and die and he'd go on and find someone else and do it again and again.

She cried again. Finally, she looked at the clock. It was the last night at sea. She didn't want to lie there anymore, wallowing in self-doubt and self-pity. The men were good, both Curtin and Del Calle were good. There were a lot of good men. Not all of them, of course, but many were good. She sat up and felt for the floor. She was weak from worry and lack of food. She hadn't eaten in more than a day. Slowly, she got up and got herself together.

Pedro del Calle had time to think as well. He thought mostly about Marta. She was the most confounding young woman he'd ever met. She was fascinating. He checked on her half a dozen times during her marathon sleep, locked away in her cabin. He even had Rebecca check in on her several times.

Rebecca was good to him. She was a lovely creature and Pedro could see why Marta loved her sister so much. She was likely the most selfless, loving person he'd ever known. At one point, when he was particularly worried, Rebecca looked at him, touched his face gently with her hand and, holding it there said, "She'll be fine, Pedro. I know she'll be fine." That was Rebecca Walsh; she was old beyond her nineteen years, kind and wise.

They all sat together for the last dinner of the cruise. Curtin and Rebecca so comfortable together, very much like an old married couple. They were soul mates, perfectly meshed, as if this had been planned for them all their lives and had finally come to fruition.

Marta could see it. She felt better seeing her sister so happy. Then that feeling of foreboding rose again and as she gazed at Curtin, she felt ill. He was leaning forward, holding Rebecca's hand. She was wearing a beautiful engagement ring, a ring that someone of Curtin's status should never be able to afford. Marta felt pain again that Rebecca hadn't shown it to her; the wonderful symbol of Curtin's love.

She started to say something then held her tongue. She'd downed a couple of glasses of wine quickly; uncharacteristic for Marta as she liked always to be in control. She saw how stupid alcohol made the savages when she was a child and avoided it except for during the most special occasions. Tonight was the exception and it had the expected effect. She became angry at Curtin again.

"So, when will you be making an honest woman of my sister?"

They all felt the barb. Del Calle looked at his hands. Rebecca spoke up before Curtin could come up with any kind of reply.

"That's ugly, Marta."

She knew it and was sorry for saying it. She didn't know why she said such things. Then went on, "Well, are you at least attempting to keep her from becoming pregnant?"

She looked at Curtin, now red-faced. He was embarrassed and becoming angry. He sat forward in his chair as Marta continued.

"She's pretty frail you know." She glanced over at Pedro. "You might end up killing her, like old Pedro did to his wife."

"*That's enough, Marta!*" Rebecca reached over, grabbed the wine glass from her sister's hand. She looked her in the eye. "That's enough, Marta."

Marta pulled her hand away, stood up. "I'm sick and tired of people telling me no, or that's enough, or to stop or shut up or whatever... I've had about enough of all of you."

She stormed out, leaving a stunned silence behind her. Rebecca grabbed Pedro by the hand. "I'm sorry, Captain." Turning to Curtin, "I'm sorry, both of you. She's having a rough time right now. She's really not like this, you know?"

"Understood." Curtin was calming down. He didn't like feeling as if he was a wedge coming between the two girls. Del Calle swallowed hard. It was a terrible insult to him, as well. He'd thought many times that he, in fact, was responsible for his wife's death and he didn't need to hear it from Marta right now.

Rebecca sat at the edge of the bed and began dressing. Curtin rubbed her back. "Going to go have a talk with her?" She nodded. "I'm sorry, Rebecca." He sat up and kissed her neck. "I'm sorry."

"For what?" She smiled and thought how much she'd rather lie back down next to him.

"For being so damned selfish. I've taken all your attention and that was very bad of me." He kissed her shoulder as she put her stockings on.

"She's good, Robert. You know she's good. And I'm sorry, but you get both of us if you get me."

"I know." He laughed. "There's an old Indian saying you know, East Indian, not Red Indian. When you marry a woman, you marry her family."

"Oh, then you are in for it, Robert Curtin." She turned to kiss him. "You're in for it."

"We should have told her about the ring."

"I know. It just, time got away from us, and then she slept for so long. I just forgot. It wasn't your fault."

She was dressed now and he stopped her. "Rebecca, before you go."

"Yes?"

"I need to talk to you about something." She didn't like his serious tone.

"What is it?" She sat back down on the bed beside him.

"I want you to go back to Maryland."

"You're kidding me. Robert, you can't be serious."

"No, Rebecca. I'm not kidding you and yes, I am serious. Something is up, something dangerous. I didn't want Marta to come down. I didn't know you at the time but now that I do, and now that we will be together forever, I don't want you down there. I don't want you in Mexico. I don't really want Marta in Mexico, but I know my chances are nil of convincing her not to go back to her ranch."

"If you've learned anything about me at all these past days, you know it will be impossible for you to keep me from the two most important people in my life. You might as well kill me as keep me from the two of you."

"I know. I knew you'd say that but I needed to try." He smiled at her and kissed her cheek. "Something bad's happening, Rebecca. I don't know what it is, but I need to do some investigating, need to do some cloak and dagger stuff. Sounds silly, doesn't it?"

"Yes. Who's doing all this, Robert? Who do you suspect?"

"Tolkenhorn mostly, maybe the government, maybe my employer. I don't think Dan George is dead, Rebecca, but I do think Marta's being lured down there. Something is up and it isn't safe."

"Marta got a telegram, Robert. Marta told me not to tell you or anyone about it. It was very cryptic. Signed by the letter Z. It read that Dan was alive and that we weren't to trust the people close to us."

She leaned forward. "Let's have a cigarette." They smoked. "What do you make of that, Robert?"

"I bet it's from Tolkenhorn. The Z means nothing, just some drama. He's a dumb ass, Rebecca, but he thinks he's clever. He wants Marta to sell, wanted me in on it. He thinks I'm with him." He grabbed Rebecca by the shoulders and looked her in the eye. "You know I'm not." He was deadly serious and she loved him all the more for it.

"With all my heart, Robert."

He thought about the ring and Marta. "Rebecca, what if I asked you to keep what we have together a secret?"

"Oh, this is real cloak and dagger stuff, Robert." She smiled coyly at him. "What do you have in mind?"

"What if we broke off our engagement?" She looked a little ill. "Not for real. Oh, my girl, I love you more than life itself. I swear to you, I love you so much." He kissed her again.

"But what can be gained of it?"

"Time. I need time to figure this out and it would be good if it could appear that I was playing you and Marta. It would look good to Tolkenhorn, but it wouldn't be real."

"And we'd lie to Marta?"

"Yes."

"I don't like that. I've never lied to Marta." She looked down at her beautiful ring. "Tell me exactly what we are to do, Robert. It's silly to say we aren't serious. She's seen us together for days, she knows me, she knows I'm not that kind of girl."

He thought about that. "Maybe tell her you called it off. Tell her we had a disagreement, that I was moving too fast, that you gave the ring back. You can't wear the ring on the ranch and let Tolkenhorn see it, that would ruin our little ruse."

"So, we can't even see each other? For how long?" She didn't like this plan at all. She didn't like lying to Marta.

He kissed her again. "I don't know how long. Rebecca, you told me about the bandits who captured you. Let me say that these people, Tolkenhorn, the people I work for, they are much the same. They don't rape literally, but they rape, nonetheless. I told you I nearly died up in Alaska. That was because they sent me on a suicide mission. They let a bunch of men go to their deaths just to potentially increase their profits. That's what we are dealing with, Rebecca.

"It's not about the land, it's not about beating them at their own game. I don't give a hang about money, really. I don't, Rebecca. It's about doing what's right. I know Marta loves the people and is a good hacendado. I know she thinks of her people first and I'm with her—and I'm with you."

"I love you Robert Curtin." She kissed him. "Have I told you that, lately? I love you."

She touched Marta's arm gently. "I'm awake, Rebecca." She didn't turn to face her sister.

"Marta, I'm sorry."

"I know, Rebecca." She rolled over to face her and her eyes and cheeks were wet. She'd been crying again and it scared Rebecca. It was not in Marta's nature to cry, and she was crying so much lately.

"Oh, sweetheart." Her own tears came now. "I'm so, so sorry. I hate to see you this way. I'm sorry, Marta."

Marta sat up and brushed the hair from her sister's eyes. "No, it's not you. You've done nothing wrong, Rebecca. This is ludicrous. I'm being absurd and I'm so sorry. Curtin's a good man. I don't know what comes over me!

"Are they all right? Is Pedro all right? I had no right to talk that way. He told me something very personal and I used it to hurt him. I'm sorry, Rebecca. You go, marry Curtin, have a hundred babies. It's what's right."

"I know, darling. But we will always, always be sisters. We'll always be together, maybe not physically, but in our hearts, darling, I swear to you."

They cried together and Marta suddenly remembered. "Let's see this ring." She grabbed Rebecca's hand but the ring was gone. "What's this?"

Rebecca reached over and lit two cigarettes. She handed one to Marta. Marta watched her as she smoked.

"I know, it's a terrible habit, you've all driven me to it." She smiled. "Marta, Robert asked me to create a ruse. We're to be married, but something is going on with this Tolkenhorn fellow. Robert wants Tolkenhorn to think that he's still working to get the ranch from you. He doesn't want Tolkenhorn to know that he and I are in love. He wanted me to lie to you and tell you that we broke off our engagement, but I'll never lie to you, Marta."

"And he thinks you're going to lie to me?"

"Yes."

"So, you're lying to him instead of me."

She hadn't thought of it that way. "Ye...s, I guess I am."

Marta grinned. "You're a sneaky one, Rebecca Walsh."

"I love him, Marta. We're going to be married."

"Rebecca." Marta smoked and blew the smoke away from them and thought for a moment. "What do we really know about Curtin?"

"I don't know. He's kind and lovely and I love him. He almost died up in Alaska. I know that. He fought like a wild animal to save me from the masher."

Marta laughed. "Masher. More of a goon."

I know he's trying to help you, Marta."

"I'm not so certain about him, Rebecca." She held up a hand. "Don't get me wrong, I know he's stealing you away and that hurts, but it has to happen sometime. We can't be a pair of old maids living together forever; we're too pretty for that."

Rebecca smiled as Marta continued. "But there's something, I can't put my finger on it. But there's something.

"I didn't want to say anything, Rebecca, but yesterday, when I was locked away, I guess Pedro was pacing around outside my door, worrying over me. He's such a big lunkhead, God bless 'im. He's sweet, isn't he, Rebecca?"

"He is."

"Anyway, he was loitering out there and Curtin came up and they were talking. I couldn't make out much but Curtin was very animated. It was strange, I never heard him act or talk that way. And I heard him say something I didn't like, Rebecca."

"Oh?"

"He was saying—and I only heard one sentence. It was like he was telling the punch line of a joke."

"What?"

"But it wasn't a joke. He said, 'Once you've got 'em on their backs, it's smooth sailing.'"

"Oh." Rebecca finished her cigarette. She suddenly felt dizzy, a little ill, and it wasn't from the tobacco.

"I don't know, Rebecca, but let's see how it all plays outs. We have each other, that's what's most important. And we know now that Tolkenhorn has lured me—us—to Mexico. Hopefully, Dan George is still alive and that, sweetheart, forgive me for saying this, that Robert Curtin *might* be on our side."

The double ruse seemed to be working. When they disembarked from the ship, Curtin was courteous and aloof. Pedro del Calle was confused. He stood by as the ladies' bags were loaded into the waiting vehicle. They were ready to make the trip to Marta's ranch. He hung back and watched with interest as Rebecca got into the big automobile with her sister and Curtin stood by. He'd made his own arrangements to get back. He walked up to Del Calle and shook him by the hand. "Captain, it's been quite a ride."

"Agreed." Pedro bowed slightly and looked past Curtin to the girls. They were ready to leave. He looked back at Curtin who gave him a weak, wounded smile.

"It's a long story."

"Any luck finding your bag?"

"No, it's gone. They looked high and low for it. They'll send it on if it turns up. If it was stolen, the thief will be disappointed. It holds only some dirty clothes and a very amateurishly written journal." He shrugged and Del Calle handed him his card.

"Keep in touch, Robert. Drop me a line and send it here, it'll find me."

"What's in store for you in Vera Cruz?"

"Whatever the oil companies or sugar companies need." He grinned a little. "Cynicism comes with the job, Robert. God help me, I'm a United States Marine."

Marta called out to the captain, ignoring Curtin. "Pedro."

He walked up and she reached out and took his hand. She pulled him close and kissed him gently on the mouth as she pushed a card into his hand. "Write, please, Pedro. Write to me."

The engine roared and they were off. Captain Pedro Del Calle stood in the road, holding Marta's address in his hand and with dust in his eyes. He headed on to Vera Cruz.

Adulio had the ranch ready. Like two long lost princesses returning home, they were greeted with great pomp. Everyone was out to welcome them. Esmeralda waited patiently, the last in line. She never looked up, always kept her head down. She loved Marta more than life itself, more even than Adulio, her husband. The first time they'd met, she became Marta's lady in waiting which pleased Uncle Alejandro to no end. She'd been with Del Toro longer than even Adulio, who took pity on her when he arrived to work the hacienda where she devoted herself completely to the bandit Jefe.

Esmeralda had been deaf since childhood and, because of this, became mute as well. She could speak, but the strange timbre of her voice made the children tease her. Eventually, she stopped talking altogether. Adulio referred to her as muñeco. She was a tiny, timid, and quiet version of Pilar, the Walsh's housekeeper and matron of the mule ranch.

Marta was never cross or mean to her; she loved Esmeralda. When she reached the end of the line she stood in front of the old housekeeper, lifted her face by the chin and smiled warmly. Esmeralda always looked the same, wearing a half-witted, impish grin. Marta hugged her servant and gave her a gift, the most beautiful shell rosary she could find in Nassau. Esmeralda looked at it, nodded her shy nod and returned her eyes to the ground.

Adulio hissed at her, poked his wife firmly on the shoulder to get her attention and demanded she show more respect. She mouthed a weak, inaudible *gracias* and looked away.

The ranch looked good, the money from the oil had come in handy and everyone was enjoying the benefits of the new found wealth. Marta would not allow any improvements to the structures. Most hacendados spared no expense in importing great pieces of art, Italian marble, Spanish tiles. The places became magnificent palaces, but Marta would not have it. Everyone lived well, in well-constructed homes. The buildings were well maintained and every one had electric lights; she would not waste money on nonsense.

She'd built a school on the ranch and the children there and from the surrounding countryside enjoyed the benefits it provided. To Marta, education was the key, she'd learned it from the old man and she'd learned it from the Walshes. It was her first priority and she worked diligently to have a first class education opportunity for all. She had her own staff of teachers and the children would be educated and encouraged to do what they could according to their talents and ambition, no opportunity was denied them.

Thankfully, the oil wells were off on the far corner of the land, a good ten miles away, and they could neither be seen nor heard. This is where Curtin and Tolkenhorn resided. It was now a little village in itself. All the gringos brought down from the states were living there. They weren't a bad lot, overall, but most had no interest in Mexico. They were there to do a job and nothing more. Many went down to Tampico as often as they could and from there by ship to home. Others took the more difficult route and rode on horseback up to Texas, then took a train to visit their homes and families en el Norte.

This suited Marta just fine. She was glad that Curtin and the other oil men weren't under foot.

She was pleased with what she found upon her arrival and was not the slightest bit concerned. Marta's great weakness was that she possessed an overconfidence that often got her into trouble. In this instance, she was overconfident in her ability to handle the threat of being lured down to Mexico. She didn't believe the mining company could touch or hurt her and in this presumption she was wrong.

She decided that she'd go along with Rebecca's and Robert Curtin's little folly, and she was actually enjoying it more than she'd imagined she would. She finally had her beloved sister back to herself and the girls were reverting quickly to their desert and Mexican ways. They'd spent so much time in this part of the world growing up that it was always a special treat for them when they returned.

Marta soon adopted her old manly dress and Adulio had gotten Pumpkin, Marta's favorite pony, in condition for her to ride. Rebecca remained a little more austere, Eastern in her habits. She'd grown so accustomed to riding English and left the big Mexican saddle in the tack room.

They'd ridden now for the better part of a week, visiting everyone who lived on the land. Marta had developed quite a status since taking over the ranch many years before. Uncle Alejandro was a good jefe. He treated his people well, with respect, and his successes in the cattle business and later, the sugar business, would never override his good senses. He'd never let making money take precedence over the welfare of his people.

Marta continued this legacy. The ranch hands loved her for it and everyone in the region knew that, whatever happened in Mexico, this little corner would likely remain unchanged. The people here were happy, they had autonomy, they each worked their own little piece of land and there was always enough left for growing an ample crop of corn.

Despite being a wealthy and powerful hacendado, Marta enjoyed hearing the stories of Villa and Zapata. It was a queer thing, as one of the great land owners, she potentially had the most to lose if they finally won the day, but despite this she was ultimately on their side. She knew that she was not a typical hacendado. She knew that so many of the peoples of Mexico, particularly the Indios, lived horrible, squalid and desperate lives. Díaz had drained so much of the wealth from the country and the Americans, Japanese and Europeans had grown wealthy, extracting riches from the land and leaving nothing behind.

She heard a man say once, that the way Díaz treated Mexico was as if he were a stupid farmer who refused to put anything back into the land. One could harvest that way for two or three seasons, extract all the riches possible from the land but, sooner or later, the land would be depleted, the soil would become barren, and eventually, it would no longer yield. A good farmer knew that part of his profits must always be used to put nutrients back into the soil, he needed to rotate the crops, let the land rest and not just suck it dry. That is what happened to Mexico. The land was sucked dry and now the peons had had enough. Villa and Zapata were their instruments and Marta could not help but be excited and hopeful for them.

Curtin was not having so pleasant a homecoming. He did not like being away from Rebecca and Miles Tolkenhorn didn't help, either. He was especially friendly to Curtin, treating him as if they'd been lifelong friends. It made him feel uneasy. And on top of this, the company had sent them a new engineer. Curtin knew the man from Alaska. He was a relative of one of the officers of the company: incompetent, stupid, and unpleasant. Now Curtin was stuck with him. There was nothing quite as miserable as having a company's operations run on nepotism. It ensured failure every time.

They'd obtained some good studies for gold in the mountains in the northwest corner of Marta's ranch while Curtin was away and the new engineer had been assigned to pursue this opportunity. Curtin tried to see the paperwork on it but the young engineer kept it from him. It was typical of the fellow, and atypical of a good team. Curtin did not like it one bit.

Tolkenhorn sensed it, sensed the tension between the two men and tried to diffuse it, albeit in his usual, incompetent style. The men glared at each other like a pair of prize fighters circling in the ring, looking for a weakness, seeking a means to land a crippling blow. Tolkenhorn threw the suitcase on the desk between them.

"Curtin, my boy. They found your case." He smiled stupidly at the prize on the young engineer's desk. "Looks like it spent some time in the gulf." It was a moldering pile of garbage.

Curtin opened it to the stench of mildew and dirty sea water. He looked through it. His journal was there, at least partially. The leather cover was intact, the pages dissolved into an unreadable pulp. He took it out and closed the case, called in a clerk and instructed him to burn the rest. It was beyond use now. He looked through what was left of his journal, remembering what he'd written about his trip south, his time with Rebecca and felt even lower. His words, memories of the most exciting days of his life, were gone. Tolkenhorn prattled on about the gold prospect.

"It's good, thinly dispersed but good."

This brought Curtin out of his reverie. He looked at the young engineer: smug, ugly, and small-minded, sitting behind his desk. The young man smoked a cheap cigar and blew smoke at his desk. Curtin looked down at the man and saw him leaning over his papers, like a child hoarding candy. In a quick movement, Curtin snatched them away as the man lunged for them, leaping at Curtin who put a palm on the man's forehead and pushed him back into his chair. "*Sit down!*"

Tolkenhorn interjected, "Easy, Robert, no need for violence!"

"*Shut up, Miles.*" He studied the reports. "You'll need cyanide." He thought about that, too. Marta's contract specifically banned it. He decided to say nothing for now. Again, he thought, no need to show his hand to Tolkenhorn or the mining company.

He went off to his own office and Tolkenhorn followed. He brought a bottle and two glasses and Curtin realized that the boozing was commencing earlier and earlier for the sot lawyer these days. The old man had changed physically in just the short time since Curtin had left for Maryland. He looked a little more yellow, especially around the eyes. He now had a visible tremor all the time. He spoke pleasantly to Curtin as he downed the first glass. "You look good, Robert! The trip did you good. Sorry we couldn't get our first goal accomplished, but at least you got 'em down here."

"Them?"

"Sure, sure. The girl and her sister."

"I don't remember you saying you wanted the sister. Why'd you say that, Miles?"

"Oh, no, nothing, nothing in it, Curtin, my boy."

"I'm not *your boy.*"

"Take it easy, take it easy." He lifted a hand, waved innocuously. "Good news about the gold, eh? This is some rich goddamned land, Robert." He saw he was not making progress and tried to change the subject. "So," his eyes became slits, "have any luck on your journey down?"

"I told you, no, she doesn't want to sell."

"No, not *that* kind of luck. You know, between the sheets; they're quite a pair of lookers."

"I..." Curtin stood up and thought about smashing Tolkenhorn's ugly yellow face. He stopped himself. He stood over the man and then picked up the bottle and threw it out the window. He looked at Tolkenhorn and, without saying a word, pointed to the door and ordered him out.

Adulio worried over the girls' saddles as they prepared, well before daylight, for a half day's hunt. "Señorita, please let me send a couple of the men with you. There's a lot going on these days. There are Federales, bandits, and revolutionaries out there. I do not think it is a good place for the two of you to roam."

"We'll be fine, Adulio. It will be a sad day when I can't go out on my own ranch without an armed guard and, besides, you know Rebecca is the best shot in the land."

Adulio looked at the completely feminine Rebecca, the least threatening human being he'd ever known. He blew air between his lips. He knew his arguments were wasted on Marta. "As you will."

They were off looking for Coues deer. The ranch hands reported an abundance of them this spring. The winter had been mild and there had been no drought now for several years. They rode along as the sun came up; Marta was in a talkative mood.

"Have you seen Curtin?"

"Yes." Rebecca smiled. They'd been sneaking visits to each other every night. He even spent one night in her bed. It was thrilling as they were afraid the staff would discover them. Curtin was nervous these days, almost paranoid. He suspected that everyone was spying on him.

"You sure do love him, don't you?" Marta was finally making her own peace with Curtin, trying hard to not upset her sister.

"More than anything." She responded automatically, without even giving her answer a thought. She considered that. It had been this way for as long as she'd known him, from the very first day when she saw him playing with the rebozo lady's child.

They played cat and mouse with a small herd all morning, they would kill only bucks as it was too early for the babies to be weaned and they did not want to risk taking a mother. It was good sport. They'd have a shot, then look for antlers. None that they had in range ever sported headgear and they ended up stopping in a shady area near good water for a long lunch.

This was when Marta was happiest. She was home, in her element. She didn't think about her days with the bandits when she was in the desert. She thought about her people. These were her people. They had lived here for the past thousands of years. The pottery shards, projectile points, pictographs, all of these artifacts made her feel at home, feel as if she belonged, she was no longer out of place or second class. She was mostly an Indian. Possibly, only the tiniest bit of Spanish blood was running through her veins. She liked being an Indian, she was proud of being an Indian and she could be an Indian here.

Rebecca took it all in stride. She had lost interest in hunting and camping when she was around thirteen. But she always went along, first with her father, then with Marta whenever they wanted to spend some time living on the land. It wasn't that she disliked hunting or rough living, it was just that it no longer— perhaps never—really interested her. That was the way with Rebecca. She was in training to be the perfect mother, always putting the needs of others before her own. She went hunting and camping with them because it made them happy. It made them even happier when she was there. Everyone loved her and felt happier when Rebecca was around.

She was, deep down, a thoroughly good person. She smiled as she watched Marta look over their surroundings. She smiled to herself, knowing Marta was especially happy because Rebecca was there. She and her sister were together and it could be seen and felt in Marta's demeanor and mood.

She looked around carefully and realized they were in the center of an abandoned home. Here and there the remnants of a wall could be seen poking from the sand, cactus and scrub brush. Rebecca wondered what had transpired many years ago when the place was the home of some ancient family. It was a good piece of desert and was probably even better a thousand years ago, even more abundant with wildlife. The family likely had no interest other than in just living; staying alive, staying fed, hydrated, together as a family. Just like it did for Marta, it made Rebecca feel connected to the land.

She sat down on the ground, near where the fire pit likely existed and closed her eyes. She imagined she could smell the mesquite wood burning, the tortillas cooking on the flat stone nearby; just over there. In a corner, a father or grandfather made arrows and in another, children were skinning a rabbit or armadillo. In another corner, an old grandmother worked on a green deer skin. She'd make it soft and useful. They'd all be talking together or maybe singing. Maybe they'd all be working quietly, waiting for the food to be ready. Afterward, they'd go out and sit under the stars and other members of their little tribe would make up a big fire and they'd sit around it and sing and just live. Just be alive.

The girls gave up on hunting and rode their horses north to the oil fields. From a rise, they looked down on dozens and dozens of wells; Robert Curtin's harvest. They weren't pretty but were necessary to the enterprise. The women looked at them and then at each other. They had mixed feelings about the blight to the land.

They rode on a little farther and came across a work party. There was a gringo, very animated, covered in oil and shouting orders to men who scurried around him under a great iron derrick. Black liquid shot from the ground and they were trying their best to contain it.

The man in charge cursed continuously as he worked and ordered his men around. He was a Canadian who worked for the mining company and reported to Robert Curtin. If he were not presently covered in the black substance, he would have displayed a head covered in red hair and lily white skin. He was a big man whose family hailed from Scotland a hundred years ago. They had immigrated to Canada to seek their fortunes.

He was a good boss and never cursed his men specifically; he simply had a foul mouth and cursed everything, all the time. He blinked hard to clear his eyes as the women approached. He held up a hand, signaling for them to stop. "No goddamned smoking, ladies!" They weren't smoking but that is how he greeted all visitors, no matter who they were. If a child had approached, he would have admonished him for smoking. It was hard-wired into him, just as was the cursing. It was second nature to him.

They continued to approach and watched, out of the direct path of the oil spray.

"Good afternoon." Rebecca nodded and gave the Canadian and his crew a smile.

"Good afternoon, ladies." He rubbed his face clean as the men got the gusher under control.

"Did you just strike oil on this one?"

"No, ma'am, it was capped, we're just harnessing up a nodding donkey to her." He pointed off in the distance at the many pump jacks working away. It did indeed look like a pasture full of giant nodding donkeys. "It's a goddamned good one." He was proud.

Rebecca grinned at him. He was a funny man. She liked the fact that he spoke so freely, so profanely in front of them. He was like a man who'd been out in the wilderness, alone for too long. He'd forgotten his civilized voice. This was the way with the Canadian. He forgot how to speak without profanity, forgot how to speak around ladies. It wasn't because he had no respect for them, he did, but because he was so wrapped up and absorbed in his work. It was nice to see.

Marta forgot herself and started for her cigarettes as the Canadian admonished her again. "No goddamned smoking, ma'am. Sorry."

It was Marta's turn to smile. "No, I'm sorry."

"It's just, goddamn, if you've ever been to a well fire, ma'am, it's a goddamned mess."

"Understood."

"I'm Marta del Toro, and this is my sister, Rebecca Walsh."

He bowed. "Ladies."

"Is the work going well, Mister…?"

"Fitzgerald, ma'am. Frank Fitzgerald." He raised a hand. "Would offer a hand, but I'm so goddamned dirty." He grinned broadly and his white teeth shone brightly.

Rebecca looked beyond him at the many jacks cranking away, a constant, not exactly pleasant, din. Clank-clank, clank-clank, clank-clank, on and on. "Does that noise ever get on your nerves, Mr. Fitzgerald?"

He looked around as if seeing and hearing the machines for the first time. "Naw, ma'am, goddamned music to my ears." He wiped his arms with a filthy rag. "It sounds like singing to me."

"Really? What music?"

"Well, hear it, *clank-clank, clank-clank*? That's really *another-dollar, another-dollar*. Goddamned music to my ears."

"Another dollar?"

"Yes, ma'am." He pointed at one of the nodding donkeys. "That there, every time it turns, every goddamned revolution, is more goddamned money pulled from the ground. Three hundred fifty goddamned barrels a day, ma'am, each goddamned donkey pulling three hundred fifty barrels a day at sixty-one cents a barrel. Goddamned music to my ears, ma'am."

Rebecca looked at the field before her. He'd gotten nearly a hundred nodding donkeys going so far, and there were more—many more—to come. She calculated in her mind. She looked on at Marta and smiled in disbelief. "*God damn!*"

They left the men to their work and headed home. It was mind boggling, the wealth derived from oil. Rebecca wondered at it. When would it ever end? Curtin told her that fields could last a year or a hundred years and he was certain Marta's ranch would likely follow the path of the latter. It was rich and it was going to go on for a very long time. She soon realized that Marta's fortune could very well be measured in something beyond millions and it was suddenly overwhelming. She looked at Marta riding next to her and thought about her sister. It would be just another burden to bear. The gods were having a lot of fun with Marta del Toro, that was certain.

Marta felt her looking at her and turning, smiled. "What?"

"Nothing." She felt like talking. "Do you realize how wealthy you are?"

"Not completely, but yes, Rebecca. Yes, I have a good idea."

"I just…"

"What?" Marta grinned, she could see that Rebecca was struggling with something. "What?"

"Nothing." She became quiet. Marta was her favorite person in the world. Marta. Why was there always something happening to Marta? Rebecca didn't look at the vast wealth as necessarily a good thing. It would be just another thing to cause her dearest sister anxiety and pain; another cross to bear. It seemed to be the girl's fate. Marta was constantly hanging onto a great pendulum, swinging from one extreme to another.

First, to be born into a bandit gang, to have such intelligence; then to be given the gift of the old man, who cultivated her great mind; then Rebecca's abduction from the train and her mother rescuing her. Why did Marta have to be there?

Marta, herself, had been rescued and given a new life. But to be so dark in a lily white world; to be an outsider. And to be beautiful, sensual, attractive beyond comprehension and afraid of love. Poor Marta del Toro; Curtin was right, she was the consummate tragic heroine.

As they rode, Rebecca continued her ruminations. They found another abandoned settlement and dismounted, looking for deer sign. They discovered more remnants of their ancestors. Why couldn't Marta have just been another peon? In a way, it would have been a better life. She could have been born into the bandit gang, but perhaps a little duller, not so precocious. She would have been one of the little girls who'd been left behind. She wouldn't have gone on the raid in el Norte, not been the little bandit boss Rebecca met when she was captured. She would have worn a simple skirt and peasant blouse and been wrapped up in her rebozo instead of carrying a six shooter and wearing vaquero clothes with her little gun rig and knife.

Perhaps, once her Mamma and Daddy had killed all the bad men, Marta could have been allowed to go to San Joachim, or some other village. She could have married a good peasant and had three or four children by now. She would not have seen the rapes and the bad things. She wouldn't have killed. She wouldn't be afraid of sex and be able to make love and have babies. She wouldn't have become friends with the old man and read the book about the circles of hell.

She would have been a simple Indian peasant woman and maybe she would have been happy. She would have been illiterate, never learned French and Latin and studied the history of the world. But neither would she have learned of condoms or bad dances and ugly songs and dirty limericks. She would have been a good Catholic and gone to the annual festival in the nearest town every year. She would have raised her children and lived out her life. It would likely have been a far easier life than what she'd been living up until now, far easier than what was in store for her for the rest of her days.

And then Rebecca thought about her own time with the bandit men. Marta had really saved her, long before her mother had arrived. It was Marta who stopped the bad men from raping her and it was Marta who helped her mother when she'd done her trick with the mock crucifixions.

So, in a way, it was all necessary, all this had to come to pass, if Rebecca was to be sitting on this horse, right now, in the year nineteen-eleven, on the ranch of Alejandro del Toro. She wondered, wondered very earnestly, whether she would have given it all up. If an angel were to come down from heaven right now and give Rebecca a choice, what would she choose? If the angel said that Marta could be a simple peasant woman, live a happy life as a peon and never know such things, but Rebecca Walsh would have to endure the bandit gang and whatever came to pass as a result, without Marta by her side, what would she choose? This made her very sad and she wanted to cry. She was giving herself a terrific headache.

They dismounted and half-heartedly looked for more deer sign. Neither of them was much interested in hunting. Rebecca wasn't even looking at the ground. She was staring into the distance, looking into the abyss of her thoughts, and could just as well been anywhere in the world.

Her musings were interrupted by a cloud of dust to the west. Both women knew by the size of it that at least half a dozen riders were approaching. They weren't afraid but it was prudent to be cautious, so they quickly mounted up. If the riders' intentions were bad, it would be better to be able to fight or run ahorse than on foot. Rebecca and Marta were not averse to either.

The group was a small detachment of Federales with two prisoners. Their prizes were not impressive, only two scrawny peons, not more than thirteen years old. They were a couple of *White Cigars*, known as such because of their white clothing and because the huge straw sombreros they wore looked like puffs of smoke. They'd lost their hats, or rather they'd been knocked from their heads in order to add to their torture. They were being pulled behind the mounted men by hemp ropes tied around their necks.

Marta positioned her horse in the middle of the road, blocking the soldiers' path. The captain rode up to her, his horse nearly within touching distance of Pumpkin. He raised his hand, a little dramatically, as if he were stopping a troop of a thousand men. "Alto."

Marta rode past him, as if he was invisible, and handed a canteen to each captive. They drank deeply as the captain lit a cigar. He was impressed with such impudence and surveyed the two beauties. They were well put together. He was not from this part of Mexico and did not know how famous they were. Marta finally addressed him. "Why are you on my land?"

"Beg your pardon?" He stood in his saddle and removed his hat. "Capitan Jose Santiago, madam."

"What did they do?"

"Subversion."

"You cannot be serious. They are children. They can barely walk. What subversion?"

He produced a pamphlet and handed it to Marta. "Against the state. Anarquistas. We found this on them."

"Nonsense." She handed it back without looking at it. "They're more likely using it as cigarette paper. They cannot even read, I bet." She looked at the older one. "Muchacho, spell cat."

He could not. Nor was he pretending.

"President Madero does not sanction such treatment of prisoners, Capitan. I know this."

"Madam, we don't take orders from that alfeñique. General Huerta tells us what to do. He is the only one keeping the country together."

"This does not seem the right way to keep a country together, Capitan. Pulling scrawny boys through the desert by their necks? Seems a waste of good Federales. You give us these boys, we'll make certain they do not become anarquistas."

Rebecca was angry at the treatment of the boys and it brought back memories of Sombrero del Oro. She slipped away as the captain was occupied with his little sparring session with Marta. The captain liked Marta and wanted to impress her with his knowledge of the revolution. It was always easy with stupid, brutish men. They could only think with their penises and it was easy to distract them with feminine charm. Rebecca rode up high on a hill overlooking the little party and uncased her Winchester. She checked the rear sight and adjusted it for the closest range. She awaited Marta's orders.

The captain leered at Marta, rode up next to her and looked her up and down, too obviously surveying her breasts. "I'm afraid that is quite out of the question, madam." He looked around. "Where are the men of your party? I'd like to speak to a man about this."

"There are no men. We are alone and I am the hacendado here." She purposefully used the masculine tense—always—when she referred to herself as the head of the ranch.

"Well, then, young lady, it would be best if you leave this man's work to men. We are pleased to make your acquaintance, but it is time we get our prisoners on."

Marta raised her hand. Rebecca fired and cut the captain's left rein. It was not a far shot, no more than thirty yards, but it accomplished its goal. The captain worked to get his horse under control, which now turned continuously in a circle, making the officer look especially silly to his men who were enjoying the spirited señoritas immensely.

Marta waited. Reaching out, she got his horse under control for him, furthering the humiliation. She closed in on the captain, looking him in the eye. "You are a nice capitan, I can see it. You don't need to die for a couple of scrawny peons." Marta pulled her big knife and cut the ropes from the boys' necks. "You go on along this road, Capitan. You will reach my ranch in another hour. See a man named Adulio. He is the overseer of my ranch. Tell him I sent you and that we'll be along shortly. Your men are welcome to rest there as long as they like, we'll even kill a nice calf for you, have a regular little fiesta. You'd like that, yes?" She didn't wait for an answer but stepped aside so the troop of men could pass. "We must finish our hunt."

She watched him take it all in. He did not like this humiliation but had no doubt that the young woman's next shot would be fatal. It was not worth all this trouble and killing a prominent señorita on her land could become an international incident.

He stood up in his saddle, once again removing his hat, "As you wish, Señorita." He called to his men who thundered past her. She could not help but notice a few of them winking at her in appreciation as they passed by.

Rebecca finally worked her way back down from her perch and began helping the boys. They were obviously starving.

Marta dismounted when the soldiers were out of sight. She kissed Rebecca on the cheek, "Lovely shooting, my dear."

"We probably won't be seeing the last of them."

"Oh, they can go to hell." She looked doubtfully at the smaller boy. He gulped water and soon began to retch. "Easy, muchacho, easy."

After a time the boys could walk. They were offered the girls' mounts and refused. They'd walk through the desert, barefoot, for the rest of their days if it meant they could follow their beautiful saviors.

That night, Curtin had a chance to interrogate Rebecca about the little excitement. He listened intently, guarded. He didn't like the love of his life shooting at Federale captains and simultaneously couldn't help being a little proud of her. "You are full of surprises, my love." She wanted him and didn't want to talk.

She climbed on and held him tightly. "Are you so surprised?"

"I am. I wouldn't be if you told me that Marta did this, but you, it's just so..." He was having trouble thinking of the words. "It's just so uncharacteristic, Rebecca." He began to worry. "And it's dangerous as all hell. Why'd you do it?"

"Those boys needed our help, and Marta needed my muscle. That bone-headed captain wouldn't give them up so easily. Now shut up, darling. Shut up."

They rested in each other's arms and Curtin was agitated again. He was so anxious lately. "Would you have shot that Federale if he hadn't given up?"

"Right between his beady little eyes."

"And the rest?"

"Only if they needed it."

"You are something, Rebecca, truly something."

"Oh, I'm much nicer than my sister, *and* my mother." She smiled at the thought of her mother.

"Really? How?"

"They'd a killed them all. Every one of them."

"Rebecca, can we please go back home?"

"Why?"

"It's just too much." He thought about what he wanted to say. "I've finally found you. I don't want to lose you."

"You worry too much, Robert."

"And you, not enough." He looked at his watch and pulled himself away. "I've gotta go."

Marta was waiting for him outside of Rebecca's room. She startled him, drawing hard on her cigarette to make her whole face glow. It had the desired effect. Curtin nearly jumped out of his skin.

"You scared me!"

Marta smiled. "Sit down, Robert. Look at this note from the captain. Pretty amusing."

Curtin peered at it, holding it up to a candle Marta lit for him.

"My dear Señorita del Toro, It was an interesting interlood today. If you ever show me such disrespect again, I will cut off your head and place it on a stake at the entrance road to your ranch, Yours humbly, J. Santiago, Capitan."

She watched the color leave Curtin's face. "Dumb-ass misspelled interlude, and he no doubt meant interaction. Simpleton."

Curtin handed the note back and Marta folded it carefully. It was just another of many trophies.

"So, you know our secret?"

"Oh, sure, Robert. Rebecca told me the very first day. Rebecca and I have no secrets, Robert. None." She lit another cigarette off her first one, smoked hard. "What are you playing at, Curtin? Whose side are you on?"

"Yours."

"Really?"

"Yes. Absolutely. But I don't care about your stupid ranch or getting rich or the revolution or whether the mining company steals the bloomers off you. I don't care about anything but your sister."

"So, to say you are on *my* side is an overstatement?"

He stood up and blew out the candle, spoke into the darkness where he knew Marta was sitting. He spoke clearly and precisely into the dark. "Yes, Marta. I'd give up your life for Rebecca's. I'd give up my own life for Rebecca's. I'd hand you over to Satan himself if it was for the welfare of your sister."

"Fair enough."

When he was gone she relit the candle, opened another note and read:

"Dan George up north, weakening. Will die soon. Federales coming to kill you, beware. Trust no one. Z."

Mexican Jousting

Adolfo, the blacksmith, looked on with interest at his mistress's diagrams. He nodded as he stroked his chin and smiled.

"And, what is the purpose of this ring tilting, Señorita?"

"Just for fun, Adolfo. Can you make these?"

"Oh sí, sí."

"Good. I want them ready for next week. We are having a tournament then, and you will be in it. Be ready." She smiled and regarded the old man. He was kind and so happy for his shop. He smiled and grabbed his belly. "Oh, Señorita, I am too fat to ride. I would need a bull and a bull would not run so fast, I think."

She loved Adolfo, who'd worked for her uncle since the beginning of the ranch. He kept the place going and could work magic with iron. Once the money started pouring in from the oil, Marta outfitted him with the best forge money could buy.

He was always working in it, to the point that everyone began to worry that he'd work himself to death. He was happiest when he was at his forge, working metal and, with the new equipment, his skill and art were now fully realized.

The girls loved ring tilting as they'd practiced it from their first year at Stonefields. Madame Boutin's little team of girls could give anyone, from Pennsylvania to Virginia, a run for their money. The girls were naturally good equestriennes and tilting was just another skill in which they excelled. Every fall it would be the same: Madame Boutin would host a great faire and the girls would all dress in the style of the English Renaissance. It was one of Marta's fondest memories.

Marta wanted her people to have some fun, do something they'd never done before and resolved, with the aid of Rebecca, to put on a proper Renaissance tournament, just like the ones they had at Stonefields. She ordered yards of brightly dyed cloth and distributed these to the ladies of the ranch, giving them picture books as inspiration. Everyone was to have a costume.

Next, she gave the participants lessons in ring tilting. Until Adolfo could make proper lances and rings, they improvised with wooden ones and by the time of the tournament, had many competent knights, male and female, young and old. It was going to be a grand time.

Next, she got all the ranch hands who could play musical instruments to learn songs of the period. Most could not read music so she played the tunes on the piano and they learned them by ear. It worked and soon, with their horns and accordions, violins and guitars, they were playing tunes a Tudor Lord would easily recognize, despite the lack of lutes and crumhorns.

She consulted with the women who were good cooks and worked on recipes of the times. The feast would be for everyone and on the big day the ranch would be adorned with streamers and pennants of every color. The men stood around, self-consciously, during their fittings, looking forlorn in their wool tights. They'd never worn such silly looking clothes and became embarrassed when the women looked at them, admiring their legs showing through the tight fabric. It was a fun role reversal and the men ultimately took it in stride.

Many of the women got a little creative in their research, going through Uncle Alejandro's library and, as a consequence, the timeline got muddled. They found some books with engravings of Hogarth's *The Rake's Progress* and were inspired to create costumes that not only accentuated, but in some instances revealed, ample bosoms. It was deliciously naughty and Marta observed as the preparations for the festivities carried on through the week. The excitement was building and everyone had difficulty containing themselves, anxious for the big day.

In keeping with the theme, she disallowed any mescal or tequila for the entire faire, replacing these instead with rum, gin, wine and ale. She didn't care if it was right for the time, it all sounded old-timey and English and it would work well enough. The people would be thrilled to try spirits that were alien to most of them. It would all flow freely but no one who was to compete would be allowed to imbibe until the jousting tournament was over. Some rings would have to be skewered and she was certain that this would be unlikely if she had a bunch of drunken knights on her hands.

She had a special outfit made for Rebecca, keeping it a secret until the big day. It consisted of a blue velvet gown and French hood of blue brocade, silver trim, and a white veil. She let her lady tailors make the neckline plunge a little too deeply and knew Rebecca would balk at revealing so much of herself. As they dressed her, she grinned as Rebecca glanced down at her chest doubtfully. Marta completed her own ensemble, topping it all off with a fuchsia cone hat to match the color of her dress. Her neckline rivaled Rebecca's.

Rebecca pulled up on the bodice, but it wouldn't budge. "We look…"

"Wonderful!" Marta was giddy.

"Ridiculous, is more like it." Rebecca acted put out but really wasn't. She was having fun.

"No, no, we don't. We look grand." Marta turned to the side and gazed into her full-length mirror. "This makes my bosom look even bigger! Wish Pedro was coming."

Rebecca regarded her and then once again looked at herself. "I don't remember anything like this at Stonefields." She looked back at Marta and pointed, guardedly. "One of your nipples has gotten out."

Marta pushed it back in and grinned. "Maybe I'll ditch this all together and go as Lady Godiva."

Marta made it a point to invite the gringos from the mining company, but did not let them know about the costume theme. She needed an audience, and they would serve the purpose. She mostly wanted to annoy and vex Curtin by showing off her sister in the beautiful and provocative gown. She did not care if it was all a great fantasy. It was fun and exciting for everyone and Marta was going to do her best to make it a memorable time for them all.

Adolfo got into the spirit of the thing and spent his time hammering away. He'd made swords and broad axes and armor and pikes for several of the men. He made giant spits to handle an entire swine and on the big day, there'd be pig roasting in every corner of the square. He made a stock for naughty children which just about everyone had to try. Marta hired photographers who came in and took pictures of every one of them. They'd all have a memento of the day. With the aid of several of the ranch's carpenters, a grandstand for the ladies to watch the tournament was built and draped with more colored fabrics.

On the big day, Curtin arrived with the entourage of mining company men. The cursing man was there and, thankfully, with the aid of many of his men, he was able to keep the goddamns to a minimum; many children were around. Marta was especially pleased about her little torture plan for Curtin, who looked on but could do nothing regarding his true love. Up to this point, he never believed Rebecca could look prettier, but now she did. The royal blue of her costume accentuated the radiant glow of her skin and her shining raven hair.

She blushed and looked at Curtin, waiting until they were alone. She looked down at herself, then cast her eyes upward, regarding her hat. "Ridiculous?"

It was Curtin's turn to blush. "Not at all." He did his best not to gawk. He felt like a schoolboy stealing glances at a classmate's bloomers. "You look, well, royal." He beamed at her. He was so much in love and, at the same time, frustrated. Every time he looked around, it seemed one of his fellow oil men was gazing at his woman, smitten as well. It was extremely off-putting; frustrating and exciting all at the same time.

Marta walked up to them. She was enjoying it all thoroughly. She was still not totally convinced that Curtin's intentions were pure and she harbored some ill feelings because he was stealing her sister away. Assuming her best poker face and adjusting her costume to show off the womanly gifts God had given her, she said, "Mr. Curtin." She nodded formally and watched him now gawk at her, turn red and avert his eyes. She looked down at herself and then back at him, looking him in the eye. "Is there something amiss with my costume?"

He shocked her a little, leaning close and whispering in her ear. "I won't forget you for this, Marta." He grinned a little cynically and looked at the gringos all around him. "I won't forget this any time soon, you little devil."

She handed him a goblet of wine, "Oh, relax, you big baby. Have a drink, try to work the knots out while you drool all over my sister." She nodded at Rebecca who'd by now begun to play with some children. "She looks good, doesn't she?"

Robert Curtin regarded Rebecca, then looked back at Marta. "As I said, I won't forget you for this, Marta." He smiled.

It turned out to be a glorious day. Everyone, especially the children, were having the times of their lives. They played and ran about in their little costumes, transported to another place and time. The school teachers had been instructing them on the history of the time and the little play would help them make sense of it all. It was fun and frivolous and just the kind of celebration Marta had planned for them to remember for the rest of their days.

Esmeralda stood by, the lady in waiting. She was dressed to match her mistress and, with her little impish half-witted grin, it was not readily evident that she liked all these carryings on; but she did. She was pleased with herself, and stole glances whenever she passed any mirrors and windows, even her reflection in the horse trough, every chance she got.

Adulio, likewise. He complained the entire way, through every fitting; complained at the itchy stockings, complained about the pheasant plume in his cavalier hat, complained that the three of them, Marta, Esmeralda, and Adulio, looked like an absurd family, ancient Englishmen in the middle of the high Mexican desert. It was ridiculously wonderful and fun and, Adulio, though he'd take it to his grave and never admit it, was enjoying it as much as everyone else.

Tolkenhorn took advantage of the excuse to start drinking early in the day. By noon he was sloppy drunk. He regarded Curtin who was trying his best to look detached from the women. He could not reveal that he was head over heels in love with one of them. He sensed that Tolkenhorn was going to start in on some nonsense and tried to drift away, but the old sot was too quick and grabbed him by the arm.

"What do ya think this cost?" The lawyer downed another glass. He didn't wait for a reply. "Waste of damned money. Look at 'em, ignoramuses. Lost on 'em. Like castin' pearls before swine."

Curtin ignored him. It was all about perception and he saw something very different. He saw a Lady of the Manor, celebrating, splurging a little. The difference was that she didn't pick and choose who'd benefit. This wasn't for the wealthy and powerful and wasn't put on to show off to other wealthy hacendados. It was a party for her people, all of her people, young and old, ignorant and well-read, the entirety of them. It was a celebration of them, of life and it all was due to the oil. The oil. The oil would—could—be used for good purposes, as long as the one holding the purse strings was good; a decent, moral, gracious and kind possessor of the wealth. And this was what the lady, the Lady of the Manor, Marta del Toro, embodied. Curtin was truly humbled by it all and suddenly lost the little enmity he had for Marta's devilment, for so deliciously, irresistibly dressing the love of his life in such a way as to drive him beyond the point of distraction.

It was time for the tournament and Marta rode first. Pumpkin was beautifully adorned with blankets and a hood matching, in color and style, her mistress's costume. It seemed the animal sensed it, sensed it was beautifully matched to her mistress and she performed likewise, she proudly pranced about and was having just as good a time.

Due to her long heavy dress, Marta was forced to ride sidesaddle, adding to the fantastical theme. She did well and soon had the medieval vaqueros primed to perform. They had quickly figured out what it was about. They were natural riders and took to the lances made by Adolfo, as easily as if they were their beloved reatas. They followed suit and in short order a close competition was in play.

Rebecca, of course, won the day. She'd been ring tilting the longest, had loved it for so many years that it was like second nature to her. She stood on a high platform, one step above the second and third place riders as Marta, queen of the faire, placed wreathes of laurel—actually Mexican Caesalpinia, an excellent substitute—on their bowed heads. The crowd cheered and as darkness fell, the festivities fully got underway.

They played and sang and danced well after midnight, outlasting the gringos who had to leave, many of them reluctantly, to continue the next day's toil in the great fields of nodding donkeys.

There was even some swordplay as two young vaqueros donned the armor cobbled together by Adolfo. Marta, like a doting mother, made them give up the steel broadswords. They'd have to content themselves with wooden ones, as she would not risk an injury to any of them. It was especially significant for Rebecca to see, the first time Marta shied away from danger, and it was gratifying, hopeful. Perhaps she was losing her fascination with death, living on the edge of reason, living for the thrill, regardless of the cost. It was a good and encouraging sign.

Just before dawn, they were readying themselves for bed. Marta watched Rebecca, by now a little sorry to have to remove the gown. It was beautiful and made her feel beautiful and now it was done, at least for another year, or until Marta got it into her head to put on another faire. Marta smiled and Rebecca saw it in the mirror.

"What?"

"Oh, nothing. You just look so beautiful."

"And you. The men couldn't keep their eyes off you."

"Hmm." She took a last look and removed the outfit. "Curtin, he was something."

"You're a real little brat for that, Marta."

"What?" She gave her Cheshire cat grin.

"You know what. You set him up, inviting the Americans and he, looking at me, couldn't touch me, couldn't even have a little taste." She grinned sideways at her sister, suddenly realizing she no longer felt uncomfortable discussing such things. She looked at the clock on her bed stand and thought it might not be too much of a stretch to see him before morning.

"Shall I go to my own room?" Marta could read her mind.

"No, it's too late. He won't be by. Come on." She jumped in bed and held the covers up for Marta. She put her arms around her and kissed her forehead.

"You made a wonderful faire, Marta. You are a good hacendado. It was like Christmas."

Marta beamed. "That reminds me. We're going to have a grand Christmas, better than what we had today. We're going to have …, have a carnival, with rides. That's what we're going to do. Yes, a carnival."

She lay back and snuggled against Rebecca's breast. She was played out. She fell into a deep and pleasant slumber. Marta was happy and this made Rebecca very happy. She kissed her sister's forehead and, she, too, fell into a deep and restful dreamland of knights and dragons and lords and ladies high in a castle keep.

VII Hunting

The summer was advancing and they'd made no further progress on discovering the whereabouts of Dan George. They'd hired a detective, an American from Texas who was Mexican. He'd tracked down the last place Dan George was seen alive, Nuevo Casas Grandes. There he found all of Dan's traps, his horse and tack. The constable assured him that Dan was not mugged or otherwise molested as far as anyone could tell. There was no sign of foul play. The patrons in the restaurant where Dan was last seen cooperated. Dan George was well known to them. He always stopped there on his way to Marta's ranch; many people liked and respected the American.

By their accounts, he was dining with two other men. They were speaking of mining business; nothing heated, all amiable. They did not think anything of it when the three men left. They figured they were simply retiring for the night. They only began to worry when his room remained unoccupied for three days. It was unlike Dan George to do anything without notifying everyone concerned. He was a good customer and always paid his bills.

Marta sent the detective on his way, up to Bisbee to report to Dan's wife. They had his traps sent back home. There was little left to do now but wait and watch.

Curtin was more often at the ranch now than at the mining office. He was constantly shadowing them. Marta was growing impatient with both he and Rebecca. They sat around as if they were attending a funeral and Marta was bored.

She sent them, separately, down to Vera Cruz. They could at least be together down there without all the sneaking around. Marta was also getting tired of looking at Rebecca's belly. She was certain it would begin to swell any day now. It certainly should with all the activity, unless there was something wrong with Curtin. But there it was, flat as a pancake, and that was vexing as well. She now wanted Rebecca to have a baby and was convinced—confident—that giving birth would not kill her.

Adulio could see his mistress growing bored. He recommended a hunting trip and Marta agreed that the change would do her good. Next morning he had everything set up, they'd take a pack mule and camp overnight. Marta looked at the old overseer and smiled.

"*You're* not going, Adulio."

He was hurt and looked down at his saddle horn but didn't say anything. She climbed into her saddle and took the man's canteens. She ordered him to transfer the provisions she'd need from the pack animal onto Pumpkin. Most of the items she would not need and refused them. She tapped her pony's sides and rode off, leaving the mule behind.

"Be back tomorrow, Adulio." She was gone.

She thought about going down to Santa Rosalia and perhaps getting into a little trouble there, maybe do some gambling. She liked to pretend to be in the old west when she was at the ranch. It was exciting and, hopefully, a little dangerous. It never turned out that way. The people didn't want to play. They just wanted to live their lives and didn't pay much attention to a sassy twenty year old Americana.

She thought a lot about Pedro del Calle. She was very sorry she made the comment about him killing his wife. That was mean and hurtful and she regretted it every time she thought about him. She hoped she'd see him again and wrote him a three page letter. It was full of sexually charged innuendo. She thought about him turning red when he read it, hoped it would get him excited and make him want her, make him come up and seduce her at the ranch. She was still bent on losing her virginity soon and she wanted Del Calle to be the one to carry out the deed. She didn't know why.

By noon it was hot and Pumpkin was limping. She was deep in the desert and in another hour it was apparent that Pumpkin was in trouble.

By the hottest time of the day she'd made it to an abandoned settlement. Uncle Alejandro had introduced her to this place. It still had intact high walls and the rattlers were abundant. One would never go hungry in the desert as long as rattlers could be found. They were bony but good eating and fairly easy to kill.

She cut some mesquite limbs and made a lean-to for Pumpkin who was now in obvious distress. The horse was not sound and Marta examined her leg. Just at the stifle she found a slight nick. She couldn't tell what had caused it. It was a curious wound, tiny, yet significant enough to render Pumpkin useless as a conveyance. Riding her home now or for the next several days would be out of the question.

She loved Pumpkin. Her parents had given the pony to her for her sixteenth birthday. She was gentle and smart and a peculiar buckskin color, the color of a whitetail deer in high summer, and that is how Marta arrived at her name. Pumpkin was pumpkin-colored.

Marta surveyed her camp. Uncle Alejandro was the quintessential bandit. He always saw terrain through the eyes of a man running from the law. He'd escaped from many and the means to do this was imprinted on his brain. He especially liked this place because it had high walls, like a fortress. With just a couple of Winchesters he could hold off twenty men. It had water, too.

So, Marta and Pumpkin were not in bad shape. She could stay here for days if needed. Once Pumpkin was better, she could walk back to the ranch or at least back to the road where a search party would surely find her.

She dug around the settlement for the rest of the day, playing like a child, exploring, imagining, discovering. It was fun as there were so many remnants of her ancestry left behind. She found half a dozen projectile points, a nearly intact clay pot and pieces of a sandal made of yucca fibers. She held it up to her foot and it would have fit. She felt akin to the owner, dead now for many centuries. Marta and the unknown sandal wearer would probably have been mistaken for sisters. Perhaps they were actually related. Maybe Marta was that woman, reincarnated, now living in the twentieth century. The fantasizing made Marta feel connected to the land, the people.

She stripped and bathed in the water running through the old place. It felt good to be out there alone in the intense heat, the blazing sun further darkening her already dark skin. She was coming to love her Indian identity more and more every day and the idea of being an Indian was progressively becoming easier to her. The problem was not *her*, it was *them*, the easterners who looked askance at her dark skin; the same dark skin as the Aztecs, the Incas, the great pyramid builders, the people who built beautiful stone structures when the ancestors of the whites who looked down their noses at her were still living in mud huts, defecating on the ground.

She reached down and scooped water with a broken pottery shard; a shard that had been created perhaps a thousand years ago. She poured water onto her raven hair, over her face, breasts, belly, pudenda. She gloried in the sensuality of it, gloried in the perfection of her body. She was beautiful, inside and out, and she was just beginning to understand and accept that. She was beginning to love herself and she wished Del Calle was with her. Perhaps one day she'd bring him here and they'd walk naked together all around the place, play and love and live and walk about as the original inhabitants had done so long ago.

By evening Pumpkin was settling down and Marta had set up a nice little campsite. She had a good fire going and plenty of wood to get her through the night. Typically, in the desert when the sun went down, it got cold. She snuggled under the blankets, naked. She liked to sleep nude though Rebecca would not have it. Rebecca thought it just too naughty to sleep without clothing of some kind but Marta was always most comfortable unencumbered by a nightgown.

She watched the fire for a while and then rolled onto her back and gazed at the stars overhead. A shooting star streaked by and she made a wish, though she didn't really believe in such things. It made her feel good, nonetheless, and she listened to the night come alive. She was never afraid when camping; not fearful of the animal sounds in the desert all around her. Coyotes started crying far off in the distance and she wished they'd come closer. She loved the coyotes and would not let them be killed on the ranch. They did no harm and there was no reason to kill any animal if it wasn't creating problems.

She drifted off to sleep and had good dreams, mostly of Del Calle, but also of Rebecca and Abuelita. She hoped that Abuelita was convinced that she and Rebecca were with the cousin in Paris. She didn't want to worry the old woman; she loved her very much. She dreamed and resolved in her dream that she would not be going to Smith College in the fall. She was going to live out her days on the ranch; run it and be a good hacendado and help to calm the unrest in her land. She was Mexican and she'd be Mexican until the day she died. She hoped that it would be later rather than sooner because now she was happy to be alive and she wanted to live a long time.

She slept well until daylight and after a light breakfast finally got moving and checked on Pumpkin. She discovered that the animal could walk better. She'd definitely not take a rider but she could at least walk. She put the bare minimum on the pony's back and left the rest. She could come back for it later, or have one of the ranch hands retrieve the items for her as it was not really so far. She carried her rifle in her hands and began to make her way back home.

It was a fine day for walking and she made good progress before the sun got too high. Off in the distance she saw a rider and, for some reason she could not articulate, decided not to let her presence be known. She settled down on a high hill after hiding Pumpkin in an arroyo and watched the rider's progress.

It was Adulio and she could see that he was tracking her. She watched him and saw something very strange. He was hunting. He had his rifle ready, carried in his hands. He never did this as there was no reason for it. No animals existed in the area any longer that were capable of doing him an injury and no wild Indians or even bandits were known to be around.

She waited for him to approach her hiding place, his eyes to the ground, picking through the desert for her sign. He was doing a pretty good job of it, too. When he was thirty feet away she called out to him and he nearly jumped out of his skin. He raised his rifle to shoot and Marta called out again.

"Calm yourself, Adulio."

He recovered. "Señorita! I am so pleased to find you. I was worried sick."

"Why?"

"I don't know, Señorita. I don't know, it maybe was una premonición? I told my wife that it was not right, something is wrong with the Señorita. I don't know." Adulio didn't look good. He was frightened. He looked terrified and she felt sorry for him. He handled stress poorly and as he got older; it weighed more heavily on him.

Marta settled him in some shade and went back to retrieve Pumpkin. Soon they were together on the trail. She looked at Adulio who now seemed to be having difficulty breathing. She stopped again and made him sit down as she wetted down some cloth for around his neck. She looked at him; he was crying.

"Adulio, tell me. What's wrong?"

He held up a hand and looked at her. Tears were tracking deep furrows in his cheeks. "Señorita, I am sorry. I am sorry. I am just so afraid. I'm afraid I've brought you to this. I'm afraid you will die."

She patted his shoulder and thought hard about their present situation. He looked as if he would fall over and expire at any moment. He couldn't ride in this condition and he couldn't pass the night this way.

She grabbed his horse and jumped on. Adulio looked at her through tearful eyes. "I'll be back with a wagon, Adulio. Don't worry. Try to rest. Try to breathe, just breathe and relax. Pumpkin will keep you company."

She was back by afternoon and he was better. The men had the wagon prepared for him and plenty to eat and drink. She left them to take care of Adulio and Pumpkin and rode on ahead, alone.

It was a strange interaction and gave her a lot to think about as she rode. Adulio was completely panicked and she'd never seen him that way. She began to wonder if she'd been too carefree about all this. She didn't want to die and she most certainly didn't want Rebecca to die. She felt queasy, a little sick to her stomach.

What did Adulio know? He could be trusted. Dan George said he could be trusted, but that meant nothing as Dan was gone. Despite the notes to the contrary, he was probably dead. Adulio said he had a premonition. Are such things real? Animals have them, she knew that. It had been documented. She read about that in history class. It happened when the Krakatoa eruption occurred. The animals knew of the impending tidal wave and headed for higher ground. Was Adulio like that? Was he like the animals? It was all very confounding to her.

By late evening she was bathed and had eaten a good dinner. She had enjoyed a brandy and cigarette on the veranda. As she undressed for bed she found another telegram that had been placed on her pillow. It read:

The horse was not lame by accident. Dan George growing weaker by the day. Z

Marta del Toro was becoming very angry. She was beginning to believe in Adulio's ability to have premonitions and she was determined to bring this to a close.

VIII Emiliano Zapata

Rebecca returned from Vera Cruz refreshed and more in love with Curtin than ever. They saw Pedro del Calle as well and were treated as royalty by his fellow marines. Rebecca was the belle of the ball wherever they went and Curtin was very proud to have her on his arm.

Marta was pleased to hear about Pedro. Rebecca reported that he could not stop asking questions about her and had four letters to deliver to her, all written by Pedro while they were there. He'd received her letter and was so happy for it that he absent-mindedly asked Rebecca to tell Marta how happy it made him feel no fewer than half a dozen times.

Marta shared the cryptic notes from Z and reported what they had learned from the investigation into Dan George's disappearance. It was at least something and the detective continued with his inquiries.

They slept together again and Marta was once again reminded how much she enjoyed Rebecca's company. She slept well after staying up long after midnight, regaling Rebecca with the story of her solo hunting trip and promising to take Rebecca to the ruins as soon as Pumpkin was recovered and fit for riding again.

Marta was up early, long before everyone else, and so as not to disturb their slumber, resolved to wash her own hair out in the clear cool of the veranda. She liked washing outside. It made her feel like she was camping, roughing it. She'd soaped up and was full of lather when she heard the thundering hooves of a significant army and worked quickly to rinse her hair.

She sensed the presence of a stranger beside her. She squinted enough to see dusty black boots and big Mexican spurs. They were big; big boots, the big boots of a big man.

She groped for a towel and could see the man was helping but not helping, teasing her. Other men were quietly laughing all around her. She was barely dressed, still barefoot and, in her haste to rinse the shampoo from her hair, had gotten her petticoat quite wet. As she stood on the veranda, the audience of the small army could easily see the gifts given to her by the almighty. She was losing patience very quickly.

"Pendejo, you might think this is funny, but I don't like soap in my eyes. Hand me my towel. Now!"

"Ah, but you must say please, Señorita."

"Please, pendejo. Please!"

"That's better." The big man handed her the towel and she was now able to see. She looked down at her naked form pressing through the sheer wet fabric and blinked twice. She recognized him immediately.

"Emiliano Zapata, at your service." He laughed and the army laughed and Marta gave him a coy smile.

"I am likely the only person to ever call el Tigre a pendejo and still be alive."

Everyone laughed again. Emiliano Zapata enjoyed a good joke and he bowed to Marta and took her hand. He looked her over. He wasn't leering, but he was obviously enjoying what he saw. He unabashedly looked at her much as he would a beautiful work of art. Emiliano Zapata appreciated stunning women and made it his policy to never try to hide that fact.

"Young lady, please get dressed. My men will not want to fight. They'll want to go for their women, you've given them such ideas."

She disappeared and ran to her bedroom. She shook Rebecca awake. "Get up, Zapata is here!" Rebecca had never seen Marta in such a state. She was star struck. Of all the people in the world, she'd always hoped to meet Emiliano Zapata. She dressed quickly and walked back to the General after ordering a full breakfast for the man and his army.

"General, I am sorry for calling you pendejo. I didn't know."

He smiled, "Oh, I was a pendejo, but I like my little joke. *Sin offender*, Señorita."

"And none taken. What brings your army so far north, Calpuleque?" She looked at the men. They were a ragtag looking bunch, but deadly and serious. They were impressive in their wildness.

Many women were along, not as camp followers or comfort women. Zapata was well known for making women soldiers, fighters, and several were officers in his army. They were lovely, every one. Like an army of Chicas, an army of replicas of their mother, and Marta was especially impressed with them.

"We were looking for you, Señorita, and... my friend, Pancho Villa, is presently in jail, so we must come up with a way to keep the Federales busy en el Norte. There is a good train coming with many things that will be interesting to our army."

"My hacienda is yours, Jefe." She waved a hand over the expanse of the land. "But I am confused. You said you came to see me?"

"I have. You are a good hacendada, madam. You are the kind of land owner we wish to have help us in the rebuilding of Mexico. Your uncle Alejandro del Toro was well known as a good man, a good Jefe, and a good provider for his people. We know you have taken up this thing. We are here to ally with you and to ask for your help."

Marta was almost giddy. The man knew her, knew Uncle Alejandro. This visit was turning out to be very exciting; more so than she originally thought. He was not here by happenstance, he'd come to see her. She squared her shoulders and grinned broadly. "We are honored to help."

The army prepared to set up camp on the ranch as Zapata and his staff settled down to breakfast on the veranda. Rebecca appeared and the men stood at attention. She looked radiant and El Tigre smiled as he smoothed back each of his long mustaches. He gently took her by the hand.

"Ah, Señorita Walsh, the stories of your beauty do not do you justice. And your shooting prowess: muy bien. We understand you severed the reins of a certain dog captain."

"Oh!" Rebecca blushed. He was a fine looking man. He was big for an Indian, with piercing brown eyes. He was much more handsome than his pictures in the newspapers. "Oh, you know this captain?"

"Oh, Sí. His brains now decorate the headboard of a certain bordello in Guadalajara."

"I see." Rebecca blushed and looked down at her hands.

Marta was less humble about the news, "I guess he won't be taking my head any time soon."

Zapata waited for them to take their seats before he took his own. An assistant took his tremendous hat as he brushed his moustaches smooth. "And how is your mother, the lovely Señora Walsh?"

"Oh, she is fine, General. She is presently working on taking over the Ottoman empire."

He looked a little confused, then shrugged. "Well, you tell her for me, please, that if she ever wants a career as a revolutionary soldier, I will make her a colonel in my little army." He grinned and looked at his entourage of soldaderas. "Señorita, if women were running this revolution, it would be over by now, and there'd be fewer of the poor, dead."

Marta smiled as she passed a plate of food. They dined and chatted through the morning. She was beginning to be comfortable with the great man. There was something about him, something larger than life and he exuded a kind of power and confidence. It emanated from him, permeating the very air they breathed. She found herself blurting out a question, "Tell me, General, are you an anarchist?"

He sat back and laughed. "Anarchist? No, Señorita. I know the papers like to call me that, especially Hearst. He hates me! Oh well, I am not very fond of him either, so I guess we are even. No, I needed help with my plan of Ayala, and I had some assistance from my friend Otilio. It is true, he is an idealist, an anarchist, but no, I am not, Señorita. I believe in your American democracy. I believe it is okay for a man to own land, even to own a lot of land. But not so much that people are starving around him. And I don't believe land should be stolen from people just because they are a little dark of the skin." He laughed and held the back of his hand next to Marta's, "Like us!"

Marta was animated and Rebecca sat back and enjoyed it. It seemed to be the first time that Marta was truly happy in a very long time. She was smitten with the great man.

He told her that he needed money and her help in the US. He needed to counter the propaganda by Hearst and other newspapers. He told her how initially he was happy with Madero, but later, the new president became bogged down; too irresolute, weak and timid. And now Huerta was jockeying for the presidency. He would have nothing to do with Huerta as he was a cruel man, another Díaz, and would inevitably continue down that same path. Mexico could not continue down such a path.

"When is the attack on the train, General?"

"Tomorrow."

"And I may come along?"

"If you wish." He looked at Rebecca. He did not like the look in her eyes. "But, I am not certain your sister thinks this is a very good idea."

"General," Rebecca spoke up. "Isn't it true that your men will not let you go into battle? They feel you are too valuable as a strategist and a leader to actually do any fighting? That you are too important to lose by charging into a battle?"

"Yes, this is true." He smiled at Rebecca Walsh. He understood her well. "This is all true, Señorita Walsh."

"So, my sister and I. We are crucial to your cause?"

"Oh, sí, very much so, Señorita."

"Do you feel it would be imprudent for my sister to go fighting and attacking a train? If she ends up dead, what will happen to all the good she could have done for the cause en el Norte and on the ranch here? We are deriving a great fortune from the land in oil and gas. Now there is talk of gold in the northern corner of my sister's ranch. Would it not be wise to keep her safe?"

Zapata nodded, concurring. "Oh, this is all true, Señorita Walsh, this is all absolutely true."

Marta was furious. She looked at the two in disbelief. "I'm sorry, but have I become invisible? Have I turned into a child and don't know it?" Her eyes flashed in anger at the two. "*I* will decide when I fight and with whom." She sat back and smoked, started to pout and then thought better of it. She handed Zapata a good cigar. He took it and three of his assistants offered him a cigar cutter. He trimmed the end and Marta lit it for him. She was no less angry, however.

He grinned as he puffed on the cigar. "And I thought all the spirited women were from the south, Señorita!" He was beginning to really like Marta. "But please, your sister is correct. May I suggest a compromise?"

"Such as?" She looked at him, still angry, not wanting to hear his suggestion, but nonetheless giving him her attention.

"You come with me, stay with me. I will be directing the battle, but as your sister has said, my officers will not let me into the fray. You can keep me company and we will do our best from afar, out of harm's way."

Rebecca sat back with a satisfied look. It was like declaring *checkmate*. This is what she did best, keeping Marta from killing herself. She caught Marta looking at her and put on her best poker face. There was no need to gloat, and if Marta lost her temper, she might just go ahead into battle to spite her. Rebecca was always a gracious winner.

Marta thought on all this for a moment. Perhaps it would be best. She only regretted not having a chance at battle. She had always wanted to be in a proper military campaign, charging through a hail of bullets, facing death head on, and this seemed to be the perfect chance. She looked at Rebecca.

Rebecca was always the voice of reason and Marta loved her for it, much as a child loves a parent for not letting them do self-destructive or stupid things. Rebecca edged closer to Marta who looked off in the distance. She would not look in her sister's direction just now.

"I see you over there, laughing up your sleeve." Marta managed a little smile despite the sting of being put out of commission. "You don't fool me for one minute, Rebecca Walsh."

Rebecca looked back and could not help a broad grin. "Sister, I have no idea what you could possibly mean."

By evening the ranch was alive with activity. The army was a festive one; they were eating well, thanks to Marta's hospitality. They were respectful of her land and kept the inevitable destruction to a minimum. An army is like a hoard of locusts, they have an insatiable appetite and leave a mess, a swath of ruin—even when not doing battle—wherever they would go.

Marta looked out over the veranda and saw many fires illuminating the countryside like giant lightning bugs rising from the ground. The dozens of different campfires represented their own little microcosm. Odors of cooking food filled the air. Each fire smelled of family recipes from the south. Here and there, excited conversations could be heard; people were singing and playing guitars and accordions. There were even a few fiddles and horns. No one fired guns or acted like fools, the way she remembered from the days of Sombrero del Oro. This was a disciplined army with a real purpose and intent. No one was getting drunk or out of order.

Zapata watched her from a distance. He'd known of this family, heard stories about them for many years. He knew of the famous Chica, the real mother of the fair one and the adopted mother of their hostess. He sensed a certain pride in Marta's countenance, the way she was looking out over his army and her land. He could not help himself, he had to engage her, and interrupted her musings. "Welcome home, Señorita Marta." He touched her cheek as she turned to look him in the eye. "Welcome home."

At full dark the girls walked arm in arm amongst the camped army. It was lovely and exciting. The army had a representation of every social stratum of Mexico. There were educated and wealthy men who dressed in tailored sack suits.

They even wore ties and collars. There were men in military uniforms, deserters from the Federale army or rurales. And there were the *White Cigars*, the poorest of the poor. They wore the simple white peasant garb of the land, atop their heads gigantic straw sombreros. Some of these had crowns more than a foot high. They wore sandals, at least the lucky ones; most had nothing at all to protect their feet.

Everyone was armed, at a minimum, with a Winchester and, without fail, the poorest peasants had machetes, the most useful—virtually indispensable—tool a peon from the south could own. The more well-to-do had a full complement of weaponry: powerful Mauser rifle, six shooters, large daga, and shotgun. They wore their cartridges on belts and bandoliers, some had as many as three, but they usually wore these only into battle, or if a camera was handy. They loved having their likenesses taken, either still or via the moving camera.

The women and children also dressed in kind. Many of the women were not warriors. Just as with the ancient armies of Europe, they were the camp followers. They took care of their husbands and children, kept everyone fed, tended to wounds, made life bearable. The children were the same. Those too young to pick up a gun were assigned the task of keeping the army alive. They foraged, hunted, cleaned, cooked, and even, on the rare occasion, played.

But it was the warrior women Marta liked and appreciated most. They were, every one of them, copies of her mother. A small army of Chicas. Many were beautiful; all were dangerous. They, too, came from all walks of life. Some wore old skirts and blouses, tattered and torn, their rebozos pressed firmly against their bodies by the heavily laden cartridge belts. The single ones ran in little gangs. They were empowered by their jefe, Emiliano Zapata. They were treated with autonomy and were not simple objects of desire; they were not there for the simple comfort or enjoyment and entertainment of the men.

They took an active role in the revolution and hoped it would finally elevate the women of the country to a status equal to men. Some would make love with the men, but on their terms, when they chose, and with whom they chose. They would not tolerate being mistreated or molested. If a man became a little too aggressive, he might find himself in significant danger. He might end up dead.

They were all gracious, welcoming and kind to Marta and Rebecca. They'd run up on them, grab them by the arm or even kiss them and call out, "Welcome home, sisters. Welcome home!" It was overwhelming, to Marta especially. She'd never been so completely accepted by any group, particularly the fairer sex. The young women of Maryland, the wealthy and educated, regardless of how open-minded, would invariably leave her out. It was hard-wired into them, they could not help themselves, they would always leave Marta out.

Rebecca watched her. She stood back and watched her sister glow, basking in the glory of being a woman, a Mexican woman, a powerful and influential member of this society and she knew what Marta was thinking, she knew that Marta was home and that she'd never, ever go back.

Marta saw Rebecca out of the corner of her eye. She looked over at her sister, misty-eyed, and gave her a smile. "Just like Mamma."

Rebecca responded in her best Mexican; "Sí, mi amor, al igual que mama."

At each little campfire, groups were engaged in singing their own corridos. The sisters wandered along, stopping here and there, and eventually ended up at the largest gathering. This one boasted a musical band with strings, a couple of horns, many guitars and three accordions. When they'd completed a particularly festive song Rebecca requested *Adelita* and they were soon playing with great enthusiasm. She looked at Marta, grasped her by the hand and they began:

> *In the heights of a steep mountainous range*
> *a regiment was encamped*
> *and a bright woman bravely follows them*
> *madly in love with the sergeant.*

Popular among the troop was Adelita
the woman that the sergeant idolized
and besides of being pretty she was brave
that even the Colonel respected her.

And it was heard, that he, who loved her so much, said:

If Adelita would like to be my girlfriend
If Adelita would be my wife
I'd buy her a silk dress
to take her dance to the quarter.

If Adelita would leave with another man
I'd follow her by land and sea
by sea in a war ship
by land in a military train...

Others soon joined in and helped them with several stanzas they had not heard before. That was the way with corridos; they took on a life of their own. Some could go on for more than an hour and never repeat the same verse twice.

They finished to applause and cheers. Many of the men threw their heads back and gave the carcajada, the high piercing screaming laugh of the people of the south. The girls were celebrities now as it was one thing to be beautiful but all together another to be able to sing so sweetly.

Soon they were given great cups of pulque and the world was beginning to swim all around them. It was one of the grandest evenings they'd spent in a long time and Rebecca hated to tear herself away, but she had to get to Curtin.

She eventually made it north to the mining camp, to her man. It was late and Tolkenhorn was drunk; he staggered out to greet her. The lovers were always formal around the lawyer, put on a show for him and Rebecca acted carefully this night. She wasn't certain why, but she didn't want Tolkenhorn to know about the army to the south. Curtin was there immediately. He couldn't bear the thought of having Tolkenhorn so much as look at Rebecca. He did his best to make certain she did not have to talk to the drunken sot.

"Miss Walsh."

"Mr. Curtin."

"How may I help?" Curtin stiffly, formally, helped her from her horse, eased her down and held her gently by the hand. Tolkenhorn babbled something along the lines of a greeting then turned and found his way back inside. They did not see him again.

"Just taking in the night air, found myself up this way and thought I'd drop in." She looked at the encampment; it was mostly dark. "I didn't realize the time. Is it too late for a visit?"

Curtin tried his best to play the part. He suppressed a grin. He was pleased that she would come to see him at such an hour and simultaneously worried for her safety. He bowed slightly as he gave his reply. "Not at all, Miss Walsh, not at all."

They wandered away from the lawyer's quarters and were finally alone. She kissed him passionately on the lips. "Big news, Robert! Emiliano Zapata and his army are at the ranch."

"You don't say!" Even Curtin was a little caught up by the celebrity of the general. He looked at Rebecca who was obviously excited. "Now, don't get too friendly, you. I've heard he's quite the lady's man."

She kissed him again. "Stop. You're being silly." He had introduced a thought and she wanted to ride back. Marta would be in the man's bed if she got the chance and that would break Del Calle's heart. "Robert, I can't stay, but I want you to stay away tonight; actually, for the next couple of days. Gringos are not popular with Zapata and his army. You understand, don't you, darling?"

"Sure, sure." He felt the old sting of prejudice. He thought about Rebecca and Marta. They'd certainly known it well enough.

She smiled at him, knowing what he was thinking. "It's not you, darling, I'm sure he'd like you. It's the oil company. It's

American business, Hearst, all the bastards who want to control this land. It's not you."

"I understand." He grinned at her choice of words, his little angel was becoming tougher by the day, or was it that she always was and this toughness was just now becoming known to him?

"And that's why I love you so much, darling. You *do* understand." She kissed him again. "I want you so badly." They kissed some more.

"What's he doing here, Rebecca?"

"He came to see us, Marta mostly, and me. He wants our help, wants us to help him in the revolution. Oh, he's grand, Robert. He's a tall man. I never knew that. He is big and nice; he jokes. He makes jokes. We're attacking a train tomorrow and…"

"Wait, wait." Robert looked her in the eye. "Who's attacking a train tomorrow?"

"We are, Marta and I, with his army." She looked at him and knew the look he was giving her only too well.

"No. No. Rebecca, no! It's no…"

"We're going to be with the general. We won't be actually fighting, Robert."

"No. This is ludicrous. *You don't attack trains!* My God, you both are insane."

"It can't be helped. I negotiated that much, Robert. Marta wanted to be in the fray. I only just convinced her to stay with Zapata. There's no real harm in it."

"And what's this got to do with you?"

"I've got to be with her, to keep her out of trouble. To make sure she keeps her word. Robert, you don't know her."

"Oh, I think I do. That's what worries me. The girl who jumped on a shark's back? Yes, I know her, Rebecca. I know her well. And you! You're both like a pair of deranged Amazons. I won't have it, Rebecca. I swear, I won't have it."

"Robert, I'm sorry." She wasn't angry, more amused. She continued in her most straightforward tone. "I didn't come to ask for permission. I came to tell you what's going on, but not to ask permission. I know you…"

"*Rebecca Walsh, I'm warning you.*" He grabbed her by the shoulders and looked her in the eye. "If you do this thing, I swear… I won't talk to you… for the next ten minutes." And he didn't. He sat down and sulked like a schoolboy. She poked and prodded and couldn't get a word from him. She sat back and folded her arms. She waited and watched him. He was resolute. He could not be moved. She finally patted his vest and found his cigarette case, took one and had a smoke. She waited, smoked, and blew smoke at the moon and waited. Finally he took out his watch, checked the time and looked at her.

"Okay, then." He reached around and kissed her on the mouth. He held her in his arms and snuggled against her breast. "You be careful tomorrow. If you get killed, so help me, what you experienced just now was nothing. I'll never speak to you again!"

She kissed him again. "I love you, Robert Curtin."

He kissed her. "What kind of world am I in, Miss Rebecca Walsh? What kind of crazy creature did I fall in love with? What happened to the obedient little woman who sat by the hearth, waiting for her man to come home?" He grinned and she understood the irony in his voice.

"Oh, you wouldn't want such a woman, really. Would you?"

"No." He thought on that and looked her in the eye. "No, I wouldn't. But it doesn't mean that my insides won't stay tied up in knots worrying over you. I guess I've got to get used to that. Living in knots, tied up in knots for the rest of my days."

She stood up and kissed him again. "Sorry about all that, Robert. You're running with wild Indians now; get used to it." She reached over and touched his face. "Gotta run, gotta get ready for the battle." She smiled and waited for the wounded look on his face. It would do him good to worry over her a little. "Stay here. I don't want the lawyer to see us when I go."

She was gone and he wondered at what had just transpired; the woman going off to battle and the man staying behind.

Tolkenhorn was still up when Curtin returned to the building that housed their apartments. He looked at Curtin with a greasy, ugly expression. Barely comprehensible, he mumbled. "Quite the li'l firecracker, isn't she?"

"Who?"

"That Walsh girl, of course. Bedded her yet?" He hiccupped, then covered his mouth.

"You better go to bed, Miles. You're drunk and I might break your nose for you."

"Easy, lad, easy." He held up a shaky hand. "No offence, but all these darkies. They can't help it. Too close to the land. They're a wild bunch."

"You're out of your element, Miles, and you are an ignorant and stupid man." He looked at the lawyer and pushed him backward, off balance. The man fell into a chair. "If you ever say anything about Rebecca Walsh or Marta del Toro again, I'll beat you 'til you can't see. Understand, Miles?"

"I understand." Now it was his turn to sulk but he suddenly remembered, "Robert?"

Curtin stopped and looked over his shoulder. "What?"

"Are you making *any* progress? *Any* progress at all?"

"Yes." He turned and looked at the old man. "I've got a plan, Miles. Leave it up to me. I've got a plan that will make all your worries go away, I promise, but you've got to give me time, you've got to have patience." He went back and held out his hand. "I'm sorry for roughing you up, Miles." They shook hands, "You know, I'm just a little on edge lately. Those two have got me not knowing whether I'm coming or going. Never had such a time with the ladies." He grinned and Miles smiled.

"I trust you, boy."

The army was ready by sunrise. Rebecca and Marta now rode with General Zapata, his lieutenants all around them. He was in an especially good mood and looked on, smiling at Marta every chance he got.

Off in a distance, a mounted man could be seen standing in the road, waiting for them. Robert Curtin stood up in his stirrups, removed his hat and bowed to the general. "General Zapata, my name is Robert Curtin and I work for Señorita Del Toro. I'd be much obliged if you'd let me ride along, sir."

Zapata smiled, looked back at the object of Robert Curtin's focus. He grinned. "Oh, I see." He looked back at Curtin and indicated for him to take a spot between himself and Rebecca Walsh. "You ride here, Mr. Curtin."

They were off and in position in short order.

Several soldiers disconnected a rail around the bend in the track. The train engineer would not see it in time. Now they waited and Rebecca was able to sidle up to Marta. "Zapata was in an especially good mood this morning."

"Uh huh." Marta grinned.

"Marta, you didn't."

"Didn't what?"

"You know what."

"Oh, I gave him something, but it wasn't *that*. Something much better."

Rebecca breathed, relieved. "What?"

"A hundred thousand dollars."

"Oh." She reached over and gave her a kiss on the cheek. "I'm glad. For Pedro's sake, I'm glad."

The train careened for several hundred yards and Rebecca suddenly felt ill. Marta held her hand tightly as she just now remembered the train wreck of a decade ago, the train wreck she helped to make happen and the train wreck that Rebecca had survived.

It was a tragic event, no matter how pure the intentions and everyone watched the awesome power of the locomotive as it drove itself into the ground. The Federale guards riding forward didn't stand a chance, and the few who survived were soon dispatched by the general's cavalry. Marta watched in awe.

The women were especially impressive to her. They were mostly poor peasant women, the ones who greeted her so warmly the night before, wearing not much more than rags, the crossed bandoliers holding the bullets for their Mauser rifles or Winchesters; each a deadly reminder of what it was all about. They were good and competent and fearless. They knew their business and knew what to do. It was all about the killing, doing more killing than the other side, killing more than the other side was willing to lose, and they were resolute in their purpose.

One car remained on the track and the few Federales still able to fight had a machinegun working on its roof. It was a significant impediment and soon many of Zapata's soldiers were pinned down. The success of the operation seemed to hang in the balance.

Suddenly, Marta kicked her mount's sides and galloped off before anyone could call her back. Zapata smiled at Curtin and Rebecca Walsh. He shrugged. There was nothing he could do, and he wouldn't have, really, even if there was.

Marta flanked them and climbed the ladder to the top of the train. The machinegun nest was spitting its deadly fire; everyone was oblivious to her actions. The Federales were terrified; they were firing desperately, trying to save their own skins and did not have the presence of mind to guard their flanks or rear.

Marta had her favorite shotgun—the pump action—the same kind her mother had used so effectively during her furious ride against Marta's father and his gang. She soon had it spitting its deadly fire, as well, and Federales now lay dead or dying around the defunct gun. She looked proudly at the general and his entourage. She held up the shotgun in victory as Rebecca sat, doing her best impersonation of their severe housekeeper from the mule ranch. But Pilar would have been proud... of both of them.

It was over quickly and now the ugliness of war was fully revealed. Zapata kept no prisoners. He could not; he didn't have a prisoner of war camp. There wasn't enough food for his own army, let alone for an army of prisoners. Soon several dozen Federales were lined up. They were offered two choices, join Zapata or die. Many chose the latter and were quickly obliged.

Rebecca was especially unnerved now. It was not because of the killing, she was used to that and expected it. But the child soldiers where almost too much to bear. Every one of them looked just like Marta had the day Rebecca met her in her captor's tent nearly a dozen years ago. She remembered it so vividly. She thought of the scars Marta bore and looked at the dozens of little children and thought of all the scars, all the sad nights ahead. She thought of the terrifying dreams waiting for these children and she wanted to cry, grab them up and take them from this terrible place. She wanted to build a convent like the one the mother superior took her to in Bisbee all those years ago. She'd build a convent, a sanctuary a hundred times that size and put a wall fifty feet high around it to keep out the war and the suffering and the horrors that no child, no adult, really, should ever know.

To Zapata's mind, no one was too young to fight and he saw the look of trepidation on Rebecca's face. He dismounted and walked to one little boy who was stripping a dead Federale. He patted the boy's head and looked up at Rebecca. "This is Juan, Miss Walsh. I found him digging through a dung heap, looking for some bits of food." He smiled at the boy who smiled back. "His diet used to consist of more shit than food."

He walked a few feet further and put his hand on another child's head. She was pulling bandoliers off her tiny shoulders and placing them in a pile. "Maria." He gently kissed her forehead and she smiled up at him, then immediately went back to the task at hand. "Maria was found at death's door. She was beaten so badly that she could not walk. Her crime was that she was dipping her fingers into a pot of raw eggs. She was hungry and could not contain herself." He grinned cynically.

"The eggs were being rubbed into the coat of a hacendado's prize racehorse." He looked up at her and she thought she could see tears welling in his eyes. "A shiny coat on a horse is so important, Miss Walsh."

Zapata remounted and rode up next to Rebecca, looked at her and said, "Miss Walsh, the newspapers did get this part right." He looked at some others, two small boys and a girl, unloading ammunition from a cattle car. "It's better for them to die on their feet than to live on their knees."

She knew that he was sincere. She understood why it was all happening but could not let it go. She wasn't trying to argue with the man but she needed to say it. "It's not the dying that I worry over, General. When they die, their troubles will be over. It is living that will be so hard on them."

With that, as if on cue, Marta galloped up to them, sliding her horse to a stop amidst them and grinning broadly. She was on a high that only battle brings.

"Well," She lit a cigarette with trembling hands. "That sure broke up the monotony."

IX Breaking Point

Miles Tolkenhorn sat and waited and trembled. He had three shots of rye to steady his nerves and wished for a fourth. He mostly never ate anything before one in the afternoon which was fine as he didn't start drinking until five. Today he'd done it in reverse and the rye was burning a hole in his gut all the way into his back. The general terrified him and always made him wait in an antechamber that was decorated with scenes of carnage. It was always hot with no air movement in the room. After another hour he was soaked with sweat and his celluloid collar was cutting into his neck. He felt as if he could not breathe. He tried his best to calm down.

The general had spent the first part of his career serving the Díaz dictatorship and honed his skill as a corrupt and sadistic government official during that time. He was initially disappointed in the exile of his boss, but later realized that there might be greater profit to him in supporting the Madero presidency. He did this with false enthusiasm and soon was given unfettered access to money and full control of the army.

Madero was not the kind of man who could control the general, and soon the general was treating the new president as his puppet. After a few months, he realized his aspirations were too modest—too conservative—and that with a little maneuvering, he could obtain a position far beyond that of Supreme General of the Federale army. He could be the next Porfirio Díaz, and then nothing but old age could stop him.

This was an appealing thought to him. He was only fifty years old, Díaz was still alive at more than eighty so, by his calculations, he could be the president of Mexico for the next thirty years if his health held out and he played his cards right.

The meeting with Tolkenhorn was just a little side project, but the idea of getting that nice bit of land appealed to him. If the lawyer could be trusted, the yield would be in the millions, annually, for years to come and that was not including the gold; just the oil and gas. He thought about the scale of his potential earnings and it soon became easy for him to measure his success in millions, tens of millions, even more. The more he thought about it, the less appealing it was for him to be pulling in his paltry quarter of a million a year. He no longer thought in pesos, but the international money of the world, the US dollar.

He was an advocate of Taft's dollar diplomacy and thought in terms of Mexico being the next United States. Not as a democracy, of course. As a monster and aspiring totalitarian dictator, democracy was a hateful concept to him. But as far as enriching himself and his cronies, he liked to think that he would someday make Mexico a rival to its neighbor to the north.

An hour later, the ambassador came in. He walked past Miles Tolkenhorn without acknowledging his presence and went into the general's office. As the door opened, an odor wafted into the room where Tolkenhorn waited. This made him even more nauseous. He was going to vomit and looked desperately for a receptacle but found only a vase and vomited into it. He felt better but now the air was full of his vomit odor, his sweat, and the stench of the general's office. He was certain he would die right at that very moment. He was certain he'd not survive this ordeal. They'd finally come out to fetch him, to interrogate and lambast and ridicule him, and it would be just fine by him if they walked up to his sweaty corpse slumped in the chair. He'd rather be dead than be here now.

But he didn't die and soon an officious little clerk came out and beckoned him in. He walked from one green cloud to the next. The general was a big man, on the fat side, with a bald head and a bottlebrush mustache. He wore big round glasses which made him look owl-like, magnifying dark mud-colored eyes. He smoked cheap cigars incessantly, had halitosis, foot odor and poorly fitting boots which gave him the habit of walking about barefoot, his mycotic toenails like the great eyes of some otherworldly beast, yellow and scabby and revolting. This is what Miles Tolkenhorn, half drunk, fully nauseated and completely terrified, encountered when he entered the room.

They put him at the center. The general was across the desk, sitting a full foot higher, his back to a great glass window so that Tolkenhorn could not see his face. It was just like his audience with Marta earlier in the year. He could not see his face and therefore could not be warned when the general opened his rotting mouth to breathe out great gusts of rotten breath.

The ambassador flanked him. Him he could see but it didn't help. The ambassador was an ugly, thin, pale man with hate-filled eyes. He was the worst kind of robber baron. He was a bureaucrat and hadn't even the brains or guts to break into business and steal his own fortune. He was simply a parasite living off the public and using and abusing his power to enrich himself. He was enriching himself now by pulling strings and making puppets like the general do the things that would make American business—and himself—prosper.

They waited. Each had so much to say, so much ridicule to heap on Miles Tolkenhorn and they both leaned forward, jockeying for the first swipe. Tolkenhorn reeled. He could not gain control of his senses and hiccupped, vomited again, this time down his shirtfront, then again into his handkerchief. He pretended it hadn't happened and used the hanky to wipe his nose and chin. The general was too savvy. He looked at the vomit puddle in Tolkenhorn's lap. Pointing at the seat accusingly, he said, *"Clean that up!"*

"Forget it." The ambassador waved him off as Tolkenhorn looked about confused, helpless, for some means to make the mess go away. He sat at attention as the ambassador continued, his seat and the crotch of his suit trousers soaking up the bilious fluid.

"What I'd, what *we'd,* like to know, Mr. Tolkenhorn, is why the deal hasn't gone through."

"I, I. We're working on it, I swear. The girl is being stubborn."

"Oh, more than stubborn." The general blew his answer and his fetid breath across the desk at the lawyer. "We've been told she's hosted Zapata and his army on her ranch, that she's gone on raids, and that she's using the money you're paying her to fund the revolution."

The ambassador spoke up, "Mr. Tolkenhorn, it is exactly the opposite of our plan. It could not be any more opposite to our plan." He looked at Tolkenhorn. "It's the antithesis of our plan."

"I know, I know." He absentmindedly wiped his forehead with the soiled handkerchief, spreading vomit across his sweaty brow.

"Slap the little bitch around and make her sign, goddamn it." The general breathed the directive at Miles Tolkenhorn on a green cloud that washed over him like a tidal wave.

"She's not the kind you slap around, General, with all due respect. She's quite independent. She's also well connected. Her family knows many people, it wouldn't do…"

"Her family! Her family! That little squaw's family was shitting on the ground until ten years ago. She's nothing. She's a zero, you stupid fool. She's got you thinking through your dick."

"Not so, sir. I swear, not so. It is very delicate. She was adopted by Americans and they've got a lot of influence in Washington. I know, sir, I've investigated. I have a plan, please, sir. I have a good plan and just need the time… and, if you please, another payment."

The ambassador leaned forward. "How much?"

"Twen… forty thousand."

"This is getting expensive."

"I'm sorry, we've got so many expenses. If Mr. Hearst would go on and buy the company, things would be much easier for me." He looked down at his hands. He was sweating the vomit away. The general became even angrier.

"God damn you, I said not to say his name. Just don't say it. Jesus, you're supposed to be a lawyer. I think your nothing but a bounder and a fool."

The ambassador stood up and motioned for Tolkenhorn to leave. "I'll take care of it." He followed Tolkenhorn out to the antechamber and lit a cigarette. He stood away from

Tolkenhorn who was by now quite the sight and smell. He did not smell any better now than the general.

"I'd be damned careful, Miles." The ambassador looked at his watch. "The general has little patience, and you're already into him for sixty. Another forty, whew, that's pushing it. You'd better produce or you'll end up in a shallow grave, if you're lucky."

Tolkenhorn swallowed hard, "What if I'm not lucky?"

"My friend," He held up a cautionary hand, "You don't even want to know about it."

For the next several days he pushed Curtin, pushed and prodded and got nothing but empty promises. He even offered Curtin money and the young engineer took it and now the money he got from the general was running out again. He dared not go after more. Something had to give but he just couldn't come up with a plan. Nothing was working. It seemed that the more dangerous the place, the more the young women liked it. Just as the general had said, his plan was having the opposite effect. It was time for something more drastic, and just at the height of his anxiety, a breakthrough occurred.

X Concerning Robert Curtin

Tolkenhorn had not visited the women at the ranch while sober. Other than for the Renaissance faire Curtin kept him away and he was just beginning to realize the place's potential. It was so austere; the young woman wouldn't waste a penny on anything that didn't benefit the stupid peons on the place. He could do so much with it, with the wealth being pulled from the ground.

The main house was situated on a high plateau and as he thought about it, he visualized a Mount Olympus. He'd build a beautiful palace; a place that could be seen from far off in the distance. It would be visible from miles away, it would be a showplace. And he'd be the man of the hour. He'd own it and would have a bevy of darkies all around to serve him: serve him food, drink, and carnally.

He could see it so clearly and it was within his grasp. He was certain it was within his grasp.

He was ready for them now. He sat in the parlor and felt prepared to share all he'd learned, all he'd discovered about Robert Curtin. He wished he could have done this all along, but better late than never. Curtin could have saved him a lot of time and trouble had he only cooperated sooner.

As he waited for them he remembered to look serious, solemn. The younger one would need that, once he'd given her the information, the news about her lover. Secretly, he was enjoying it. He hated them. He hated them because they were wealthy and had the upper hand and were not white and were so damned smug and superior. They—*she*—wouldn't be superior once he'd finished giving her this news. He could barely wait to see the look in her eyes, watch the color go from her face. Perhaps she'd even faint, oh that would be good, she'd faint and he'd catch her, be the fatherly figure and help her in her hour of need.

Marta and Rebecca entered the room, shook his hand and sat on either side of the tea table laid in his honor. Marta held nothing against the man. He tried for her ranch and lost, there was no need to throw salt in the wound. She leaned forward and gave him a friendly smile. Rebecca followed suit.

"Ladies, I do apologize for not coming to see you sooner. I'm certain everything is in order with the operations and the payments?"

"Adequate, Mr. Tolkenhorn." Marta watched him fumble with the documents on his lap. He wouldn't look her in the eye and it made her wonder at what he was playing.

"I, I don't quite know how to say all this, ladies, but, well frankly, we've had a bit of an embarrassment as it concerns the mining operation."

"Oh?"

"Mr. Curtin."

"What's wrong with Robert, eh, Mr. Curtin?" Rebecca sat up straighter in her chair.

Tolkenhorn began to explain when Esmeralda entered the room to replace a bouquet of flowers. He looked at the two women and held his tongue.

"It's all right, Mr. Tolkenhorn, she's stone deaf." Marta smiled at her housekeeper and nodded for her to continue.

Tolkenhorn smiled politely at the servant and continued. "Well, ma'am, no harm, but it appears Mr. Curtin is quite the scoundrel."

"How do you mean?" Rebecca demanded.

"Well, ma'am, ladies, oh, this *is* very embarrassing. We've been taken in. The dirty kike has taken us all in. Oh, I'm sorry for using such an epithet; not generally in my nature."

"He, he told me he was a Catholic." Rebecca thought this was all perhaps some sick joke.

Tolkenhorn, reading her mind, put up his hand. "I know, I know, we all thought it as well, thought a lot of things about Robert Curtin, or whatever his name is. He's apparently not even an engineer." He removed the packet from his lap and placed it on the settee beside him. "I've brought everything he left behind. Seems our men were onto him and he vamoosed in the middle of the night, even emptied our safe, but he left a lot of his personal effects."

"And why are you telling us this, Mr. Tolkenhorn? What's it to us?"

"Forgive me, ladies, but I'm an old fool. I'm not dead... or blind. I could see the attention he was giving you, Miss Walsh. The terrible things he said, I feel just awful the way he's done you wrong." He looked at her and then away, embarrassed for her. "Well, it's a pity. I liked the man, at least the man he portrayed. Appears he's got a family, well, here, you look."

He handed a portfolio of photographs over. It included one of Curtin standing with a woman and a man, wearing a yarmulke. It was Robert Curtin, all right. Then more photos, a heavy woman with dark hair accompanied by two children. There were notes, letters, documents all corroborating Tolkenhorn's story.

"Not to appear indelicate, Miss Walsh, but he was a bit of a braggart, as well. Last night, in his cups, he really showed off. He regaled us with stories of how he'd strung you along, telling you that you'd be married, and eh, other things." He blushed and averted his eyes. "Bragged about, eh, being …, being intimate. He joked that he even made reference to Christmas morning, as if a Jew would know of such things." He hesitated when he saw the look of mortification on her face. "I'm sorry, ma'am. I shouldn't have brought that up. I know that was very personal." He looked down into his lap, in deep thought. "He even gave you a ring, I believe."

Rebecca sat, dumbfounded. But here it was, right in front of her. Robert Curtin was not a Catholic looking for a mate. He was a married man, an opportunist, and she felt that she might fall over. How could it be? She'd heard of confidence men, heard how they would prey on wealthy women such as herself. Madame Boutin even gave a lecture on it. She could not believe how good, how convincing he was.

"And Dan George, do you suppose he was involved in Dan George's disappearance?"

"I'm sure of it. He tried to do away with you, Miss del Toro, we know that for a fact. And the men up in Alaska. We know

now that he wasn't so innocent in losing his work party. That's what put our men onto him."

"How so?"

"Oh, he found a good strike up there. But as they say, dead men tell no tales. He got rid of the men in his work party when…"

No, not that." Marta was annoyed at his silly prattling on about Alaska. "Trying to do away with me, what do you mean?" Tolkenhorn was the most annoying man she'd ever known.

"The man on the boat, the one Miss Walsh so bravely dispatched, he was not just a stowaway, ma'am. He was hired by Curtin. Curtin was planning to lure you out and the man was to attack you. Curtin was to pretend to fight him and you were to be killed in the process. They even had a boat waiting. The man was supposed to jump overboard and Curtin would look like the great hero, fighting the brute, throwing him overboard, never to be found again. But it all fell apart. Curtin tried to manipulate it so that he would leave you at dinner that night, Miss Walsh, and escort you, Miss del Toro, out where you'd be isolated. There were to be no witnesses and then the attack would occur. But it got muddled. He was especially annoyed at the way all *that* turned out."

"But, but he fought so well."

"Yes, he said that, too. Said he had to make it look good, had to be a bit battered himself. It was all planned."

Marta was annoyed with him again. No matter how hard she tried, she could not help being annoyed by this man. "So, he bragged about murder and conspiracy and doing all these things and you just sat there, you old fool, just sat there like a bump on a log and let him get away?"

"*Madam!*" He was hurt. "*Look at me.* I'm an old man. Robert Curtin might have looked mild, but I can tell you he wasn't. He…" the old man choked up a little, then recovered, "he scared me so."

With trembling hands he picked out his cigarette case and passed one each to the ladies. Tolkenhorn looked especially wounded. "Oh, he was a cocky one. He bragged that he convinced you to keep the affair under wraps when you landed in Tampico, made it look like you weren't involved up on the ranch. Spider, he's a doggone spider is what he is." He looked at the two and continued. "I told him not to meddle in your affairs. I told him that you didn't want to sell, Miss Del Toro."

He turned his attention to Rebecca, suddenly remembering something. "That was a cruel, cruel incident with the cigar band, Miss Walsh. He romanced you. He made it all sound so sincere."

He looked at her with watery eyes, "I'm not ashamed to say, it made me cry a little when he bragged about that. Terrible, terrible!" He reached for his handkerchief and dabbed the corners of his eyes.

He went back to addressing Marta. "He said that if he couldn't beat 'em, he'd join 'em. I think those were his words. I think he considered himself so smart that he could even get away with bigamy. I've heard stories of such things in the past. A man I heard of had four wives, all over the country, set up homes in…"

Marta stood up. The dolt was giving her a headache, droning on so. "Well, that's all well and good, Mr. Tolkenhorn, we're obliged for the information."

He stood up and took the photos from Rebecca's trembling hand. He reached over and touched her lightly on the elbow. "I'm mighty sorry about all this, ma'am. Mighty sorry." He was gone.

Marta reached for her sister. She looked terrible. Rebecca held up a hand. "I'm going to go lie down for a while." She looked around the room as if searching for something, some joke. Maybe Robert Curtin would jump out from behind a door and yell that is was a late April Fool. But he didn't. All she saw was Esmeralda, mindlessly clearing the tea service away. It just made no sense.

She went to bed and thought it all through. He must have been describing his real wife that day, the so-called Catholic wife he dreamed up when he was young. The big, big-breasted woman. No wonder he could describe her so well. She was real. His real wife. And the ring, she remembered now that he'd taken it back. It was a sloppy fit. He even took a ring that fit her properly so that he could have it sized when he went down to Tampico for supplies. So really, he didn't actually give her a ring at all; he'd stolen one from her. And now the comment to Pedro that day on the ship, *getting them on their backs*, it all made sense. It all made sense and he was a scoundrel. He was not the love of her life and he was perhaps even a murderer and was most definitely a thief. He even tried to kill Marta. She wanted to cry but she didn't. She was more angry than sad; heartbroken, yes, but not despondent. He was a son of a bitch and a bastard but he would *not* break her. She felt exhausted from the stress and shock of it all and soon, mercifully, fell into a deep sleep.

Marta was lying next to her after midnight. She snuggled up to Rebecca and held her like a child. "I'm sorry, sweetheart." She could feel Rebecca's face wet with tears. "I'm not going to call him names. I'm going to pretend that he died. Robert Curtin was a real man, a good man and he fell into a mine and died. That's what happened, darling. That's what happened." She held her more tightly. "We'll even have a full funeral for him if you want, if it'll make you feel any better. I'll even have the boys make him a nice coffin, if that's what you want. Whatever you want, my darling, whatever you want."

"Thank you, Marta. That's sweet of you. I didn't need a 'S*ee, I told you so'* lecture. Not that you would. He was a tricky fellow, no doubt." She laughed a little, ironically. "The devil actually gave me a ring, then stole it back and stole one of my rings to boot! And that man who attacked us. A hired killer. Well, I guess he didn't hire one big enough for us, eh?"

She felt better talking about it. She was so sad, like when someone died, and Marta was right, Robert Curtin had died. He was a real and living human being, the loveliest man to ever breathe air and now he was dead. She patted her Marta and finally had a good cathartic cry.

Miles Tolkenhorn did not like the visitors. The general should not have come. He paced about filling the room with his rotten breath as he walked unsteadily in his ill-fitting boots, peering through his owl-eyed glasses. Tolkenhorn could only imagine the stench at the end of the day when he finally took those boots off. The ambassador was there too. They were pacing, both of them pacing and waiting for the one man who supposedly had the plan. When he arrived, Tolkenhorn was flabbergasted. "You!"

The man ignored him, looked through him and at the other two men. "Why's *he* here?" He looked on with disgust at the lawyer.

"It's his office and he's got the information from the mining company." The ambassador blew smoke as he replied. He looked at Tolkenhorn and gave a solemn side to side movement of his head. "Doesn't look good, Miles."

"What, what doesn't look good? I've been working this thing, I've been doing a good job."

"Enough." The general looked at Tolkenhorn's desk, paged through the documents. "Here's what we're going to do."

It went on like this for several days. The girls stayed together and said little. Rebecca ate almost nothing. They both would have looked more natural wearing black. Rebecca now had the habit of walking around the ranch, head down, saying nothing, oblivious to everything. She felt leaden, like everything, walking, even breathing was a nearly insurmountable task.

Marta watched her from a distance, knew there was little she could do. She resolved to just be there, ready to offer any assistance, any words, an ear or any kindness that she could. She thought a lot about Robert Curtin. She honestly liked the man and, although at first was pleased to hear what Tolkenhorn had said about the engineer, soon regretted it. She was a good and loving sister and it was abundantly clear that the anguish Rebecca was suffering was significantly greater than the benefit Marta could ever derive from Robert Curtin being a black-hearted scoundrel.

Marta thought about the time on the ship, how both happy and sad she was to see her little sister being swept off her feet. She remembered taking his measure, deciding whether or not he was worthy of such a prize. She had her doubts. She felt good about that. She was a good judge of character and Curtin had pulled the wool over her eyes for a while, but not completely. She felt a little smug about that. She always knew there was something a little off, a little rotten, about Robert Curtin.

She was so sad for Rebecca. Rebecca *was* the marrying type and now she might give birth and have a bastard baby and have a much more difficult time finding a husband. She quickly dismissed that. They'd just do like all the other wealthy people who got tripped up. She would be packed off to a spa, maybe to Switzerland for her confinement, have the baby and call it a cousin when she returned.

Rebecca would probably not go for that, though. She was too pure. She would rather live in shame and alone than ever lie to her baby. She'd openly be the child's mother and that was that.

And then, the realization of this made Marta even happier. Maybe they'd all be together forever, just the three of them, Marta and Rebecca and the baby. Hopefully it would be a girl. She loved all children but never could envision either herself or Rebecca giving birth to boys. Her fantasy babies were always girls. They'd be three happy little ladies living together forever.

She'd teach the baby girl to be naughty and Rebecca would teach her to be good. They'd create another one of them out of the child; another Chica. She'd be smart and beautiful and fearless. They'd teach her to ride and shoot; to operate a machine. She'd drive the automobile everywhere. She'd go to Stonefields and they'd stay at Abuelita's house and visit her every chance they got. Marta was actually getting excited at the prospect of this fantasy baby that she was sure was going to come.

She thought about Pedro del Calle. Was he a liar, too? Maybe he was just a brush salesman or some other kind of oaf and a lout. Maybe he'd bought or, worse, stolen that marine uniform. Maybe he had no education and maybe he didn't even like women. That would be just her luck, to be stuck on a romantic voyage with a homosexual. It was all so bizarre and the more she thought about it, the more her mind wandered and the more preposterous and fantastic her theories became.

She didn't grieve for herself, though. She was happy at the outcome. She was definitely *not* the marrying type, she was certain of that. She felt a sense of relief and even stopped thinking about doing *it*, now. It was as if the removal of both men from their lives had taken the burden away. She no longer thought or worried over sex and this was a significant relief to her. She wasn't ready for such carryings on and she'd just as soon not think about men at all.

But even at this, Marta's self-imposed celibacy—at least in her mind— didn't last. Rebecca spent so much time alone now, wandering the ranch and going out for solitary rides, that Marta soon found herself bored and restless. Rebecca wouldn't even sleep with Marta these days, preferring her own room. But despite this, she was confident that Rebecca was on the road to recovery from her grief. She knew Rebecca was strong enough not to be paralyzed by it, she wouldn't be in a depressed mood forever and this was a great relief to Marta.

She was bored as all hell and decided she needed a little trip to Tampico, perhaps even to Vera Cruz. She sat quietly at breakfast, across from Rebecca and daydreamed about it. She felt her sister's eyes on her. She looked up and smiled. "Eating a little better?"

Rebecca had. She would take at least some food now at every meal. She wasn't eating enough, but at least it was something. She smiled at Marta. "Yes, better. Marta, I'm just a horrible stick in the mud. You look like you could jump out a window, you're so bored."

"Funny you should say that." She lit a cigarette and worked on it. "I was thinking of running down to Tampico, some errands, just to keep busy. Why don't you come along?"

"No, darling. You go. Go on, I'll be all right. I think the trip'll do you good. Why not go on down to Vera Cruz?" She gave an impish smile. "Bet Pedro would like to see you."

"You can read my mind, can't you, darling?"

"I can."

She set her alarm clock for extra early. She would get an early start and, with a specific plan in mind—a specific purpose—she felt good; comfortable, and sleepy. She drifted off and thought of Pedro, the captain of marines. She wasn't kidding herself. She wanted to see him. She felt she had to see him for some reason. She didn't know why, but she missed him terribly and resolved to make it her first priority.

At around two that morning, the sound of shots woke her and she dropped, instinctively, to the floor. She soon realized she was lying in glass. She reached up and retrieved a pistol from under her pillow. She carefully crawled to the wardrobe and grabbed her shotgun. Glass cut into seemingly every part of her body.

She waited a moment for more shots to come. She looked at the pattern made by the shattered glass and surmised the shooter fired from just outside the window nearest her bed. Now she heard the sound of running footsteps and shouting. Several of the men from the ranch were rushing to her aid, guns ready. Suddenly, they were in her room.

She was bleeding. Blood was mixed with glass and ground into the carpet. Esmeralda was there, concern on her face. Marta called out, "I'm all right. I'm all right, just a few cuts from the glass. I'm not shot. Where's Rebecca, where's Rebecca?"

"I'm here." Rebecca was now standing over her, a pistol in each hand. She looked wild, ready for battle. She looked at Marta and began taking inventory of her wounds.

"What happened?"

A ranch hand called out from the yard. "Señorita, out here, out here!"

It was Adulio, bloody and beaten, but likely to survive. He looked up, bewilderment in his eyes. He looked at the sisters and smiled uneasily. "It was that engineer. I saw him. He was prowling around the veranda and he had a gun. He fired through your window, Señorita, and I tried to stop him. I didn't have a gun and he hit me. When I was down, he fired at me, but missed. He must have gotten scared and run off."

They smoked until morning. Rebecca spent most of the time picking glass from Marta's backside as Esmeralda assisted. "I wish you wouldn't sleep naked. Look at this mess." They finally finished and washed the wounds clean.

Marta gave her a little smile, "I don't usually plan to roll in glass of an evening. Sleeping naked is not usually such a dangerous proposition." She gave Rebecca a little wink, "Unless a man with a gun is around, and I don't mean the kind old Curtin used tonight." Rebecca slapped her on an uninjured part of her behind.

They were interrupted by a knock at the door and Adulio came in. He was bandaged around his head and some blood had seeped through. He had the beginnings of a black eye and his jaw was swelling.

"Thank you, Adulio. I truly thank you." She stood up to shake his hand and he waved her off.

"It was nothing, Señorita, nothing. But the men have insisted; they are all taking shifts and will be guarding you and Miss Rebecca when you sleep. They know you need no guarding otherwise. If the coward had tried this when you were awake, we all know we'd be digging a hole for him this morning."

"Go to bed Adulio. I don't want to see you for the rest of the day. Rest." She patted his hand and felt guilty for treating him so roughly during her camping trip.

"As you please."

Over breakfast, which Marta ate and watched Rebecca sip a little coffee and pick at an egg, she brought it up.

"What do you say about a little ride in the machine, down to Tampico? Just the two of us?"

Rebecca looked at her, trying to make sense of what her sister had said. She was so distracted with her own thoughts these days that she only ever heard a fraction of what was spoken to her. She was too embarrassed to continuously ask Marta to repeat everything. She was now even more disturbed and distracted. How could he? How could Robert Curtin try to assassinate *them?* She was convinced that she would have been next, had Adulio not foiled the attempt. My God, the man *was* a monster, a genuine monster. She finally focused. "Oh, no, no Marta, you go. I'm not up for it."

"That's okay, I don't really much feel like it either."

Rebecca was fully engaged now. It would be better, safer, if Marta was off the ranch, she was certain of that. Curtin would likely not know she was gone and he'd probably lie low, with the whole ranch now on full alert. They'd both be safe, she at home and Marta in Tampico. "You go, Marta. Go. Please. I'm just not going to be much company now. You should go. I'll be alright here."

So she did and the ride down was pleasant enough. She'd taken some purchasing chores from Adulio so at least her trip had some real purpose. It was nice to be conducting some mundane business as it kept her mind off all the things that had been vexing her for so long.

There was big news in Tampico. It was good to hear so much about what was going on in Mexico and around the world. The raid on the train she attended with Zapata was big news. The rail cars were apparently filled with weapons from the US and it was a great scandal. There was talk of a congressional hearing and the US ambassador to Mexico had to do a lot of damage control. It definitely was a powder keg down here and Marta was a little excited by it. She liked battle, she could not deny that. It was the purest act she'd ever committed—mortal combat—and it was when she felt most alive. Everything seemed to pale in comparison to fighting.

She spent the day wandering about, going here and there shopping, doing the business of the ranch and wondering about the revolution, thinking about battle. Before she realized it, she found herself at the dock, purchasing passage to Vera Cruz by mail steamer. She'd done this a few times in the past and enjoyed it. She suddenly wanted to see Del Calle.

It was an uneventful trip and she spent most of it chatting with the crew. She usually avoided the officers. Most of them were too busy and, frankly, boring. They all did the same dance, sizing her up, carefully selecting their words. Was she a lady? Was she loose? Was she a high-class whore? Marta was difficult to read and gave a very unorthodox first impression. Most educated men did not like it.

But the working men liked her well enough. They could see that she was different from them and it was clear to them that, even if she were a high-class whore, she was beyond their means. It was easy after that. Knowing where they stood made it easy. They never had to worry about bedding her and once that was out of the way, some true human interaction could follow. She could chat and tease and engage them in a way that was not possible for them with other women. It was not just her charm and beauty that made her such fun. Marta genuinely cared for people. She talked to them, not at them, and she was engaged. She would tease, but they'd never be the butt of the joke; she did not tease at others' expense. She respected people, all people of all color and station in life, and they responded in kind.

She wanted to know what it was like for them to make their way in life; survive, go on day after day when the same boring tasks stared them in the face. She knew she was privileged and with privilege and wealth came the greatest benefit, the benefit of not having to do boring and mundane things in order to get by.

She thought about this as she regarded a man dutifully scraping a rail on the forward deck of the ship. He was working diligently and singing to himself. She could just barely hear the song. He looked up at her and bowed his head slightly, then went back to his work.

"Ola, Señor."

"Señorita." He smiled broadly and returned his attention to the rail.

"How long have you been working on this ship?"

"Twenty-three years, Miss."

"And this is what you do?"

"Oh, sí. I do this, and painting, scraping and painting and all the things that must be done to keep Mother at bay."

"Mother?"

"Oh, sí." He looked up at the sky, "Mother Nature. She is hard on a ship. She makes us pay dearly for the privilege of traveling her waters."

"So, when you finish scraping and painting, then what?"

He looked down at the rail, looked forward at the yards and yards to go, shrugged and looked at Marta. "Start over."

In Vera Cruz she hired a taxi and called on Captain Pedro del Calle. He wasn't in and, instead, was greeted by a sergeant with great chevrons covering his biceps. His uniform was so crisply ironed and creased that she thought it might crack apart at too much movement. He seemed to be having the same thoughts, as he moved very little. He moved only his head and mouth as if too much movement would untuck the crisp shirt from the crisp trousers and he'd have to excuse himself, run back to his squad bay and rebuild himself for the day.

He looked at her and did not smile or speak beyond what was required. She was nearly a head taller than the man and, when she looked down on him, she looked at the top of his nearly shaven head. He was a fascinating man as he was two shades darker than Marta and he spoke with a heavy island accent.

He attempted to disengage. He wanted to go about whatever task he had in mind, as there were many. He was the top sergeant, which meant he did all the work while the officers signed the documents, taking credit for the work. He was the one who ensured that the officers moved up the ladder to eventually become majors and colonels and perhaps, even generals. He was at the top of his game and it was abundantly clear why. He did not have time for Marta del Toro.

"So, you work for Pedro?" Before he could answer she thrust a good Cuban cigar in his face. She'd already lit her own and the pungent odor was distracting him. He couldn't pass it up.

He looked at the cigar worth half a day's pay and regarded the young lady in front of him.

"Yes."

"Like that cigar? Romeo y Julieta. "

"Yes."

"From your homeland?"

"Yes."

"Can you answer in more than one word sentences?" He amused her.

"Yes."

He stood up and went to a file cabinet, pulled open the middle drawer and produced a bottle of Vat 69. He poured for both of them and they clicked glasses. "Your health."

"And yours." She drank it down in one swallow and firmly set the glass in front of him. She appreciated the significance of such a gesture. The top sergeant did not do this for just anyone.

"That's some of the shittiest Scotch I've ever had."

He ignored the insult and poured again.

"What's your name?"

"Sergeant Ramirez, but I'm called Top."

"No, your Christian name."

"Alonzo."

"Alonzo. That's a nice name. Why would they refer to you as a child's toy?" She knew the answer, but wanted to tease him a little. He understood and would have smiled if it were in his nature, which it was not.

"I'm the top sergeant." He regarded the many stripes on his uniform sleeve.

"Okay, Alonzo. What do you do for fun around here?"

He wanted to get back to work, then thought better of it. No wonder the Captain had been so distracted all these many days. "This is the United States Marine Corps, madam. We have no fun here."

"Oh, come now, Alonzo. You've got to get the knots worked out somehow. What do you do, when you're not doing this?" She looked down at the mountain of bureaucracy on his desk. It was an absurd collection of redundant paperwork. It was vital to the operation of the military, the government, the machinations of a great monster serpent that existed for the purpose of waiting to unleash a fury that may or may not ever be required. Hurry up and wait, hurry up and wait. Since waiting was too tedious, it had to be filled with hours upon hours of mindless, useless completion and duplication, writing and rewriting of forms. And this is what Top Sergeant Alonzo Ramirez did with great purpose and efficiency.

In his formative years as a marine he filled his days cleaning and polishing, ironing and folding, creasing and flattening all manner of things: uniforms, shelter halves, bedclothes, rifles, bayonets, boots, leather belts and hat brims and holsters. Year upon year, cleaning things that were already clean, straightening things that were already pin neat, and finally— finally—after twenty three years, he'd arrived, to this; to the constant, endless, unimportant paperwork of running a battalion or regiment, or company or squad of US Marines.

When the cigars were smoked and half the Scotch gone, she had him. He was talking freely and relaxing a little. They had the place to themselves. The captain was not there and, as it was Sunday, he'd let the men go to chapel. Most of them did not care one way or the other about chapel, but at least in chapel they could not be ordered to do something. It was the one afternoon, the few hours in a week, when they could be fully assured that no command would be barked at them, no order would be given to perform some mindless, silly, redundant task.

"Alonzo, I need to learn about your weaponry."

He looked up at her, regarding her and the question. "For what purpose?"

"The revolution. I'm going to fight in the revolution, on the side of Zapata, of course. I need to know about your weaponry. You might, *we* might—I'm an American as well as a Mexican—we might be sending weaponry down from the north and it might be used against the revolutionaries. I need to know what we're up against."

"Do you think I'd look better in prison stripes?" He once again glanced down and regarded his great chevrons.

"You're already in prison." She moved her eyes over his desk full of paperwork, "What would be the difference?"

"There would be. Trust me, there would be."

"Do you think our rifles, the Springfields are better than the Mausers?"

"No, neither better nor worse. The same." He stood up and Marta thought that she'd gone too far. She thought that he was going to grab her by the arm and throw her out. Instead, he put on one of those ridiculous hats Pedro wore in Nassau. It looked better on Alonzo. "Come with me."

They rode in a little truck for a half hour and were soon at a firing range. Here and there men moped around, trying their best to look busy enough to avoid being assigned work. Several of them saw the top sergeant and began to move away. It was an interesting little dance and Marta enjoyed it. Alonzo was wise to them, halted them and spouted orders. They jumped, just enough, not too much. Jumping to attention was only for the officers and Alonzo was the Top, but he wasn't an officer. They took heed to what he was telling them and dispersed, not so much out of reverence for the man, but more in hopes of getting away from him before he could come up with more tasks for them to perform.

In short order, Marta had a dozen weapons laid at her feet, everything from hand guns to machine guns and anything in between. She smiled when she considered the shotgun. It was just like hers and she was pleased that her mother knew so much, that her mother had chosen one of the guns of the US Marines.

Top Sergeant Alonzo showed them all to her in detail, taught her how they operated, what ammunition they used, what each weapon's effective range and specific purpose was. He gave her particular instruction on the machinegun. She could tell it was his favorite and she almost asked him about his time in battle. She wanted to know how many men he'd killed. But somehow, it didn't seem appropriate, and she kept quiet on this subject.

When she thought the lesson was complete, he surprised her by scooping up the machinegun and placing it in her arms. She cradled it like a newborn babe. He grabbed some ammunition and the gun's tripod and instructed her to follow him.

With great precision and purpose, he assembled the gun in a field. Off in the distance some targets could be seen, lined up shoulder to shoulder, white pasteboard representations of human beings, a couple of feet apart from each other. He checked the gun out and was satisfied that he'd assembled it properly, handed her cotton for her ears and beckoned her to sit beside him.

"Now, the trick with this weapon is to not shoot too fast. The barrel will burn up and then it won't do you any good."

She paid attention, nodding and taking it all in. She leaned close and put a hand on one of his chevron covered biceps. "I see, Alonzo."

He racked the first round in the chamber by pulling the swinging arm down under the barrel and checked the range. "Point blank up to one hundred fifty yard, then you fix the sights according to the range of your target, here. Make sure there's nothing under the barrel when you set up, or the operating arm will dig into the ground. That's why we call it a potato digger."

"I see."

"Don't just hold the trigger down. Like I said, you'll burn up the barrel. And besides, you'll miss more than you'll hit." He pointed to the targets. "See 'em? First mistake is to press the trigger and roll along from left to right. The gun'll rise. You might hit the first one, but the rest'll get away. You'll just be sending rounds over their heads. Little bursts. That's what's wanted. And always, focus on the front sight."

He demonstrated to her, bap, bap, bap. He moved to the second target, bap, bap, bap; on to the third and so on. He showed her his work and all the targets were hit, as he planned, three rounds in each, all fatal. "If you're loaded with Dum Dum's, they'll need a spoon to carry what remains away."

He was testing her a little. Wanted to see how she'd react and he was impressed.

"May I give it a try, Alonzo?"

He moved the gun and tripod a little farther down range, identified three fresh targets and set her up, ready to fire. She was as a good a student as the top sergeant was an instructor, and she was soon firing with deadly effect. It was a hellish machine and Marta loved it dearly. She was very happy with the outcome. She kissed him on the cheek and he did not mind.

On the ride back she decided to ask him. "What do you think of Del Calle?"

"He's an officer."

"What's that mean?"

"He's an officer. I don't mix with officers and they don't mix with me."

"You like him?" She cut the tip of a new Cuban for him and lit it, stuck it in his mouth as they drove. She had a cigarette. He smoked and regarded her question. She was a strange young woman, sure enough. He found himself speaking without thinking.

"He's the best officer I've ever known. He's a good man."

"Were you with him in battle?"

"Oh, yes."

"And he did well?"

"He did well." He looked at her. She would be good enough for him. "He's not been himself, though."

Marta became a little concerned. "Oh?"

"He's been distracted." Alonzo drew in a deep lungful of cigar smoke and blew it out, off to his left.

"Oh?"

"He's been distracted by you."

She got a good room in the Hotel Vera Cruz and had a bath. She smoked three Cubans while she soaked and thought about Top Sergeant Alonzo Ramirez and Captain Pedro del Calle. She was now back to square one. All the talk and worry over Curtin and the thoughts, the dreams of spinsterhood with Rebecca, melted away. It was too much. She felt tingly again when she thought of Pedro. Now she had discovered for sure that he wasn't a brush salesman; he wasn't a phony like Curtin. She already knew, really, that he wasn't. But now she had learned what a good man he was for certain, verified by Top Sergeant Alonzo. Old Alonzo wouldn't lie. He couldn't lie. He was a machine, a machine of the Marines, he was hard-wired to work, not lie, not let his emotions rule him and he told her, in so many words, that Del Calle was in love with her.

Now what was she to do? Would it be she who left Rebecca? Would Rebecca be the solitary creature, living out her days, caring for her bastard baby and Marta the one to live the dream, the wonderful fairytale story with her knight in shining armor? The knight wearing a silly campaign hat? Would she become a soldier's wife?

The military base was horrible, ugly. Everything was so poor looking. The military was a terrible place to raise a family, and if the wife wasn't in the hellish places with her husband, they'd be apart for months and months, perhaps years. She didn't like the sound of that at all. She was confused now. Doomed. And then she had another thought. How could she run the ranch and have babies and run all over the God forsaken hellish places that marines were sent? She couldn't. What, then, *could* she do? Women did not tell men where to live or what to do. It was the wrong way round. A woman followed her husband, helped advance her husband's career.

Now she felt completely miserable. The ranch was where she belonged. Zapata saw and knew it; Adulio told her as much, everyone saw it. She was vital to the place. It was her home. It was what she would do—her destiny—and now the thought of having a man, any man, not just Del Calle, was likely an impossibility. Could she perhaps find one of the men on the ranch? That seemed unlikely. There were many good men there and Marta was no snob, but they were not educated men, they were not worldly men. They couldn't match her intellectually, not even remotely. She knew well enough she'd absolutely have to have that for a marriage to endure. She'd need an intelligent, learned man.

Her mind drifted to the night before. She regarded the scratches from the glass all over her body. She thought about what it must be like to die; to get a bullet through the brain while sleeping. What would happen? It seemed like a pretty good way to go, much less painful, likely, than most deaths, and in bed, while asleep, dreaming.

She remembered she was having a good dream when the shot woke her. She was dreaming about being intimate with Pedro. Would she just go on dreaming when she died? Would that be heaven? Would heaven be like the best dream she ever had, and just go on and on? Would she live the dream? Would it all come together, all the hopes and wishes be fulfilled? That would be a nice heaven to live for all eternity.

Or would she just be dead? No more dreaming, worrying, having fun, having sadness; just a deep black void of nothingness. That didn't seem so bad either. Maybe, like the old saying goes, all her troubles truly would be over. She didn't know, but neither end seemed so terrible to her and she realized that she was not afraid to die. Bring it on, bring on the worst possible, because she was ready for it and she'd handle it, defeat it. She would endure and survive.

She felt like crying again. She often felt like crying these days, but she didn't. The water was cold and she was cold. She snuffed out her cigar and got moving, dried off and got dressed. She wanted to go home.

XI Rebecca's Ride

Marta awoke and Rebecca was not in bed. It was nearly five. She looked over at her nightstand, another telegram, it read:

31° 6'N, 107° 58' 48"W
Z

She found Rebecca out by the stables, looking off into the desert, not really looking, her mind was on Curtin. She hated to disturb Rebecca but the message was just too compelling. "What do you make of this?"

Rebecca looked at it, handed it back. "Don't know. We don't even know who Z is. Could be Curtin, could be a trap." She looked at Marta and then into her cup. "I'm so tired of all this, Marta. Why's it happening, why us?" She looked tired, haggard, even old. "We're good people, Marta. You're the best hacendado ever. We're moral, kind, we look out for people, why is this happening to us?"

"Because of money, darling. It's always because of money, the greed, the expectation that money will bring a person happiness and power. This ranch is literally sitting on a gold mine. It's black gold and gas and crops and yellow gold, probably silver too. It's too much for an Indian to own." She smiled and pulled back a strand of Rebecca's hair. "I don't know anymore, Rebecca. I don't know if this is all worthwhile. This country, maybe it's doomed. God played a bad trick on Mexico by putting all these riches under it. It's all just so much fuel, fuel for the devil's own hell fires. Perhaps all of Mexico is doomed, from back before Cortez, back when the Aztecs were so greedy and the gold had hold of them too. I just don't think any peace and justice and freedom is ever in store for our Mexico." She smiled but was not happy. "You know, we could go back home, go to college and live well, like a couple of princesses all our lives. We could go to Europe, leave all of North America to the scoundrels and greedy bastards. Mamma and Daddy have been in Europe for more than a year and are so happy there. We could spend a lifetime there and not experience it all. We could have such fun. We could go to Italy or Spain, anywhere south. We'd be accepted there. Some of those people are as dark as me!" She gave Rebecca a little smile. "We could not bother to ever step foot in Mexico again. I wonder." She turned and left her sister, went back, wanted to do something, could not decide what, she'd had such a headache these last days.

Rebecca watched as Marta walked away. It was not Marta's walk. It was a defeated walk and she didn't like it at all. She turned and called on the groom to get her best mount ready. She went to Uncle Alejandro's library and pulled out the most recent atlas, found the coordinates, got her guns, got a compass, and off she went.

She rode north for most of the morning, up to the far reaches of her sister's land. It was mountainous up there and no one ever went there except to hunt late in the season. Uncle Alejandro had done some mining there many years ago, but the gold was thinly dispersed in the rock and he had no interest in using mercury or other poisons to extract it. His men had a couple of shafts dug and this is where the coordinates took Rebecca.

It was an eerie place, desolate, dusty, dry. The shaft's entrance was foreboding, as if entering it would be like walking down into one's own tomb, into the devil's lair. Her keen eye discovered some recent activity as there was an abundance of fresh footprints all around. She took her shotgun and also a small flashlight which she soon discovered was not needed. There were fresh ones at the entrance. She chose one and moved ahead. At fifty feet an iron grate blocked her way. The old mine shaft was being used as a dungeon.

"Hallo?" She called down and waited, listened intently and was startled by a voice behind her. She turned to see a young man, fit and dirty and wearing a six shooter, standing at the entrance to the mine. It was his footprints, his flashlights that she had only just discovered.

"Oh, hello."

"Miss, Walsh?" He smiled. "Sorry, ma'am didn't expect anyone, especially *you* out here."

"What are *you* doing out here?" She recognized him as one of the men working for the oil company. She never liked him, he was always leering at her and her sister. She absentmindedly pointed her shotgun at him and once she realized, did not change the muzzle's angle. There was no need to be too friendly to him just now.

"Just, just checking, ah, just checking the entrance, ma'am. Been folks poking around lately, I guess trying a little prospecting."

"There's still gold, I understand."

"Oh, yes ma'am. An energetic fellow might pull a few dollars a day out of it, if he worked hard enough at it, broke his back for it." He grinned and was leering at her again. He noticed the gaping bore of the shotgun and it looked more deadly with the barrel cut down. Another gift from their mother, cut down Winchesters for their sixteenth birthday.

"That grate down there, it's locked. Do you have a key?"

"Oh, sure, ah no."

"Well, what is it, do you have a key or not?"

"I, err, I do, but there's no point in you going down there, ma'am." It was his weak attempt at forcefulness and it did not work.

"Open it." She started heading for the grate as the man plodded along behind her. The lights from their flashlights caused shadows to dance, strangely, irregularly around them. At one point Rebecca swore she saw a man's face on the other side. She stopped and held the light to the lock, waited for the man to catch up and turn the key. In an instant a voice cried out, from deep on the other side of the grate, a familiar voice, one with significant anxiety in its cry.

"Rebecca, watch out!" She turned in time to deflect the blow from the flashlight, pushing the man off balance. She swung her shotgun, catching him on the top of the head, dropping him as if he were pole-axed. Dan George emerged. He looked a wreck.

"Thank you, Dan." She reached through and grabbed his hands, shook them briefly, turned and retrieved the key. She opened the lock as the man on the ground began to regain his senses. Dan George was on him, over him and in one resolute motion kicked him across the face. The bad man went limp once again.

Dan found another key in the fellow's pocket and uncuffed himself, put the shackles on his captor and relieved the henchman of his gun and gun belt. Dan was now armed and they would not molest him again. He smiled down at Rebecca Walsh. "Darned good to see you, Rebecca, darned good to see you." He shook her hand, then absentmindedly grabbed her up in his arms. He held her tightly and kissed her cheek.

"Is Marta alive?"

"Oh, yes, she's fine, Dan. We're all fine. We thought you were dead, but we kept getting messages that you were still alive. We worried so, Dan. We hired a detective, he lost track of you in Nuevo Casas Grandes. It was Curtin, wasn't it?" Dan looked at her, not certain of her meaning.

"No." He took her by the hand and brought the flashlight to bear. "Follow me." They walked another hundred yards down the sloping corridor to an antechamber. He grabbed her by the hand and led her around a corner, held the light high, "I think this might be someone you know."

"Robert!" She needed no prompting. He looked like hell. They beat him bloody, echoing his threat to Tolkenhorn the night before the Zapata train robbery; *I'll beat you 'til you can't see...* and that's what they'd done to poor Robert Curtin.

He sat up straight and leaned forward, looked at her sideways. "Hello, my darling."

"Robert!" She hugged him gently and worried over his wounds.

"How do I look?" He grinned and his front teeth were gone. "Think it'll leave a mark?"

"My God, what did they do to you?"

Dan interjected, "our boy up yonder, it's a kind of pastime for him."

"So, I guess you're not a Jew."

He looked up again and smiled. "What do ya have against Jews, Rebecca?"

She smiled, embarrassed, "Oh, nothing, nothing at all, got cousins who are Jews," she blushed. "Tolkenhorn told a big story about you. Said you were a Jew, not Catholic, said you were married with two children, even showed me photos. Robert, he had one of you wearing a yarmulke."

Curtin smiled his toothless grin. "Son of a bitch bastard. Those *were* my photos. Remember my friend Abe, the reporter, we called him about the turtles? He's my friend from college. He's a Jew, I attended his wedding. We all wore them, out of respect for his faith. And the other photos, my sister and her children. God damn that son of a bitch."

"Oh, Robert. He was convincing, he told me things, told me things that only you and I would know. He said you'd gotten drunk of an evening and bragged about what you did to me." She looked down and blushed.

"My journal! Rebecca, you remember one of my bags was lost? It had my journal and it was recovered and sent on to my office, but Miles got it first. Everything was waterlogged, all my clothes were ruined and what was left of the journal was just a cover with all the pages ruined, unreadable, just a pile of unreadable pulp. He must've stolen the good pages and replaced them with the ruined ones. That old bastard, he's smarter than I thought. He went through it, read it. I'm sorry, Rebecca, I shouldn't have written in it. I'm sorry. It was a thing I picked up in college. Just write everything that happens to me. I'm sorry. They were never meant for anyone to see."

She kissed him gently on the few spots on his face not battered. "And you didn't really steal my rings? And you really didn't hire that man on the ship to attack us? And you didn't shoot through Marta's window and try to kill her?"

"God no!" He looked at Rebecca, mortified. "He told you all that? Jesus, Rebecca, you must have thought me a monster!"

"I did. You broke my heart, Robert Curtin."

"Do you still want to marry me?"

"With all my heart."

They walked out together, steadying Dan George. He had difficulty seeing as he'd been a captive in the mine for so many days. They dragged the henchman in and locked him away. He'd do no more damage now. They intended to leave him when Rebecca had a thought. She motioned for her companions to stand by and dumped a bucket of what she thought was water, immediately realizing it had been used for a chamber pot, on the man's head. It had the desired effect and he suddenly awoke, sputtering and spitting the contents of his former captives' bladders.

"My God, why'd you do that?" He looked up at them, dumbfounded.

Rebecca took out a cigarette case and handed everyone but the captive one. She smoked as the man blinked; his hands shackled behind his back so that he could do nothing but let urine run down into his eyes. It was not a comfortable feeling.

Rebecca spoke and blew smoke into his face. "Tell me what you know about me…, what's your name?"

"Dobbs."

"Mr. Dobbs."

He was becoming angry at his situation and looked on her with disdain. "Nothing, don't know a damned thing about you, lady."

"Well, no matter." She pulled her big hunting knife and began playing with the blade's edge. She kept it, as her mother had taught her, razor-sharp. "Tell us everything you know."

He smirked. "That's easy. Don't know a thing. Don't have any idea what's going on." He looked away, smugly.

"Oh, I doubt that. You're in congress with that lout Tolkenhorn, and I hear he's a lawyer and a drunkard and a loudmouth who can't keep his mouth shut. You've heard some things." She reached over with the knife, toward his face as he stiffened.

"Get that thing out of my face, you don't scare me, lady. You're a lady, I know that, you're not going to hurt me."

She pushed him backward, pressed her knee into his gut and shaved off his left eyebrow. "Yes, it's good and sharp."

"Mr. Dobbs, it would be a good idea if you told me everything you know. It's true, I'm a lady, but I have a lot of Indian blood in me," she looked up and gave Dan a wink and a knowing smile, "bandit blood. You see, my mother was a woman very famous in these parts for many years. One time, when I was a little girl, I was kidnapped by a band of cutthroats." She reached over and shaved off his other eyebrow. He looked strange now, as a man with no eyebrows always looks strange. "And, you know what my mother did?"

"No." He was sulking now, blinking to remove the remnants of the urine and now brow hair from his eyes.

"She cut the leader's goddamned head off." She looked on at Curtin and Dan George. "Hold 'em down, boys."

Curtin was shocked, Dan George was not. He nodded, commanded Curtin to obey with a look and they held the man in place.

"You're bluffin'," the henchman announced with uncertainty.

Rebecca reached over and smoothly sliced into the man's neck. He screamed in pain and panic.

"Oh, God, no! Stop, stop, I'll tell you. I'll tell you everything I know!"

She stopped, the blood ran freely and she looked on at the damage she'd done. "Good man. Good. Thank goodness I haven't gotten to your jugular, that would be the end of you for certain. Now, tell me, tell us what you know."

He was panicked now and began crying like a baby. He had difficulty catching his breath, "Oh God, oh Jesus, that hurts, my God, I'm dying, you've killed me!"

"Oh, stop it, you big baby." Rebecca took a long draw from her cigarette and stuffed it in his mouth. He sucked on it as if it were a pacifier. "I hardly broke the skin."

He began to calm down. "They're tired of Tolkenhorn's lack of progress. They found out he," he nodded at Curtin, "was playing them, that's when they put him in here for me to guard…"

"And beat." Curtin sneered at the man.

"And now they're planning to finish you all off, you, your sister, everyone on the ranch."

"Who, who is going to do this?"

"A general, don't know his name, and some American fellow, a bigwig in the government. They want to get the land, they're going to make it look like the revolutionaries went in and killed a bunch of Americans, they're trying to get the US army in here, get the US to take over in Mexico. You all are going to be, wait, wait, someone said it, you all are *the Maine*. Don't know what it means. But that's what they said."

Dan George grinned cynically and looked at his companions, "*Remember the Maine.*"

Curtin finished it for him, "*to hell with Spain.*"

Rebecca sat back and thought hard. "Goddamned Hearst. Got us into a war in Cuba with his yellow journalism, now he's trying the same with Mexico. They say he owns half the country down here as it is. If the revolution is a success, he stands to lose big. Greedy bastard."

"Yes, Hearst, Hearst, that's what they kept saying," the henchman was pleased with himself for adding this bit of information.

"So, when's this all happening, Mr. Dobbs?"

"Don't know," he looked at the knife, covered in his own blood turning menacing in Rebecca's hand, "I, I really, honestly don't know ma'am." He was suddenly respectful to Rebecca Walsh. "But sooner than later, maybe even tomorrow, probably tomorrow, ma'am."

She finished her cigarette and the men left their captive lying on the dirt floor of the mine. The wound on his neck was beginning to clot. Rebecca poured a canteen full of water on him to clean him up a bit. She looked on, doing her best impersonation of her mother. "I'm not going to kill you...today, Mr. Dobbs." She leaned forward, close to his face, "But if you ever do harm to any of mine again, I'll cut your head off and use it for a football."

He swallowed hard. "Yes ma'am."

In a few days, or perhaps a week, Rebecca would send someone to retrieve him.

They found the henchman's camp, took his mount for Dan George to ride. Robert and Rebecca rode together and he held her gently the entire way, now and then kissing her long delicate neck. "I've missed you, Rebecca Walsh." He suddenly thought of something. "I remembered to grab this when they took me away," he reached down his shirt and pulled up a string from around his neck, two rings hung together. "I got your ring resized, and here's the other." Now they were a perfect fit.

She rode on admiring her new ring. She'd forgotten how beautiful it was. "Robert?"

"Yes, darling?"

"Don't be hurt, but, Robert, this ring. It's far beyond your means."

He laughed. "You can say that again."

"How'd you get it? Not on credit?"

"No, no." He shifted and pressed himself more tightly against her back. "My old mother, she told me that there was a rule, a rule that must be followed and that was that a man had to give his wife a good ring. I've been saving for a long time, Rebecca. Wiped me out, but I got you a dandy. A ring my mother would have been proud of." He laughed at the thought of something, "And besides, the money I took from Tolkenhorn more than paid for it. Hah! I beat that bastard at his own game at least in that respect." They rode on a bit further and Curtin continued. "Rebecca?"

"Yes, darling?"

"Would you have cut that fellow's head off?"

"No." she felt the sense of relief course through his body and continued. "But *he* didn't know that." She reached back, over her shoulder and touched his face. "Besides, he didn't really get me riled. I wouldn't have even killed him, probably." She grabbed for another cigarette and lit it. "I've got to be really riled to do something like that." She grinned. She felt like her mother saying that.

"Rebecca?"

"Yes, darling?"

"Remind me every day to never ever cross you or ever get you riled. Remind me of that for the rest of our days."

Dan George stopped and waited for them to catch up. "Folks, where are we going and what are we doing?"

Rebecca grinned. "I'm working on that."

Dan smiled back. "Well, there's no law to help us. This little drama goes deep. Old Tolkenhorn, typical lawyer, couldn't keep his big mouth shut, I heard him mention the general and the ambassador, too. That boy Dobbs was telling the truth. They're all in it."

Curtin smiled at Dan deriding his own profession, "Yea, when they thought I was unconscious I heard a thing or two also. Rebecca, I've been playing at being a spy for you and Marta," he felt his jaw, "not a very effective one, but the big scheme was to get the ranch from Marta, then sell it to a certain rich and powerful newspaper mogul, name rhymes with thirst."

"Just as the kid said." She sounded old saying that. Rebecca had aged a decade in the past week.

Curtin continued. "Rebecca, there's a lot of oil under that ranch, and in those mountains, where you rescued us," he stopped and had to kiss her for that "there's a lot of gold, but they're going to have to do a lot of extraction. It's going to spoil the whole region. The aquifer for this area is fed from those mountains. I told them that Marta wouldn't go for it."

"As did I." Dan looked on so as to comfort Curtin. He knew what the engineer was thinking, that somehow he was the cause of all this. "I told them she wouldn't let them spoil the land. The gold is really the issue, and the fact that they, the general and Tolkenhorn, and the ambassador wanted to get it from Marta and resell. It's a lot of money, Rebecca." He hesitated, "but I guess the biggest prize is political. Can you imagine the hoopla? They'd use you and Marta as martyrs. It's not a problem if poor Mexicans are slaughtered by the bushel, but a couple of rich and beautiful American debutantes, well, that would get us into it down here and good. Son of a bitch probably has glamorous photographs of you two all picked out for the front page." Dan continued. "The general's probably preordained as the next president. Dictator's more like it, but men like Hearst, they miss Díaz. They miss that old coot, because they could get so rich by him. Madero wants a democracy, and that won't ensure a big payoff for them, and, if the socialist get in, they'll really lose big. Can you imagine? Hearst would have a fit! They'd nationalize all the businesses, the oil, collective farming, my God, he'd have a stroke over all that."

Rebecca thought for a moment. "Come on, I've got an idea."

They ended up in Nuevo Casas Grandes and settled in for the night. Dan George got a telegram to his wife. The men got cleaned up and a change of clothes. Dan had many friends in this town, as he had wherever he went. Rebecca had a plan. "Gentlemen, here is what we must do."

They ended up in a rough saloon on the edge of town, her companions looked out of place, Rebecca did not. She still wore her hunting outfit and sombrero. Dried blood from Dobbs had gotten smeared on her blouse and she had a bit of a glint, a fight, in her eye. They stood at the bar and ordered mescal.

Suddenly Rebecca held up a glass and blurted out, "*Viva Zapata!*" And a chorus went up around her. She ordered drinks for the house and held up another. "*Viva Villa!*" and again, the same reply.

She sauntered over to an old man sitting at a corner table. He'd said nothing when she'd raised her glass. She asked permission to sit with him and he stood up, bowed and removed his hat. They sat down together and she leaned close to his face. "I need to get a message, an urgent message to Emiliano Zapata, Señor." She presented him with her card.

"I know you, Señorita Walsh, and I know your sister. Come with me", he stood up and extended his hand, as if to show her the way, "I will help you."

She left Dan and Curtin and followed the man through several dark alleys, through the roughest part of town. They finally arrived at a warehouse, to a secret room at the back of the building. Several men were in the room and when she entered, they all stood up, removing their hats. The old man became animated and spoke quickly to several of the men, the network was kicked into motion. He offered her some American whiskey and they drank to the revolution. He assured her that everything would go to plan, that Zapata's army was not far away and that the general would be notified by midnight.

She shook his hand and looked him in the eye. He had a kind face and sad eyes. "You do not look happy, Señor."

He smiled a little self-consciously, "It is a great tease, Señorita, a great tease, the fates are playing with us, letting us dream, but I fear..." he looked down at the glass of whiskey, "there is no real story of David and Goliath." He gave her a look that made her want to cry. "It's just a fairytale, and fairytales, well, they never come true."

Rebecca had not returned to the ranch. She was gone, off on some adventure and it was full dark and Marta was worried sick. Esmeralda tried her best to calm her in her simple, almost infantile way. She turned down her bed and waited nearby. She would likely be needed by the end of this night.

It was so uncharacteristic of Rebecca to do such a thing. She was always the careful one. She was always the prudent and levelheaded one. Now she was gone, no one knew where she'd gone, only that she was dressed for desert travel, for hunting, but she'd not taken her hunting rifle, only her six shooter and shotgun and a Winchester. It made no sense.

At ten o'clock she called Adulio, ordered a search party.

"Where are we to search, Señorita?"

"*I don't know!*" She snapped then regretted it. She took a deep breath. "If I knew where to search, I wouldn't need a search party, Adulio. Send the men out, send everyone who can ride. Someone saw her go north, go north. Find her."

"As you please."

By one o'clock he was back to her room, standing in the shadows. She did not see him there. She looked up with a start. "Adulio, you scared me."

"Did I? I didn't think anything scared you, princesa."

She looked at him askance. "Princesa? Since when did you start being so jocular, *and* familiar, Adulio?"

"Oh, you *are* a princesa, but your story is not going to have a happy, princesa ending." He stepped out of the shadows and she could see that he was holding a gun, pointed at her. She looked over at her own revolver under her pillow, too far away to reach. She always kept several guns around the room, and Adulio knew this. He held up a hand. "I will only kill you quicker if you try to fight, princesa."

"So, you are in with Curtin?"

"Hah! Curtin, the errand boy. Curtin is not your problem. Your problem goes much deeper, my child." He lit a cigarette and smoked. He looked angry and evil but his unsteady hand betrayed him, showed that he was not so much in control. He was terrified and she knew it.

"Why are you doing this, Adulio?"

"Because it is my right. M*y right!*" His voice grew louder but he didn't care, no one was around to hear him. His wife sat, like a dummy in the next room, could hear nothing, could not hear this story of betrayal.

"For half a lifetime I served that bloated pig, that worthless peon. The great Alejandro del Toro got a little jingle in his pocket, got some good clothes, got fine soaps and perfumes and looked the gentlemen. No matter of soap can wash it away, princesa, no matter of soap can wash that stain from the skin." He pointed at her dark complexion. "My family should have had this land. *My family*, pure blood that could be traced to Spain, not you Indios, you dirty worthless creatures. Cortez should have killed you all, should have spread the smallpox to every one of you. But now, finally, the revolution, the final best excuse to kill you all."

"I think Zapata and Villa might have something to say about that, Adulio."

"Hah, more dog Indios, they will be defeated, they and all you dark savages. And you. When I learned that he was giving this all to you, well, I decided, I would get it, I'd get my revenge and I'd be the rightful owner some day."

Marta reached out, palm open, "Give me a cigarette, Adulio." He complied, handed her his case with trembling hands and watched her smoke. She worked on a plan.

"Adulio, you are as dark as me. Who's to say you are not one of these terrible indios you claim are such a scourge?"

He became furious, "I am not a goddamned Indio! I am dark from my ancient Castilian blood and because the sun has baked me, all the hard years of toil, working for your so-called uncle, working and slaving for *him*, and now *you*."

She smirked and shrugged, regarding her cigarette. "Look like an Indian to me."

"Enough!" He pointed a trembling finger at her, looked on her, hate in his eyes, "You are so arrogant. You seriously did not think I got you to come here so that you could be the hero, save the day. A woman? A woman is nothing but a beast of burden, exists for nothing more than to serve a man, have offspring, provide a little pleasure. You are *nothing*; you are worth less than a good horse or mule. I brought you here to kill you, get rid of you, so that you will no longer stand in my way, my right to this land. *And*, you will serve another interest, but I will not bother telling you about it, you aren't worth the time it would take to tell, but just know this, princesa. You will help,

help to end this absurd revolution. You will help to put the peon back in his place, back where he belongs."

She shrugged and ignored his long diatribe. She looked him in the eye. She began to speak and he cut her off.

"Enough, you little bitch!" He smoked and shook. "I've a plan for you."

"Oh, come on now, Adulio, share it with me, let me know what is to be my fate. You at least owe that to me."

He looked on at her, angry that she was not afraid, angry that she was not on her knees. She should be groveling at his feet, instead she was humiliating *him*, as she'd done all the time he'd known her. He would enjoy killing her, he was convinced of this. He thought and regarded the tip of his cigarette.

"Perhaps it is just as well to tell you." He looked at her and grinned a demented grin. "I will. I will tell you. You will not see the morning, princesa, but you will not receive a bullet. No, you will be hacked to pieces with the machete, the tool of your hero, Zapata and all the worthless bastards who follow him. The newspapers in el Norte will have a field-day, a rich American, murdered by Zapata's army. Something will need to be done. Within six weeks, the American army will occupy the entire land, and this ranch, all of it will be mine. This ranch will finally be in the hands of a worthy hacendado, and I will run it accordingly."

"What if I don't let you *hack me to pieces*, Adulio?"

He pointed the gun at her head. "I don't think you have much choice, princesa."

She sat up a little straighter and calculated the distance between them. He was shorter than her, yet stronger. He was a tough old bird and it would be touch and go.

Just as she transferred her weight, like a panther, ready to spring the sound of a shot tore through her eardrums and she looked down at herself for a wound. She looked up at Adulio staring stupidly, a chunk of face gone, and now torrents of blood running down. He dropped to his knees, waited, looked up at the princesa with vacant eyes.

"I guess you didn't understand Zapata's words, Adulio." She stood over him and looked down on him in her best, most superior attitude. "He said it was better to die on your feet, Adulio, not on your knees." With that, she pushed him on the forehead and he fell over, dead.

Esmeralda looked on with her impish grin. She stood resolute in the doorway, the smoking revolver in her hand. "My God he was an annoying bastard."

Marta smiled at her servant. "Esmeralda, you've been tricky."

"Sí, Señorita, I can hear okay, and I can talk. And this excremento has been planning to do this for a long time, but I could not tell you so well. I could only tell you with my little notes, I am sorry, Señorita, please forgive me."

"So, you are Z?" Marta lit another of Adulio's cigarettes. Handed one to Z and they smoked over the dead man.

Esmeralda regarded the corpse at her feet. "I always hated him, you know. He used to walk around our room ranting about you and the ranch. Of course he didn't know I could hear. He would look at me," she grinned, "it was hard to pretend I couldn't hear him. And he used to abuse me."

Marta looked up at her, pain in her eyes at the thought of the old woman being mistreated. Esmeralda waved her off. "Ah, Señorita, he had a little pencil, pequeño." She held up her fingers a couple of inches apart, "and that was when it was happy." She grinned and looked at the dead man at her feet. "And then, he could never get it to work. I'd have to lie back and wait and wait and wait until he was finished. Most of the time he just had to give up. It was very boring, Señorita, and I could feel nothing. He could never even give me a child." She drew a deep breath in and spit on Adulio's back, then remembered where she was. "Oh, lo siento mucho, Señorita."

"Nada."

"He was a bad man, a coward, he tried to kill you four times, but he was too estupido to make it work."

"Four times?"

"Sí. He hired that man on the ship, the stowaway, but Rebecca got him. Then the Federales with the boys, that was his little scheme, but again, Rebecca foiled that as well, and the Federales lost their nerve. Then when you went hunting and he cut poor little Pumpkin's leg, to make her lame. Oh, Señorita, he was so angry when you would not let him go along. He was going to escort you into the desert and kill you, but you would not let him go, he was angry, he had to bounce up and down on me for that one." She smiled cynically. "Then the next day, he went out after you. He was going to stalk and kill you, but he lost his nerve when you discovered him." She looked down at her hands. "I was going to try to stop him that time, but he beat me and I could not wake up the next day." She looked at Marta as if her mistress were a priest in a confessional. "I'm very sorry, Señorita, very sorry for that." She worked on her cigarette.

"You must have been in much danger all these years." Marta looked on at her servant with a sorrowful look, imagining spending a lifetime with a monster.

"Ah, sí, he did beat me many times, he abused me often, and, I must admit, I was a little afraid." She looked up from her cigarette. "It is a strange thing, Señorita," she looked down at the corpse, "he does not seem so powerful now, but he, he had a hold on me. He, I don't know why, but it is why I could not tell you outright, why I could only send you little clues. I don't know what came over me, I guess, it was just he had some power over me for so long. All his scheming, I guess I thought he was much bigger than he was." She blew smoke at him and shrugged.

"One things for sure, he was a tricky bastard." Marta looked down at the dead man. "He had a little fit out there, crying like a child. I felt sorry for him."

"Ah, he was crying, that is true, and the tears were real, but he was crying at his own cowardice. He was so terrified of you, Señorita, and he cried at his own lacking of cojones. He had little balls."

"Old bastard." She grinned a little at Esmeralda's insult.

"Sí, and then the night he shot through your window."

"He?"

"Oh, sí. He did that. He was so terrified that he could not shoot straight. He missed you. The ass could never shoot well. He could shoot standing inside a mine and miss the wall, I think."

"But he was beaten, bloody."

"Oh, sí. He was so scared that he ran right into a column on the veranda, then fell off the porch onto his face. He threw his gun away and had a good alibi."

"I see." She smiled at her servant. All these years, she loved her, but she never thought much of Esmeralda, thought of her more like she would a loyal, dim-witted dog. "Z." Marta lit another cigarette and blew smoke at the ceiling. "All these years, you never talked? Was that not difficult, Esmeralda?"

"Bah," she waved her hand, "too much talking goes on in this world, not enough listening, Señorita. I like to listen much more, but no one knows I'm listening." She worked on her cigarette and continued. "When I was a little girl I got very sick and it made my hearing go away, but little by little, it came back." She looked on at Marta and smiled. "I guess I liked being deaf. I liked that everyone thought I could not hear, I used to hear a lot of things because of that, and..." She hesitated a moment. "No one expects much of you when you cannot hear. They think you are stupid."

Marta smiled at her. "Z."

"Sí, my little sister, she could not say my name, she always called me Z. No one knows that but you now, they are all dead, my sisters and brothers and parents. All dead." She crossed herself and kissed her fingers.

"Esmeralda, how did you get the telegrams to me?" This was particularly confounding to Marta, as Esmeralda was essentially a captive on the ranch.

"Oh, that is not so hard, Señorita. I have a cousin in Tampico, he works at Western Union. He's part of the network."

"Network?"

"Sí. We have a network all over Mexico, boys, women, men, children, we are Zapatistas and Villaistas, we can get news and messages out better than can the mail system."

"I see." She was amused. Esmeralda was a sophisticated revolutionary and all along, right under Marta's nose. It was fascinating.

"Sí. So, I can get a telegram to anyone, anywhere, in one day or even less, if the boys are running fast." She finished the cigarette and looked on at Marta. "Señorita, we have much to do. I know that Rebecca has found Dan George and Robert Curtin." She watched Marta's face. "Sí, they are good, Curtin is a good man, not bad, and not a Jew. He is as Catholic as us." She regarded her comment and looked up at Marta. "Not that a Jew is bad, I don't even know a Jew. But this Robert Curtin is not one." She began pulling out Marta's hunting clothes. "Here is what we must do."

XII Vengeance

By morning, Rebecca, with the love of her life and her old friend Dan George, was approaching the ranch from the northwest. High on a hill, they watched as a troop of Federales moved up the main road from the south. Here they waited and watched.

There were at least three hundred of them, led by the general with the round glasses, and with Tolkenhorn riding nearby. The lawyer looked miserable. He hated horses, hated to ride and he hated any kind of danger. The ambassador rode up next to him, smirked and looked over at the hapless man.

"Now we're going to show you how to take the candy from the child." He sneered and rode on.

They could see Marta del Toro sitting on a horse on the little plaza at the entrance to her hacienda. She wore the outfit of her land: a straw sombrero and fancy vaquero clothes, two silver six shooters strapped around her waist and her favorite shotgun in her hands.

She was an arrogant little bitch, the general thought as he rode up on her, his men now fanning out, preparing torches. Marta's eyes widened.

"If you are going to take my ranch, why ruin it, general?"

He smirked. "Oh, we are just clearing the pigsties." He regarded her fine, albeit plain, home. "So that a proper palace can be made."

"Oh?" She pulled out a couple of big Cuban cigars, her favorite Romeo y Julietas and handed him one. She clipped the end of her own and began to hand him her cutter. She looked on in disgust as he, like an uncouth animal, savagely bit the end of her expensive gift, spitting the tip onto the ground. He next began licking it all over like a ravenous dog, spittle freely running off it as he stuffed it into his fetid mouth.

"*Putz,*" she muttered, and stared at him through a great cloud of smoke. "It seems that it would be more fitting then, for you to dig a big hole."

"How's that?" She was an appealing Indian, well put together, and he thought he might rape her before finishing her off.

"Yes," Marta continued, "A big hole in the ground. Then you can have all your men gather 'round the hole. They could drop their trousers and shit in it. That would be a more fitting home for you, I think."

She puffed on her cigar and looked him in the eye. She continued. "My mother, she always taught me, before you kill a man, she would say, always offer him a way out. Always offer him his life. That's the Christian way. That's what Jesus would do."

She positioned the shotgun, got ready and then continued, "Well, General, I'm offering you and your men your lives. Go ahead out of here now, just ride away and you may live." She regarded him and smiled. "No. I see it on your arrogant, stupid face. You aren't going to ride. You choose to die, here and now."

He smiled. Then lost the smile and looked at her, stared through his bookish round glasses. "Before this day is done, I will make you cry like an infant. You will wish that you'd been properly prostrated before me when I rode up here today. I will make a tobacco pouch of your womb and decorate the entrance to my new home with your head."

"I'm sorry, General, but I disagree." She reached down with her free hand and patted below her belly. "My little box will be staying put, safe and sound, right here." She leveled the shotgun and fired, hitting Tolkenhorn through the head, spraying brain and blood on the men behind him. The lawyer pitched over onto the ground as the others looked on. She glared at the general. "I'll kill you last, pig. I want you to see what Emiliano Zapata does to your army before I send you on to hell."

With that, she wheeled her horse and galloped off to the side as, at her cue, hundreds of *White Cigars* appeared on the rooftops, behind walls, through windows. And then, El Tigre himself emerged in his lovely dark suit, replete with oversized beaver sombrero, crossed bandoliers and sword. He looked magnificent on his white charger. He gave the command and a great scythe of bullets cut through the unsuspecting men.

Everywhere they dropped, shrieking and crying out in pain and fear. The torches tumbled onto the backs of their mounts, men and horses running like giant flames, screaming and shouting. The confusion was intense, incomprehensible.

Marta, now off to the side and out of the direct barrage, replaced her fired load of buckshot and gripping her reins, rode amongst the surviving would-be assassins. She rode up to each of her victims, oblivious to the danger. She was in kill mode now, like her mother, like her ancestors. She was a warrior and she practiced her craft with great skill and precision. She shot man after man, working her shotgun as her mother had taught her. As she loaded and reloaded, she thought about her wonderful, fearless mother and, for the first time, fully comprehended and appreciated the value of Chica's advice and training during those summers when they'd returned from school.

She was a splendid rider and galloped amongst them, headlong, too fast, too furious. She remained unscathed, able to carry out the maximum carnage possible.

This was her land and she was defending it. She was like a mother bear. She was the mother whose children were good people who worked the ranch. Even more, she was the mother defending all the victims of all the ages; the peons and dispossessed and beaten and downtrodden. She was shooting the bad men, punishing them and exacting revenge for all the victims of the ages and she was doing it very well.

She felt more alive now than she had since the day she first met her mother those many years ago. She suddenly realized, in the span of a heartbeat, that she *was* her mother: she was Chica and she was very proud.

She slowed and then stopped momentarily to take stock of the battle. Zapata's men were ruling the day. *It would be over soon*, she thought. Suddenly, the staccato sound of a machinegun could be heard, off in the distance. It was a potato digger, just like the one she had fired in Vera Cruz with top sergeant Alonzo. It was hundreds of yards away, raining death upon her beloved people.

She considered the terrain and her options. If it wasn't silenced soon, many of Zapata's army would lose its most precious commodity: warriors. She galloped over to her general, her hero, and gave him a friendly salute.

"General, dynamite, if you please."

He handed her three sticks, fused and ready to go. She puffed her cigar energetically, the tip now glowing red. She rode off, thundering toward the terrible machine.

The shooting team was locked on, the trajectory right for maximum destruction. They didn't see the solitary rider coming. Marta lit the fuse, watched as it caught and started to hiss, waiting until it burned down a mere fraction of an inch from the dynamite stick and threw it high into the air. She watched it tumble end over end like the relay baton she used back at Stonefields School every autumn. It struck the loader in the leg, bounced once and landed in the shooter's lap. It exploded and they all blew apart, mingling gun and steel and lead with bone and blood and offal. She rode up on them, firing her shotgun at the last man. He was terrified and too disoriented to defend himself. He stood there, waiting quietly, like an animal gone to slaughter. It was his coup de grâce and Marta willingly obliged.

The general with the round glasses and rotten breath was a good rat. He kicked his mount with his ill-fitting boots, scurrying away, abandoning his men. He had learned early on how to save his own hide and this is how he'd become a general.

Rebecca saw him. She watched him ride toward them down the dusty road. It would eventually take him south, toward Mexico City. She reined her mount, touching its sides and before Robert Curtin could protest or call out, she was off, galloping down the trail toward the fleeing coward of a man.

She was on him in short order and uncased her Winchester. Guiding her mount with her knees, as her mother had taught her, she pointed the rifle at the man's back and squeezed the trigger. Her shot went wide; she'd pulled it. She always pulled a little to the right when shooting on the run and the bullet tore a trench along his uniform coat, lodging itself in the back of his horse's head. The creature crumpled and the man tumbled over onto the desert floor.

Curtin was after them. He had a poor mount, an old tired horse and was not a good rider. He pushed the poor creature as best he could, seemingly in slow motion, but, as if caught in a nightmare, could not move quickly enough. Rebecca stood over the general. The miscreant sat, looking about, reorienting himself, his round owl-eyed glasses dusty and crooked on his face. He smiled broadly at his captor. "You'll never get away with this, my dear. No matter what you do, you'll never get away with it."

She smiled coyly. "What is that old saying, General, '*Dead men tell no tales*?'" She butted the Winchester into her shoulder and looked down the barrel. Even at close range, she used her sights.

"You are no killer, young lady, no executioner; I can see it in your eyes." He grinned, his eyes two slits behind the dusty lenses. He looked evil and she suddenly remembered her tormentor from years ago. He was the clown man, come back to haunt and torture her.

She became infuriated. He was right, of course. She lowered the rifle and looked back as Curtin called out.

"Rebecca, stop!"

It was just enough time for the general to make his move. He pulled his pistol and fired. Rebecca was shot. She lay on the desert floor with a hole through her breast, blood pouring freely from her body. The color fading from her porcelain complexion; she would not last long.

"Oh, God, no!" Curtin grabbed her and held her, oblivious to the danger around him. The general walked up to them; coolly, casually, as if he were taking a mid-morning stroll. He grabbed the reins of Rebecca's mount, preparing to ride. He looked at the lovers, the dying princess and the broken-hearted suitor. His mouth turned up in a satisfied grin.

He threw his leg across the saddle, agile for a fat man. He looked down at them, pointing the pistol at Curtin's head and tipped his head solemnly from side to side, "Too soft, too soft."

The bullet tore open the top of his skull and he dropped down beside her. He convulsed twice as blood covered his owl-eyed spectacles. Dan George holstered his pistol and rode up on them. He looked at Curtin and gave him a slight smile. He spoke to Rebecca who was gazing skyward, scared and pale as parchment, the pain intense and nearly unbearable.

"Oh, it's just like mine, darling. It's just like mine." He stuffed a handkerchief into the gaping wound and scooped her up, carrying her back toward the hacienda, to her room overlooking the road south; to her comfortable bed where Zapata's surgeon could do his best work.

Dan hid his fear, speaking softly in her ear as he ran. He was not at all certain she would live and he felt that he might fall apart. He held her tightly and spoke words of comfort and reassurance to her as he would to an injured child.

The fighting had died down. Most of the Federales were dead, a few lived but most of the wounded would not survive. Few of the freedom fighters suffered more than sunburn, it was a good day.

They began the ghoulish and inevitable battlefield scavenger hunt, removing rings, gold teeth, watches, money, guns, ammunition, swords, knives, bayonets. The machinegun could be salvaged and two children used dead soldiers' uniforms to wipe the mechanism clean before the blood of Marta's victims could begin to corrode it beyond repair.

The ambassador could not be found and this they deeply regretted. It would have been a grand coup to bring him to justice now.

They all waited, impatient, outside Rebecca's room. Robert Curtin, the young engineer, the man who'd proudly declared that emotions never ran his life sat, broken, crying now, nearly inconsolable. "All my fault, all my fault." He sat forward with his head in his hands, his eyes red from crying so hard. Dan George patted him on the shoulder.

"Come on now, man, you've got to be strong; be ready when she needs you."

Zapata was respectful and kind to Marta. He could see it in her eyes. She was not easily shaken, this one, but her most favorite person in the world was lying in the next room. They did not know if she would live or die. She held Zapata's hand and he covered it, patting her gently with his palm.

"He's the best surgeon in Mexico." He waited for Marta to look up. "I only just captured him a few days ago. I told him I'd shoot him if Rebecca did not make a full recovery."

She smiled a weak smile and looked into his eyes. "General, if she dies …, I don't know, I don't want to live." Curtin heard her and his tears began to flow more freely. He wasn't embarrassed. He didn't care who saw him cry.

An eternity passed and the surgeon finally emerged from her bedroom. He looked tired. He looked at Zapata and then to the others. "The wound is clean and the bleeding has stopped. She will likely lose some use of one lung, but they'll live."

Marta jerked her head up. "*They'll* live?"

"Young lady, your sister is going to have a baby."

Curtin was now with her. She opened her eyes and smiled, put a hand to his battered face. She breathed uneasily.

"Rebecca, I'm sorry. I'm sorry. It seems I can't do anything right by you."

"Oh, I don't know. You gave me a baby. We're going to have a baby, Robert."

"I know. When did you know?"

"For a while. Probably from the first time we were together. All that practice for naught." She smiled. "I have to tell you something, Robert." She was getting tired and the morphine was working on her mind. "I'm not … I don't blame you, Robert. I should have shot him. I should have, but it's not in my nature, Robert. They all teased me, my mamma and daddy and Marta. They all said I was the civilized one. It's not your fault, Robert. No matter what happens, you have to know it's not your fault."

"Rebecca." He was crying, nearly out of control. "The doctor said you're going to be all right. You're going to be all right, Rebecca. Please, please rest, just rest. I'll be here if you need me. Just rest."

"One more thing, Robert." She tried to get more comfortable. "What did you mean when you told Pedro, on the ship, when you said, '*Once you get them on their backs it's smooth sailing?*'"

His mind struggled to remember, to think back to that day. He smiled. "Turtles, darling, I was telling him about the turtles and my friend Abe. He said he'd use it for his headline, to get the word out about the cruelty, to give the public an understanding of the horror we saw."

She smiled and drifted off. "Turtles."

Marta and Dan George rode through the carnage with General Zapata. It was sad to see so many dead. Even if they were Federales, they were still Mexicans. It hit home that it was just another ugly, bloody civil war, brother against brother and now the US would be there, like a meddling, troublemaking neighbor. England did it to America those many years ago, and now it was America's turn to torture the people of Mexico, strengthen the brutes and bullies so that the freedom fighters didn't stand a chance.

Dan George looked up at the sky. There was enough time if he left now. "Better be getting home, folks. Not certain I'd be popular in these parts, knocking off a Federale general."

Zapata held up a hand, "Not to be a glory hound, but if you please, Mr. George, I'll take credit for him. It will exonerate you and give my friend up en el Norte something to write about in his newspapers. He will be another notch on my Winchester's stock. I make an extra fancy one for generals."

Dan bowed to Marta and kissed her on the cheek, "Okay by me." He turned his mount. "Boss, tell Rebecca I said goodbye and thank her for saving my hide. You Walshes are always getting me into and out of danger. I hope sincerely, now that you're in your proper home, you'll no longer need my services and go ahead and fire me." He grinned and she understood. This was the second time Dan George nearly gave his life for the Walsh family.

"You're fired, Dan." She waved him off, "Adios, Dan. God bless you."

She smiled at the thought. It had, finally, fully sunk in. First Zapata, now Dan George, they knew where she belonged. She looked around at the scarred walls of her hacienda. They were battle scars and she'd never have them repaired. They were the reminders of this scarred and battered land; the strife, the suffering, the unrelenting toil that was required to live in this place. She was proud to live here, proud to be given the honor of caring for it and the people on it. This is where she belonged and she'd be here for the rest of her days, whether that amounted to the next hour or the next fifty years or beyond. She was home in her Mexico.

Dan George interrupted dinner as he sauntered in through the front door of his home. He walked through the waiting room, the examination room and then, finally, into the dining room. He breathed in all the old familiar smells; the leather chairs, antiseptic, alcohol, and Ging Wa's cooking. He was greeted by his beloved family. Ging Wa could not contain herself, and it was pleasant for Billy Livingston and little Bob to see her so animated.

They were always cool to each other in public, as it was their way. Sometimes people wondered if they were actually married. She had gotten his telegram and knew he was all right. She had her cry then, in private, but now it was just too much for her to contain. She jumped from her seat at the table and grabbed him firmly around the waist. Because of his extraordinary height she could not reach any higher.

Little Bob followed. He appeared to have grown an inch since Dan last saw him. "Pop!" He could grab his father a little higher and all three stood together, in a small group, while Billy tried to leave.

Dan didn't look up from his wife and child. Rather, he just called out to his old friend. "Supper's not over, Billy. Please, have a seat."

Billy sat back down and grunted at his plate. He didn't like being there. He felt that he was spoiling the family reunion. He waited, uneasy, and Dan finally disengaged. He stroked the heads of three dogs and a cat as he made his way to the table, finally reaching over to grab Billy by the hand.

He sat down. "It's good to be home."

They both looked him over, clinically, now. Ging Wa was shocked that the man, who was slim to begin with, could have lost so much weight. He looked old, gaunt, more wrinkled and his hair had gotten greyer. His eyes shone, though. He was alive, happy, not emotionally touched by any of what had happened to him. Dan George was a tough fellow and he'd survived his captivity in the old mine very well. He looked at his boy who was devouring the food on his plate. Ging Wa smiled.

"I can't keep food in the house."

"How are the girls, Mate?" Billy was relaxed now that he'd been ordered back to his chair. He looked at Dan and did his best to hide the worry over his second best friend in the world.

"They're good, Billy. They're both going to need you, though."

Billy looked up from his plate.

"They're going to need a good man to birth babies down there." Dan smiled at his wife. "Lots and lots of babies."

Ging Wa became a little rigid in her chair. "I don't know about that." She looked on as the three of them looked up from their dinner. They'd not heard this tone but a couple of times in their lives. Dan grinned, sheepishly.

"We just got you back. I don't want Billy down there now. I don't even think those girls should be down there right now. It's a holy mess, just too much."

Dan thought about the battle, remembered shooting the general through the head. He grinned at the thought of his wife not knowing the half of it. "Marta fired me." He tried to assuage her fears.

She went back to her meal. "Those Walshes." She grinned. "The most confounding people I've ever known."

Billy grunted. "You can say that again, Ging Wa. You can sure say that again."

Rebecca Walsh sat on the veranda growing her baby and healing her lung. No one was to smoke in her presence, ever again. Robert Curtin waited on her constantly. She was now beginning to take on the glow of pregnancy and he was astounded that she could possibly look even more beautiful; but she did. He resolved to make certain that she'd never again leave his sight.

She had a good view of the road from the veranda and watched the approaching solitary rider with interest. He was a big man, wearing military clothes. He was not a Federale. She suddenly called out, "Marta, Marta!"

"What is it, darling?"

She pointed and smiled.

Marta looked toward the rider as he approached the little plaza. She turned her head slowly from side to side. "Still wearing that silly hat."

Pedro del Calle dismounted. He climbed the stairs and gave Rebecca a hug. He shook Curtin by the hand.

"Major." Curtin looked on, nodding at the new insignia as Del Calle scoffed.

"Yes, well, Napoleon had it right; *a soldier will fight long and hard for a bit of colored ribbon.*" He grinned, "Well, he got it almost right."

He turned to Marta. "So, this is the famous hacienda of Marta del Toro?"

"It is." She hunched up her shoulders and grinned. She loved seeing him. She was so pleased that he was there. She began beating the dust from his back and removed his hat. "You are a mess. You should have let us know, we'd have sent the machine for you."

"Oh, those things'll never catch on. I'll take a horse any day."

"I'm glad you're here, Pedro." She welled up a little. "I'm glad you're here."

"Are you, Marta?"

"I am."

Robert moved Rebecca inside and the two were left alone. Marta looked out at her land. She was proud of it and pleased to show it to Pedro del Calle.

"Here long?"

"That's up to you."

"Oh, the United States Marines don't have a say in it?"

"Not anymore. I'm through. Resigned, obligation's up and I'm finished with them."

"And now what?"

"Came here looking for work. Know anyone who's hiring around here?" She reached over and kissed him gently on the cheek. He kissed her back, passionately, lovingly, on the mouth.

"What can you do?"

"Oh, lots of useful things: sail a boat, wrestle sharks."

"Any good at taming wild horses?"

"Perhaps." He kissed her again. "Marry me."

"Is that an order or a request?"

"Take it as you will. What's your answer, woman? I need to know, right here and right now."

"Yes."

Epilogue

There was a double wedding on the Del Toro ranch. Marta created a new cattle brand with bull's horns on one side and a road on the other, melding the two family names. Pedro worked hard to catch up with Curtin and Marta del Toro did not mind at all.

The Walsh family was finally home from Europe and, including Abuelita, soon forgave the little trick played on them by the girls. Even Pilar made the journey down from the mule ranch and soon became fast friends with Esmeralda, her counterpart to the south. They shared stories about the girls and looked on proudly as the two beauties walked down the aisle. No one minded that Rebecca's dress bulged in the middle. As with every decent wedding, they all had a good cry.

The girls each received a special wedding present from Chica. A gold locket with the inscription: *Be kind, for everyone you meet is fighting a hard battle.* Each locket also had the following note:

My Lovelies:

This is a gift and a reminder of all the good things that have come from this saying which is the thing that your daddy, my Arvel, has lived by all his life. It is the reason why he made a wild Mexicana bandida fall in love with him one day when we met and he lassoed me and knocked me to the ground, ha ha. It is what we have tried to teach you during all our time raising you and hoping that you would turn out to be the wonderful ladies you are. We are so proud. Keep living the saying, girls. It is a good saying and it is importante to know that everyone is fighting and they need a little kindness and understanding in their fight through life. Your daddy and me, we are very proud of you. Make many good babies and make them happy. Make sure they know the saying by heart. Make it in their hearts.

Love, Mamma.

Marta dismissed the mining company and Robert Curtin created his own. With the incredible yield from the mines they soon had everything they needed to do a first class extraction of the riches from the land. Emiliano Zapata and—now that he was out of jail—Pancho Villa would benefit as well, as Marta and the family became devoted revolutionaries. They'd do their best to stop the rape of Mexico and, hopefully by example, show that the rich could be just and decent members of society.

Rebecca took charge of their little school and tirelessly worked to help others in the region. She made it her goal, her purpose in life, to modernize education and healthcare in Mexico. This she found more valuable than studying art and literature at Smith and she never looked back.

Chica and Arvel spent more time in Mexico now. They had grandchildren to spoil and Arvel, heading into his seventh decade found sitting around the veranda more and more appealing these days.

Chica was more energetic and became instrumental in teaching the White Cigars how to fight. She worked tirelessly to get the ragtag army to kill well, with maximum efficiency. She advocated for her sisters in arms and regretted that she was so old. She would have made a formidable soldadera.

Abuelita worked quietly from Maryland, exercising her influence when she could. It was an uphill battle. There was just too much money at stake for the influential and powerful of America to worry about the injustice in the land. The profits were too dear, too great to risk in the event that the socialists or anarchists should gain a foothold to the south. And it was that sort of thinking that would make it possible to lose. Democracy would work, if only they'd give it a chance in Mexico. All too often the brutish totalitarians and dictators were chosen over what was right and just.

Abraham Myer did some good work on the New York Times, making known the cruelty suffered by sea turtles just for the enjoyment of the well-to-do. His article, 'Once You Get

Them on Their Backs' was a hit and both disgusted and mobilized many interested in the welfare of all creatures, whether they served as pets, beasts of burden or even table fair. The New York Supreme Court would eventually hear the case and it was gratifying to think that something would soon be done about the barbaric treatment of these majestic creatures.

Marta learned that she really did love men and she'd content herself with one and only one. She was a good hacendado, wife, and mother. She learned to love others and, more importantly, learned to love herself and recognize that she was truly, a genuinely good person. She learned to forgive herself for her deeds as a young bandit and she learned—fully appreciated—that it was a good thing to be happy.

And she was, for the rest of her days.

Maria's Trail
The Early Adventures of Chica,
Heroine of *The Mule Tamer* Trilogy
John C. Horst
© 2012 John C. Horst

I Curanderas

The child watched the curandera work on the old woman. The hovel was dark and hazy with smoke from the old healer's cure. She leaned close to her patient as she spread the mixture of ointment and dirt and saliva onto the woman's chest. In a little while the invalid would be resting again and the girl was hopeful as she watched the witchdoctor gather up her belongings. She followed her out into the little yard.

The curandera was even more frightening in the daylight and she stank of her treatments. Her breath was bad. It reeked of the various things she smoked and blew onto her patients. The little girl looked at the medicine woman scratching her backside as she pointed to the remaining chickens. The girl complied. She didn't need to be told, she knew that the payment would be dear. The sick woman had no earthly possessions, money, jewelry or any goods of consequence. The little girl didn't know what they'd do without chickens as now there'd be no eggs.

"She is beyond my help." The curandera eyed the chickens doubtfully. The little girl wondered why, then, she was being paid. The curandera looked at the child and wagged her head slowly from side to side. "There is another, in the next village, who will help her but it will cost more than chickens."

"How much?"

The healer tipped her head toward the hovel. "More than she has in the world."

"How much?" The child was precocious and the healer gave her a weak smile.

"Let her die, child. Let her die."

"How much?"

"Ten centavos."

The little girl kept her face stone-like. She calculated in her head. She'd never heard of such a sum.

She thought hard and replied without thinking. "Will you fetch her here? I will get the money."

The curandera became severe. "I will, but if the payment is not made, it will not go well for you or anyone who lives here. You understand, child? You understand that if the debt is not paid, it will not go well for anyone here?"

"I understand."

The other one would be here in three days, she promised, as she tied the chickens together by the legs. Now, added to the curandera's odor was the stench of chicken manure. She was gone.

The little girl prepared the last of the eggs while the old woman slept, covered in the strange thick paste. She'd begun stinking from being ill and the treatment made her nearly unbearable. The child was diligent in keeping her clean but now this seemed impossible. The curandera gave no instructions on how long the unguent must stay. Would it dry and peel off, would it continue to stink? The little girl did not know.

The old woman stirred momentarily, but drifted off again and the little girl began taking an inventory. She dug up the treasure the old woman kept hidden. She had her dowry necklace. The little girl put it on. The old woman used to pull it out every so often and put it on the child and now she looked down at it, hanging low. It was big and the child was very small. It was supposed to be hers one day. It had old coins and they'd be worth something.

She dug some more. There was a gilt mirror and hairbrush. The bristles were mostly gone and the gold had mostly worn away, only a metal color showed through on the high spots and sides. But it was beautiful and one could still see a reflection in the glass. It must be worth something as well.

Then there was the old woman's work. She'd made some good baskets before she'd gotten so ill and they must be worth something.

She thought about the amount she needed. There were the two goats. They'd make it all up but then they'd have nothing. The chickens were gone and if the goats were gone there'd be nothing left. She thought about this. If she didn't get rid of everything, the old woman would surely die. But if she did get rid of everything, the old woman would perhaps live but they'd have nothing to live on. It was a significant problem.

"What are you doing, child?"

The little girl looked up. The old woman was awake. She took the string of coins from around her neck and moved over next to the old woman. She gave her a drink.

"Wash this from my body, Hija."

"But it is the cure."

"Bah. Take it off. It stinks of shit."

The little girl complied and the old woman did not stink so. Her breath was still horrible, not like the curandera's, as the old woman did not smoke, but of some kind of dreadful odor that the little girl did not know. It was the smell of impending death and there was no way to take it away.

"But you will perhaps die."

"When?" She laughed a little at her own joke until she saw the effect it had on the girl. She reached up and touched her gently on the face. "What are you doing with these things?"

"The curandera cannot heal you but she can bring in another. They need payment to heal you."

"Hah." She thought of how to break the news to the girl. She was already weakening from the little bit of talking she'd done. She breathed deeply and her chest rattled. She coughed and spit into a rag. "You keep them safe, child. Keep them safe." She looked at the mirror and brush and asked the child to bring them to her bed.

The old woman looked them over as if she were trying to remember them. She held up the mirror and looked into it. She then looked at the child. "See this, Hija, see what is in there?"

"Me."

"You remember this, child. There is no one else in the world. No one else will take care of you in the world. Only this." She pointed at the little girl's reflection. "Never forget that, child." She pointed again. "This is the only one who you can rely on and trust. You remember that, child."

She fell back and rested her hands by her sides. The little girl took the mirror and brush; she covered up the old woman and hid the treasures. Gathering the water jars, she walked outside.

It was getting late and a few people in the little settlement milled about. The mean man was there and he saw her. He sauntered up to her and looked her over dismissively.

"Is she dead yet?"

The little girl didn't want to answer, but he was important in the little settlement and she wanted no trouble.

Before she could speak the important man's wife interjected. "Don't talk like that to the child."

"Whore's spawn."

"Stop it." The mean man's wife was not so mean and the little girl could not understand why she was with him. The mean man's wife walked up to the girl and regarded her. She brushed back her long black hair and put her hand to her cheek. "How is your old mother?"

"She's not her mother. She's an old woman." The man spit tobacco juice as he spoke. "She's the whore's spawn," he pointed, accusingly and self-righteously at the child.

The wife took the girl away from the mean man and they walked a little way to the well. The girl worked and the woman watched her. "What did the healer say?"

"To let her die." The little girl filled the jars. "But I told her to get another healer. She's coming in three days."

"I see." The wife sat down and looked at the child. She was smart this one. She'd survive, but it was sad to see that she'd have nothing when they'd finished. The old woman would be dead in a week, probably, and then the girl would have nothing and the woman's husband would not let her live in the hovel alone. The child interrupted her thoughts.

"Where can I sell some things?"

"What things?"

"Just some things. I need the money for the second healer."

"Nuevo Casas Grandes would be best. There is a man there. He has a store. He would buy some things I guess."

The little girl turned and slowly walked away. She was thinking of all the things she needed to do. She was soon back at the shack. She'd never been to Nuevo Casas Grandes but knew it would take a whole day to get there and a whole day to get back.

She thought about the old woman being alone for two days. The mean man's wife would not help her. She couldn't help her as the mean man would not allow it. She decided she could make up food for the old woman and leave it nearby, within easy reach. That would not be a problem. She'd likely soil herself though. She'd have to lie in her waste for two days.

She looked outside and reasoned that it was too late to do anything now. If she worked late into the evening, she'd have everything prepared and could leave before sunrise in the morning. She'd be back in time for the healer and have the payment. It would be enough, it had to be enough.

She worked and the old woman slept.

Nuevo Casas Grandes was overwhelming. She'd never seen so many people and she soon realized that she was not dressed anything like them. She wore, literally, rags and was barefoot. She knew well enough that she'd not be taken very seriously in her present state.

She spotted a stable. She washed in the trough and braided her hair. She adjusted her rebozo to cover the top part of her dress and carefully cut away the ragged part of the skirt. She could do nothing about her feet but wash them the best she could. She pulled out the mirror and looked herself over. She didn't look so bad now. At least she was clean.

She surveyed her treasures. The goats traveled well enough and she could not believe that all of it would not be enough for the amount needed. She decided to hide the necklace and looked around.

There was a spot at a corner of a building with loose rocks and earth. She looked around to see if anyone was watching her and saw no one. She dug a little hole and hid the necklace there. If worse came to worst, she could always try and sell it to make up any shortfall.

She was ready now but a bit shaky. She wasn't hungry, but the thought of going into the grand and fancy store and talking to a stranger, selling her pathetic goods, made her shake. She resolved to eat a little and drink from the trough. That helped the shaking to stop. She looked at her reflection in the water and thought about what the old woman had said. She took a deep breath and let it out. She was ready now.

She tied the goats to the post outside and entered the store. It immediately made her shaky and dizzy again. It was more than she could take in; the odor of the fresh straw from new brooms mixed with finely dyed fabric, new leather and chemicals, coffee and candy and so many odors she'd never known. She looked around at dresses and fabric for rebozos and fancy hats. It was the most beautiful place she'd ever seen.

A man was behind the counter. He looked at her and smiled. She did not expect that. She expected someone like the mean man and he wasn't anything like the mean man. She suddenly felt a little fluttery in her stomach; as the man seemed to be good and kind.

"Well, young lady." He looked behind her and all around for an adult and realized she was all alone. This made him even friendlier. "How may I help you?"

She looked at him and hesitated, she couldn't seem to find her voice. He looked like a nice man. He had a big smile and good teeth. They weren't stained or black or missing anywhere. He wore a white high collar around his neck made from a material she'd never seen before and a colorful cravat protruded from the collar. He wore a vest that matched his trousers and his sleeves were clean, everything was clean. He looked through little oval glasses and he had no hair on his face at all. His face seemed as smooth as a lady's. She was very impressed with all of this.

"I have things to sell and was told to see you."

"I see." He beckoned her to the back of the store, to his desk where she could sit down and not have to reach up high to the counter. This made her fluttery again; she knew this part of the store was not for customers. He was a very nice man.

She sat and pulled the items carefully from a sack. She then laid the sack down, as it too was for sale. She'd have no use for a sack if he would buy the other things.

He looked them over carefully.

"And two goats." She turned her head, then pointed at the front of his store.

"I see." He picked up the useless items and turned them over in his hands, as if he were regarding some great heirlooms. He did not look up from them but asked her, talking toward the items as if they'd give him the answer to his questions, "Why do you need to sell such things, child?"

He finally looked up, looked into her eyes with a tenderness she'd never known.

"The old woman, eh, the woman who cares for me." That sounded silly because she'd been caring for the old woman for more than a year now. "She's sick and I need money for the curanderas."

"I see. And your mother or father, cannot they do this? Cannot someone else help you in this?"

She answered automatically. "There is no one else."

"I see." The man became animated. He was excited and suddenly sat back in his chair. "Well, let's see," he stroked his chin and regarded the items. "I have no use for goats, so I can give you nothing for them. He picked up the brush and mirror. "The bristles are gone and the finish is gone. The mirror needs to be re-silvered. So, I am sorry, but no, they have no value."

He watched her face fall. She was about to tell him about the necklace when he continued. "How much do they need?"

Te…twenty centavos." She didn't know why she lied to the nice man, but thought it would be better to start high. He laughed as he could see her little lie, and then grinned a fatherly grin at her.

"Twenty centavos! A king's ransom!" He stood up and held out his hand. "Little girl," he stopped himself and walked away. She watched him as he retrieved a box and opened it. She could see great piles of paper money and coins. He laid out ten centavos before her. He went back to the box and gathered more coins. He placed another pile of coins next to the first one. She could not understand why. He smiled and continued.

"The pile on the left is ten centavos little one. The pile on the right is one hundred." He stood up again and walked to the front of the store. He turned the sign around and locked the door. He returned and picked out a pretty blue dress hanging on a rack and held it up to her, under her chin. "Lovely, lovely. And just the right size."

She suddenly felt weak again, like her legs were made of lead, like something had happened to them and she was afraid that she would not be able to move them when it was time to leave. She didn't like this and wanted the man to stop. She found she could not speak; blood pounded in her chest and ears and was giving her a headache. She could only watch him, wait and see what he was going to do next. He sensed this, too, and continued.

"Little girl." He held up his hands ever so kindly. "I will not harm you. As God is my witness, I would never harm you. I, I lost my little girl and my wife and, I, just want to be nice to you."

She relaxed and he continued. "I will give you all the money on the desk," he looked at the two piles of coins, "and this lovely dress and some shoes if you'll just be nice to me." He patted her gently on the cheek, "And you can keep all your treasures."

She regarded him. He was nice. She did not understand his kindness. It was confusing, but she'd known some kindness like this before. Wasn't the old woman kind to her for the same reason? The old woman took her in because she'd lost all her children, and her husband was dead. Wasn't this the same thing?

She felt the flutter again. It was going to be all right. He'd even picked the dress that caught her eye when she'd first come into the store. It was as if he knew what was in her mind. Then she thought of the money. A hundred and ten centavos! And she could keep the goats and the mirror and brush and the necklace.

It was overwhelming and she was more than a little proud of herself. She'd make the old woman well and they'd be fine. They could buy extra goats and more chickens and they'd be good through winter and beyond. She smiled at the man and thanked him.

He jumped up and patted her gently on the knee. "This calls for a celebration, my little one. A celebration!"

He looked about, not certain what to do next. Then he remembered and, pushing the dress on her, pointed to a little room. "Go, go change, child."

She did and when she returned she looked very pretty. She was quite pleased with herself, despite the fact that she was still barefoot. He'd laid out some things on the desk, a fancy drink of yellow liquid and some candy and a cake. She'd never tasted anything so wonderful in her life.

He chatted constantly but she couldn't respond. She listened and ate and drank. She looked down at the pretty blue cloth covering her legs and she became dizzy with the excitement; overwhelmed and happy, warm and tingly all over. She wanted, for some reason, to sleep.

II Alone

She awoke and it was hot and nearly dark. Something liquid was splashing her and now she looked up and something wet was thrown into her eyes which burned terribly. Some had gotten into her mouth and it tasted horrible. She squinted and could see the man. She could see that she was in the desert and he was ranting and speaking so quickly that she could not make out what he was saying. She cast her eyes about to see who was there for him to speak to, but no one was there, just his horse hitched to a wagon. He was splashing her with coal oil from a metal can and it was getting everywhere and she looked down and she had her old dress on and she wondered at that, as she remembered having the pretty blue one on before she fell asleep. Her old outfit was now getting soaked with the rest of her.

He backed up and tripped, spilling coal oil down his front and now he brushed at it as if he could wipe it away. He no longer looked happy and friendly. Now he was wild, like an animal she'd once seen with hydrophobia and it scared her very much.

He turned and put the coal oil can in a wagon and then came back. He picked at his vest pocket and found matches. He was going to burn her up and she knew it. She thought desperately, thought about what to do. She could not run, he'd catch her and her legs were giving her pain and her feet suddenly hurt. He was striking the match now. It would engulf her and suddenly she knew. She learned from a young age how to throw things with precision, she'd killed rabbit and chickens in the desert this way since just about the time she could walk, and she knew this was her only chance. She picked up a fist-sized rock and threw with all her might, striking the man in the forehead.

He dropped as the match ignited and it now lit his soaked matching vest and trousers, he was suddenly a giant flame and he screamed and ran in circles, nearly ran toward her then changed direction. He ran toward the desert and finally after a hundred or so feet, dropped and continued to burn. He was finally dead.

The horse pulling the wagon panicked and also ran wildly into the desert and after a time she realized that she was all alone and it was fully dark now. She did not recognize this place so surmised that she had to be somewhere other than southeast of the town as that was the route she knew and she'd never been on the road nearby. She slowly got to her feet and stumbled to the burning corpse which was by now devoid of most of its flesh, the face gone, now nothing more than a red burning skeleton and she realized that this did not scare her but actually made her feel good. He was a bad man and this was the first of his kind that she'd seen get what he deserved and she couldn't help be a bit proud of the fact that she'd made it happen to a certain extent. No one could say that she'd killed him or burned him up, she just stunned him with the rock, but he was dead now and he'd died a fittingly horrible death and she was partially the reason it happened.

She sat down next to the corpse, upwind as she didn't want to smell like greasy burning human, but she was suddenly very cold and the corpse gave off a fair bit of heat and she warmed herself and the coal oil dried from her dress and she became sleepy. She slept next to the shopkeeper until morning.

When she awoke it was full daylight and the corpse was burned out. Nothing much was left but a skeleton and she regarded him again. She could recognize him. His nice teeth were recognizable. She needed to urinate and did and had to push extra hard as things were bound up down there and something popped or tore and she looked down to see that her urine was reddish and she realized then that he'd been up to no good but that she'd been so sleepy from what he'd given her to drink or eat that she didn't know. She was glad of that and now she looked down to survey her dress and saw blood on it and further surmised that she'd been bleeding at some point. What he'd done to her made her bleed and made her very sore. He was a wicked man and she looked on the corpse again and was glad to see him in such a state. She was glad that he was dead.

She got her bearings and began walking toward town. She was famished and had nothing but her soiled dress and needed to get her things. She wondered if the goats were still tethered to the post out front of the burned man's store. She found some water and drank until she was full and washed herself and it burned and stung very much and she felt down there and could feel that her body was torn and that it would scab over then open up whenever she urinated and wondered how it would ever heal.

She soaked her dress where it was bloody but it wouldn't come out. It had dried there and was fixed. She'd have cut it away but her knife was gone, so she resolved to continue walking in her bloody dress. There was nothing more that she could do.

She arrived to town at midday and the goats were gone. She checked the store and it was locked. She checked the windows and could not open them. She sat down and was shakier than before. She began to doze again when a man on a horse rode up and dismounted. He tied his horse to the post she'd used for the goats the previous day. He wore a uniform and a sword which bounced about on his side. He walked past her and pulled on the store's door, then peered in while knocking. He turned and regarded her.

"What are you doing here?"

"Waiting."

"For what?" He looked around. "Where's Sanchez?"

"I don't know. I don't know who that is."

"The shopkeeper."

"He's...I, he's not here, but he has my things. I need my things."

The rurale regarded her. He looked at her dirty and bloody dress. "What have you gotten yourself into?"

She realized that she might not want to tell him much. "Chicken blood."

He shrugged and shook his head. "Big chicken."

He began to walk away and she decided that he was her only hope. She called out to him as he mounted up. "That man, Sanchez, he has my things. I need to get inside."

"You, peon, have no business with Sanchez. He's a respected shop owner. You come back when he's here, don't bother me with such things, child."

"But he took..." she thought better of it. "He has my things, it is my right. And my goats are gone."

"Hah!" He sneered. "You have no right, child. Go back to your hole in the ground, go back home." He was gone.

She did as she was told, automatically and by sundown she was nearly home. She walked without thinking and was so hungry now that her stomach ached constantly. She drank a few times through the day and that helped a little. By full dark she was just too tired to go on and resolved to lie down for a while. She thought that she would only rest for a little while and then go on.

But she didn't wake up and it was full daylight by the time she got moving again. She worried over the old woman and wondered and hoped that she was okay. She did not know what she'd tell the curanderas. She wanted them to treat the old woman but now had nothing to give them. She decided that she couldn't worry about that now. She decided now, after all that had happened to her in the past two days, that she'd not worry about things that she could not control, but that she would resolve, from now on, to control as many things as she could. She also resolved to trust no one, as the old woman had told her, except herself. She could rely on no one in the world and that was the way things would be from now on.

She saw smoke off in the distance, in the direction of the hovel, and she hurried on as best she could as such a large fire made no sense to her. She finally arrived to the hovel burning, the mean man and his wife and the curanderas looking on. The mean man sneered. "You are late."

"Where's the old woman?"

The mean man's wife pointed at the hovel and the girl looked at them. "Why?"

The mean man spit tobacco at her feet. "She was dead when they came to treat her. They said it all needed to be purified and we burned it. She's gone, child."

The little girl watched it burn and was eventually alone. The curanderas left and the mean man and his wife went about their business. She watched the little hovel fall apart and watched now as the foundation was revealed and she remembered everything she could about her time there. She could not say that any of the times were really good, but they were her time and the old woman's time, and sometimes she was a little happy when she made the old woman smile. She never went hungry and the old woman was good to her, better than any other human being had been and now she was dead. She thought about crying but didn't. She lay down in the shade and fell asleep until the mean man's wife nudged her awake. The wife was nervous and looked back at her own hovel often as her husband would be cross if he knew that she was helping the whore's spawn, but the woman was good and she could not help herself.

She had food for the girl and sat beside her as the child ate. She reached over to touch the girl's hair and the child recoiled, pulled away and put several feet between them. They were both shocked at this behavior.

"Take these things, child." She gave her a bundle of old clothes wrapped in a rebozo along with a knife and a flint and steel. At least the child could make fire. She gave her a sack of tortillas and some dried beans and a water gourd.

The little girl looked the things over and then into the woman's eyes. "May I live with you?"

The woman looked away, at the burned remains of the hovel. "No, child. You may not and you may not stay here. He won't allow it." She regarded the child's dress and the bloodstains. The bastard missed nothing, she thought, looking back at the hovel where her husband was likely eating, gorging himself while this little one suffered. His mean, beady little eyes saw everything.

"He says you are no good, that you are the product of a whore and now you've been spoiled." She looked away and the little girl saw that she was crying. She felt sorry for the woman even though she was not going to help her beyond the little bit that she had. She stood up and brushed her skirt off. She looked down on the woman's head, grabbed her new kit and was gone.

She walked back to the town as she now remembered the necklace she'd hidden. She needed to get it as it was the only thing she had left in the world, other than her kit and her clothing that was of any tangible value. She at least was not hungry and this helped her progress a good deal. She killed a rattler with a rock on the way and made a fire and cooked it. If she could do this regularly, she could save the tortillas for when she was in the town as she did not know how long she'd be there or even what she'd do after reacquiring her necklace.

She was just outside of town at dusk and decided to bed down in the desert. She felt safe in the desert and vulnerable in the town. That was curious to her as she thought a lot about her little time in the town and the shopkeeper and the rurale were not good to her. It seemed that the desert was safer as it had no people in it.

She made a fire and found water and filled her gourd and settled down for the night. She'd made her camp in an arroyo so that her fire would draw no attention. No one taught her this, but it was reasonable to think that it would be best to remain invisible. She found an armadillo and killed it with a blow from a stick and ate it. At least she was not hungry and she was safe. She was alone and she missed the old woman, but the thought of being alone did not bother her as much as she thought it might.

Before going to sleep, she had to urinate and it hurt again, but not so bad as before and she no longer bled. Her wound was healing and now she went to sleep.